Mischiefs
and
Miseries

a novel of Jamestown 1607

K. K. BRUNO

To Michael —
a fellow
writer!

Best wishes —
KKBruno

PublishAmerica
Baltimore

© 2006 by K. K. Bruno.
All rights reserved. No part of this book may be reproduced, stored in a retrieval system or transmitted in any form or by any means without the prior written permission of the publishers, except by a reviewer who may quote brief passages in a review to be printed in a newspaper, magazine or journal.

First printing

All characters appearing in this work are fictitious. Any resemblance to real persons, living or dead, is purely coincidental.

At the specific preference of the author, PublishAmerica allowed this work to remain exactly as the author intended, verbatim, without editorial input.

ISBN: 1-4241-4367-5
PUBLISHED BY PUBLISHAMERICA, LLLP
www.publishamerica.com
Baltimore

Printed in the United States of America

To Jack and Evan

Acknowledgments

All writing is collaborative, and in my work I enjoyed the help of many volunteers who offered fine suggestions and enthusiastic encouragement. I will be forever grateful to Cathy Jones Gunderson, Susan Schultz, Kathy and Megan Early, Heidi Kunz, Mike Polizzi, Cathy Tobia Naylor, Thad Tate, David Meadows, Jim Rubin, Doc Schneider, Susan Prock, and Edward Wright Haile for their support in all stages. Any errors at this point are mine alone.

In specific, I owe much to my husband Jack and son Evan, my dearest treasures, who willingly and cheerfully forgave my lack of attention to life's little details as I worked the manuscript, and who are personally responsible for setting me on the road to authorship.

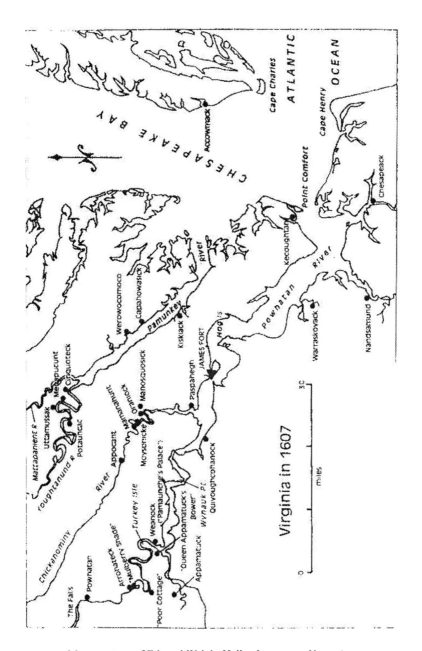

Map courtesy of Edward Wright Haile, *Jamestown Narratives*

Pronunciation Guide

    Since Algonkian was not a written language, and English spelling was not standardized until the mid-18th century, definitive pronunciation of the Indian names and words below is almost impossible to come by. Here is the best guess we have to date, based on the written records of the English.

Arrohattoc	Air-uh-HAT-ick
Amonute	Ah-mon-OO-tay
Chickahominy	CHICK-uh-HAH-min-ee
Kecoughtan	KICK-uh-tan
Matoaka	Muh-TOE-kuh
Nansemond	NAN-se-mond
Nevis	NEE-vis
Opechancanough	O-pe-CHAN-cuh-now
Pamunkey	Puh-MUN-key
Pasbehegh	PASS-buh-hay
Pocahontas	PO-cuh-HON-tus
Powhatan	Pow-HAT-in
Rappahannock	Rap-uh-HAN-ick
Werowocomoco	Wair-uh-wo-COMB-a-co
wingapo	win-GA-po
Wowinchopunk	Wow-IN-cho-punk
Zúñiga	Zoon-YAY-gah

"Into what a mischief and misery had we been given up…"

William Strachey, *True Reportory*, 1625

Foreword

London, England, December 1606. One hundred and four adventurers aboard three ships – the substantial *Susan Constant*, the middle-sized *Godspeed*, and the frighteningly tiny *Discovery* – were part-owners in a Venture intended to bring easy riches in the form of gold from Virginia.

About half were gentlemen, many with war experience; about a quarter were craftsmen and artisans; and the last quarter were laborers, probably servants to the gentlemen. The adventurers' goals were to find gold, gold, and more gold; a safe and quick passage to the South Sea; and, if Providence allowed, the lost Colonists of Roanoke Island – all the while spreading the Anglican form of Christianity to the New World. All were volunteers, all were joint-stock owners in The Virginia Company, and all had aspirations of unimagined wealth. Many also longed for the glory wedded to great adventure. Above all, however, hovered Profit.

Malcontents, followers, natural leaders, weak leaders, risk-takers, hopeful youths, Protestants and even a few Catholics: all were part of the first expedition. It is unclear who intended to stay permanently in this business settlement called Jamestown. It is very clear few survived to talk about it.

History provides little beyond certain factual matters, and even those must be taken cautiously because the Venture had its own sort of Public Relations to promote in order to survive. John Smith in particular was not above embellishing a tale. Still, the men who crammed themselves into the tiniest of ships to cross the Atlantic did so with an unwavering willingness to seek out a New World and to mine it for God, Glory and Gold, though not necessarily in that order.

The following tale is true in so far as dates, places, major characters and central events are concerned. I have taken liberty with characterization, because, for most, names are all that appear on the written record. John Smith, because he published eleven books and numerous films carry on his legend, is the most widely known and yet descriptions of his character vary greatly. To some he was annoying or obnoxious. To others, he was right when being right meant the salvation of an enterprise and later—although undreamed of by him or his colleagues—a nation. He dared damnation by his fellow colonists, the Virginia Company and King James to do what was right.

Sailing for Virginia:

John Smith   Twenty-seven years old and son of a Lincolnshire yeoman, Smith earned a Captain's rank and coat of arms fighting the Turks in Hungary. He possesses a commanding voice and presence, and knows the value of military discipline, strong leadership. Despises weakness especially when it inhibits progress. He understands men and their natural inclinations. Straightforward, righteous and clear-minded, he is a threat to lesser men.

Christopher Newport   Successful privateer and sole commander of the Virginia expedition while at sea, he stands at the helm of the *Susan Constant*. With this voyage to Virginia, Admiral Newport is forty-six years old, but he will cross the Atlantic three more times before his life is over, a feat at which many younger men balk. Well-known and loved for his excellent seamanship, his fairness and his ability to judge men accurately, Newport bears an empty right sleeve as a reminder of his days battling the Spanish in the West Indies.

Edward Maria Wingfield   At forty-seven, an old man compared to most of the adventurers. Distinguished in birth and fortune, he sees little reason to explain himself to anybody and is keenly aware that his investment in the Virginia Company is one of the most substantial, and that he is the only one of four principal investors to actually join the expedition. Has seen military action, but mostly in Ireland and in a limited fashion, primarily because he was captured and imprisoned for a goodly length of time. This does not make him popular with the men. Many of the gentlemen admire his dedication to the written instructions for the Venture. He brings along two servants and a brace of mastiffs, Phoenix and Phaeton.

Bartholomew Gosnold   *Godspeed*'s captain, thirty-five, older brother to Anthony who is also on the expedition, and distant cousin to Wingfield, he's sailed to the American coastline before. He, along with Wingfield, is one of the prime movers pushing for an effective colony in the New World. His experience, levelheaded reasoning, and friendship with Smith endear him to the crew and adventurers. A solid, capable man of intelligence and wit with wife and family in Suffolk, he's not likely to stay in the Colony.

John Ratcliffe   *Discovery*'s captain despite a sore lack of
sailing experience; violent fits of anger give little recommendation for him as
a leader and leave his compatriots wondering how he won the position in the
first place. At thirty-three, he's neither young nor old, says little and does
even less.

Gabriel Archer   Gosnold's recorder for the 1602 voyage to
New England, this is the first of two trips to Virginia for him. A thorough man
who's thoroughly ambitious, he sees himself in command of the Venture
once it makes a settlement on land. His law background will be of use, though
he doesn't know it yet.

John Martin   Roughly the same age as Gosnold, but
without the purse or birth. A former artillery officer with a Captain's rank, he
has brought with him his son, a sturdy man still in the flush of youthful
enthusiasm for daring adventure. Inclined to sickness and arguing over
picayune matters, Martin can't understand why the others don't take him
seriously. He dreams of large profits; how they are obtained is of small
consequence to him.

George Kendall   Silent, moody, handsome, and cold, he has
an infantry background. A Captain by rights, he brings military experience
but little in the way of comradely charm or leadership ability. Owes his
position in the Venture to having once been in Lord Salisbury's employ and,
not insignificantly, being cousin to Sir Edwin Sandys, an influential backer of
the Company. Gold seems to be his goal in coming to Virginia.

Robert Hunt   With his personal library in tow, Hunt, a
venerable priest in His Majesty's Church, is ready to spread the Anglican
Good News to the Naturals and keep the flock under his watchful, pastoral
eye. Never a sailing man, he takes the voyage hard and is grateful for every
day they spend ashore while crossing. Portly, thirty-six years old, he's not
prepared to labor extensively but cheerfully offers advice when he thinks it
will help.

George Percy   From a family that would have been kings
except for an historical twist of fate, Percy is the eighth son of Henry, the
eighth Earl of Northumberland, a Catholic. With so many brothers ahead of

him in line to inherit, the twenty-six-year-old Percy must find a way to make his fortune on his own. The Venture comes along at just the right time. His record of loyalty to the King is untarnished, but because his brother Henry, the ninth Earl, and two other brothers are in the Tower for conspiring in the Gunpowder Plot of the previous year, he has little hope of being disassociated from his family while in England. He is happy to be as far away from brotherly troubles as possible and still have his birthright recognized, however minimally. Tall, reedy, poised and dense, with a face only his mother could love.

Stephen Halthrop   At twenty, young, hearty, eager to earn a fortune in gold, Halthrop admires John Smith's courage and bravado. He emulates Smith in every way possible.

James Read   Broad chested, lean, and muscled as only a blacksmith can be, Read joins the Venture for the lure of easy gold. At twenty-five, with no wife or children, he's free to go and stay, if he finds Virginia to his liking, but without women there, he probably won't. As the only blacksmith in the group, he will be plenty busy and he likes it that way.

Matthew Scrivener   Young, open and confident, he arrives with the First Supply as a new Council member. He is quick to understand the men he meets and finds Smith's practical nature and tenacious spirit appealing from the first. Capable and full of potential, he yearns for adventure as well as gold, but keeps a cautious profile in the wake of a factious Council.

Living in Virginia:

Powhatan   Sixty-year-old ruler of many tribes in the Chesapeake Bay area; he is crafty and wary of the English, and attempts to be friends with the sickly, rag-tag group who may very well die without his help. He is tall, strong and powerful, with a plethora of wives and children scattered about the land, thus tying local tribes to him and his authority. When he realizes that the English will not only stay but come in waves by the hundreds, it is too late for him to stop it, even if he could.

Pocahontas   Ten, maybe eleven years old when she first encounters the English, John Smith in particular, she is one of the many children fathered by Powhatan, and, since the Powhatan lines of succession do not flow vertically but horizontally between siblings, she is not the Princess the English imagine her to be but a normal, inquisitive youngster with a penchant for cartwheels. An emissary for her father, she happily visits the English and plays at the Fort.

Opechancanough   Younger brother to the powerful Powhatan, he is about forty years old, quick to anger. He feels the English have no place in his world and despises the white man from the beginning.

Mosco   Youthful French-English man who has lived with the Potomac Indians as one of their own since northern Indians in Canada killed his family and took him hostage. He is content to live as a Potomac but is intrigued by the English ways. His language abilities make him a unique translator.

Chapter One

A Midnight Departure

Two men eyed each other from opposite sides of a heavily scrolled mahogany desk littered with parchment and inkwells. Air thick with burning incense and candles cloaked a clandestine and sensitive negotiation.

Pedro de Zúñiga, Spain's ambassador to England in London, smiled stiffly at the English gentleman, a well-dressed, neat man of thirty odd years with serious eyes and terse style.

"They sail tonight?" asked the ambassador in surprise.

The gentleman blinked and tilted his head once in assent. "The Virginia Company keeps its secrets well, when it wants to." He did not like the ambassador's formal smile, but he had not expected a warm reception; he did expect to be paid.

Zúñiga, middle-aged with the swarthy look of his Spanish ancestors and a balding pate, gave an almost imperceptible nod to his clerk and offered the gentleman a cup of Spanish wine.

As they drank a toast to the Pope and to success, a priest in stole and alb entered the offices.

"Ah. A blessing before you take leave," declared Zúñiga.

The gentleman was still kneeling on the cold stone floor when a shuffling noise diverted the prayerful attention of the three men.

Rising, the gentleman took a large bundle from the clerk, inspected inside to see that all was as it should be, and closed it again with smug satisfaction. "This will do. His Majesty is most kind."

"The other half will come to you upon your return," said Zúñiga.

The pay was large, the risk was small, and the gentleman could not think of a better way to serve his Faith than to help stop Protestant expansion. Nothing would interfere with that mission, that he swore.

Leaving by the back door, he disappeared into the bitter, damp December London night and, after depositing the bundle in the appropriate place, made his way to the East India docks where those aboard the *Susan Constant*, the *Godspeed* and the *Discovery* awaited his return.

John Smith, one-time captain of Hungarian and Dutch forces, threw his tired arms and legs in one long, joint-cracking stretch and rolled his aching shoulders. The quarters on the *Susan Constant* were hardly commodious; his elbow smacked into the head of the boy next to him and his feet brushed against the shoulder of another companion.

Smith turned over, wishing for sleep that would not come.

His thoughts turned to his home in Lincolnshire, something he had not recalled in years. The farm, now in his sister's trust with her husband managing all their concerns, reminded him only of how little profit there was in the life and how he had longed for adventure, to be more than a field hand with a family to feed and never enough in the family purse. He had gladly left home at sixteen, willing to go anywhere and do just about anything, so long as it was legal. With a soldier's love of open spaces and constant movement, he had ended up in Hungary, Turkey, and Ireland. Now he was on his greatest adventure yet, on a ship to the New World where gold paved the streets and a passage to the South Sea begged to be discovered.

A rush of excitement surged through Smith despite his attempts to force sleep; he wanted, more than anything else in the world, more than life itself, to be the man who discovered the South Sea Passage.

He sighed. In the darkness of the ship's belly he could barely make out the outline of bodies and goods crammed together. He pulled his blanket closer and breathed deeply into the wool to warm his nose and lips.

"Captain?" The voice, high pitched and worried, came from the boy next to him.

"Aye, Sam."

"Shall we be off soon? I can hardly bear the strain of waiting any longer!"

Smith threw his young page a smile. Fourteen is an anxious age even if you are not about to leave your home and all that is familiar for God knows how long, maybe forever. "Patience in all things, lad." Aye, Smith, he told himself. Patience. "The Admiral promised we would be off at midnight, and I take him at his word, as he is a man of great honor. It cannot be half-past eleven yet. Listen for the bosun's whistle and the cast off order. And say your prayers, like a good lad. I promised your mother, and I won't have her call me a liar."

He heard Sam breathe easier and the sibilant rhythm of private orisons. A vow is a solemn thing and Christian he shall continue to be, Smith thought, adding his own petitions for a safe crossing and mild weather, though he truly had little hope of the latter since they were so very late in departing. Drunken sailors on another ship had rammed into the *Susan Constant* while she was tied to the dock and cost the Company both time and money in repairs and investigation by the Admiralty Board. Now, in mid-December, the Atlantic would be at her roughest, coldest and most heartless. But we are off indeed, thought Smith, as the bosun's shrill whistle pierced the cold air. Midnight had arrived.

Anticipation and excitement stirred his innards in a familiar dance. Every adventure of his life had started with the same pent-up thrills, and he knew sleep would not be a companion tonight, not for him, not for any that lay on the three ships that crept out of East India Docks and toward the savage and untamed land of Virginia.

Chapter Two

Stalled

"Tell 'em about the time you was almost turned into a Turk by a bonny Turkish lass, Cap'n." Jehu Robinson gulped his ale as he winked at John Smith, snorted, then swallowed hard to force the brew down.

Spirits had been high upon sailing from London until lackluster winds or windless storms commanded that the three ships remain anchored miles off England's coast, within sight of land. Bad weather was not to be sailed through but endured with sails furled and anchors dropped, and the *Susan Constant*, the *Godspeed* and the *Discovery* had been stalled for almost six weeks. Such situations required light entertainment to hold the men together or heavy hands would be needed to keep them apart.

Smith well knew the value of diverting the attention of restless, bored, and confined men, stuck indefinitely with morale souring as quickly as the beer.

Stroking his narrow, chestnut beard and oddly flared moustache, he considered the invitation. His thick, wavy nutmeg brown hair, longer than was popular, refused to stay slicked back, though he often ran his square hands through it as he did now. Hazel eyes, shrewd and clever, surveyed his audience and sized up their willingness to hear, yet again, the tale as he had so often told it before.

Surrounding him, all fifty gentlemen in the Company's retinue—save the two captains on the other ships—reclined, leaned or perched upon crates, barrels, and casks filled with personal belongings, guns, ammunition, food, medicines, tents, tools, cups, platters, kettles, jugs, copper and beads to trade with the Naturals, and Master Hunt's beloved books—supplies enough to build and live in a settlement until replenishment arrived from England or the Naturals were subdued into working, if they preferred that path to trading their food.

Those who had heard Smith's story before tried to move away and yet the quarters were tight, and none but the crew was allowed above decks at the moment. Still, many of the bored travelers happily indulged in another incredible Smith adventure.

Smith, eyes turning to glittering crescents as he laughed, alighted from the barrel in the dimness to tell the story of his capture by the Turks, his subsequent sale into slavery, the beautiful woman who had wanted the English slave for her husband, and his ultimate escape by the daring dashing in of the heads of her brother and two servants in a field. At the conclusion, a few of the listeners cheered, slapped their thighs and the bulkhead in appreciation and waited for more.

"I see, Master Smith, that you have not lost your gift for embellishment. The last time you told this story your 'two servants' were not near enough to speak of, let alone kill." Edward Maria Wingfield, patentee, had been relegated to the lower decks during daylight hours, and now sniffed into a finely embroidered handkerchief as he looked down upon Smith.

Smith took the older man's preoccupation with his handkerchief as a social slight, but it could easily have been a sign of age, or a reaction to the animal odors wafting from the deck below. Whatever the cause, Wingfield seemed uncommonly prone to dabbing his aristocratic nose, especially when Smith was at hand.

That others found Wingfield admirable was to be expected: he was well born and moneyed, enjoyed many favorable connections in London and other European cities, could boast of minor military service in Ireland and the Netherlands, and was willing to voyage to Virginia when all the other patentees or major stock holders would not or could not. Indeed, Smith could well understand how Wingfield was highly regarded by the Virginia Company and Englishmen in general. But Captain Smith had other criteria for assessing a man's worth and Edward Maria Wingfield possessed none of these. To say the least, he was too portly, slow, overdressed and effeminate. And he never responded reasonably to reasonable questions.

Before Smith could reply, a gurgle and a lunge from Master Hunt parted the two men.

The pastor stumbled toward the ladder. By the time the sputtering man reached the top, Smith had forced open the hatch and was reaching in to help Hunt to the open deck. Frigid air shocked them as they pushed toward the side. Hunt, his hand covering his mouth, staggered to the rail just in time to pitch his wild vomits into the black sea. When his efforts were spent, Hunt's gentle brown eyes, ever thankful, closed in tired misery. He and Smith returned to the middle deck, Hunt leaning heavily on the stronger man's arm and shoulder, letting Smith guide him to a straw mat near a small air hole in the bulkhead. Master Hunt sighed, mumbled something that sounded like a blessing, and then drifted into a troubled sleep.

Smith, looking about for Wingfield, found the man had moved to the ship's farthest corner, engaged in deep conference with George Kendall, a moody man usually with little to say—and that was just as well, for when he did speak Smith always felt the urge to strike him. Kendall's perpetual expression, handsome though it may have been, was one of having just stepped in something unpleasant. Smith picked his way over, made himself comfortable nearby and began great preparations for a nap.

"I agree. Yes. Yes." Wingfield nodded as he spoke. "I will speak to Admiral Newport about returning Master Hunt to shore tomorrow. He cannot possibly endure the crossing and his home is but ten miles from the shore we see from here. This will leave us, of course, without the inspiration and spiritual guidance of the King's Church, but I am certain we can manage until the first supply ship arrives with another pastor."

Kendall's reply was so low that Smith could not hear it, but that didn't matter. Smith thought about the years England had been at war with Spain over religious differences, years pitting newly founded Anglicans against the corrupt and centuries-old Roman Catholic Church. England's victory over Spain had been a victory over Papists, but England had her own Catholics.

Master Robert Hunt, sole administrator for the Anglican Church on the expedition—an expedition whose purpose in part was to Christianize the savages before Spanish or French Catholics could have a go at them—was about to be conveniently removed from the party.

Wingfield should have been aware of the seriousness of such a move, but Smith couldn't be sure of that. Hadn't the old man already declared himself leader of the expedition when everyone knew the Charter called for elections in Virginia and not before? Wingfield believed that his social rank and his substantial portion of funds for the Virginia Company entitled him to more power than the Charter—or Smith – were willing to grant, especially here on the sea with the damned coast of England still in sight.

I must speak with Admiral Newport before Wingfield does, thought Smith, but when?

The galley fires dwindled as the men aboard the *Susan Constant* fell asleep in the still, bitter January night. Snoring filled the spaces between men and cargo. Amid the reclining bodies, someone's voice, soft and low, sang in the night:

In Scarlet town, where I was born,
There was a fair maid dwellin',
Made every youth cry Well-a-way!
Her name was Barbara Allan.

Smith and Wingfield planned their petitions to Newport as they drifted off, other men dreamed of loved ones left behind, and George Kendall smiled in the darkness.

With the dawn came the abrupt clanging of ship's bells and the general stumbling of men to the top deck for nature's necessities, a brisk walk about, and eventually, the morning meal of salted pork, sea biscuits and beer after Morning Prayer led by an ill-looking Hunt.

Admiral Newport, tall and elegant, stood at the helm, his left hand pressed tightly into the small of his back. He rarely missed his right hand, so long ago blown off in military action. He watched the stiff bodies trying to both huddle against the cold and stretch sore arms and legs. Grumbling and sidelong looks were meant to signal the Admiral of their displeasure, but he registered no outward response.

Ignorant bastards don't even know when they're well off, thought Newport. A day or two of not standing at all on *Discovery* or *Godspeed* would put them to rights.

Moderate winds had appeared just before dawn, winds without storms in the offing, and Newport pushed aside thoughts of discontented men to consider getting under way again at long last. Food and beer were running out, becoming infested with vermin, or merely turning stale and inedible. With favorable weather they should easily make it to the coast of West Africa—to the Canary Islands—in a few days where fresh meat and fruit could be brought aboard and the men could enjoy the warmer weather. The chance to wash soiled clothing, bodies, and spirits would be most welcome indeed.

"Begging your pardon, Admiral, but could I speak with you for a minute or two in your cabin?" Smith was polite but firm.

The two men entered the small cabin to find Wingfield already present. Smith was surprised; Newport was not. Wingfield as patentee had privileges not permitted most passengers.

"Good day, Master Wingfield. I was just about to confer with Captain Smith on an urgent matter."

Wingfield ignored the implied message to leave. "I have come to speak with you about a matter that does not concern Master Smith. He should return to the deck and wait to be called."

Not moving, Smith said, "I believe our concerns are one and the same, at least in part. Have you come with regard to Master Hunt?"

A flicker of annoyance crossed Wingfield's face.

"If indeed these conferences are similar in nature, I think it best we meet together, here and now," said Newport, taking his seat beside the desk and motioning for the two men to sit as well. "I have decided to make use of the favorable wind which has blessedly come our way. We have little time to waste. Now, then, what is your business?"

Wingfield spoke first.

"Surely you have noted the misery which has afflicted poor Hunt every day since we set sail. Others, true, have also been sick, but none so relentlessly. We are anchored within reach of his home county and I am here to suggest, with only his health and well being in mind, that we be merciful and allow him passage to land. His constant ill health does him or anyone here no good for he has been unable to fulfill his clerical duties. It would be judged a kindness to release him from his obligations."

Newport said nothing, but looked to Smith for rebuttal. He was not disappointed.

"Yes, but Master Hunt has made it plain to me that he would rather die of sea sickness than give up the mission on which he has been sent. He does not mind the situation as much as Master Wingfield seems to, and if he does not, then we should not. I say let him stay until such time as he requests transfer or return passage. Each man here travels voluntarily and paid for the privilege. Master Hunt deserves our respect for his wishes."

The two petitioners waited for Newport's answer. Wingfield, certain of the power he wielded as patentee, brought his linen handkerchief to his nose and eyed the top of Smith's head. Smith kept his eyes on Newport.

Newport leaned back in his chair, drumming the desk with the fingers of his remaining hand, and thoughtfully considered both men.

He knew both well – too well, perhaps – and while he admired the younger Smith's courage and easy connections with most men regardless of class, he sometimes wished the barrel of a man were more…tactful. As for Wingfield, snobs were insufferable, especially the ones who let social rules interfere with common sense, but he was a powerful force in the Virginia Company's band of profiteers and as such needed to be taken seriously.

Newport could, of course, call in Hunt, but time was pressing and the good of the expedition came before a silly quarrel over one man's puking.

He rose from the desk. "Moving Master Hunt to the coast would require at least a day's transport. As I have just said, we are about to get under way on our original course. We will be landing in the Canary Islands in a few days time and Master Hunt – all of us – will benefit from the respite we'll gain there. Since Hunt has not asked to be relieved of his duties and sent home, nor has his behavior warranted removal for cause, I see no point in delaying the expedition further."

Wingfield's eyes narrowed, and he turned to give Smith a disdainful look, but Smith had vanished before Newport's last syllables had formed frost in the air.

Chapter Three

A Hanging

Smith settled in next to Captain John Martin, a sickly man whose son was a lad of eighteen with an air of practicality and common sense. Smith approved of the lad but despaired at the elder Martin's frail frame and weak appearance. Although cheerful and pleasant company with a reputation for distinguished military service, Martin in his present state wasn't the kind of man Smith would want to rely on in the heat of battle or in the presence of imminent danger, both of which could be counted upon in savage Virginia.

Martin's son, Will, tall and straight, preferred reclining to standing in a perpetual stoop here between decks, and so lay on his back with hands under his head. He eagerly anticipated the adventure before them and was more than willing to learn from John Smith all that could be learned by listening and watching.

Also admiring of Smith's bravado and good sense was Stephen Halthrop, whose elbows were now digging into Will's side. Not yet twenty and from a conventional mercantile family, Halthrop found Smith exactly the kind of man of action he had always wanted to be. Smith would no more find joy in checking ledger books and supervising clerks than he did. Furthermore, Smith's candor and easy-going charm were refreshing amid those who kept close to themselves out of prejudice or fear; fear of what Halthrop couldn't be sure, but fear it was.

Halthrop turned on his side, placed his hand on the side of his head and addressed Smith. "I was beginning to think we'd never see the end of England. What are the Canaries like, Captain? Are there savages there? Will we stay long? Will we all go ashore?"

"Well, now there's a fine set of questions. I don't know exactly what we'll find because I have not come further south than we are right now. This is all as new to me as it is to you. Savages? Likely not. The islands have been under Spanish rule for some time." Smith put his hands under his head and raised his knees.

"Spain? I know we are at peace, but the war is barely over! Is it not a hazard to stop there?"

"Not when money is freely given and taken for goods received. It appears a mutually beneficial trade is enough to keep politics at naught."

"Captain?" Will leaned closer. "I've been asking around and it seems to me every man jack of us is after gold. If we all go looking for gold once we're in Virginia, who will be guarding our base?"

Smith looked past Captain Martin to Wingfield who was far enough away that he couldn't hear Smith's reply. "Not everyone will be looking for gold."

"But that is the Company's aim!" exclaimed Will, shocked.

"If everyone is in search of gold, there won't be anyone left to tend the settlement and that, as they say, is no way to run a colony. We'll be divided, I'm sure, so that some will be out, some will stay behind and that's not altogether a bad prospect. Gold for the Company is gold for us all, remember."

Smith shifted his weight and waved a well-muscled hand as he continued. "I am more interested in finding the South Sea Passage. Think of the possibilities! Gold in your pocket will make you no different than any other Englishman of wealth. But to have your name writ in the pages of history as the one who discovered the shortest way to the South Sea! Think of Drake! Of Cabot!"

Smith paused to let that sink into the fertile, open minds around him.

"I want to be the leader of the expeditionary forces, and I could use useful lads like you to come along and explore with me. Are you interested?"

The gleam in their eyes shone through the dim light around them.

"Wingfield is looking at you like you owe him money, Captain." Halthrop's voice was even and low.

"Oh, he always looks that way at anyone who does not have 'Esquire' or worse after his name." Will's tone was impatient. Still, Smith decided it was time to change the subject and suggested that they begin Algonkian language lessons from Richard Hakluyt's book. So far, few were interested in learning the language or even parts of it, but Smith reckoned it would be useful when they would inevitably want to confer with the Naturals. He had often wished he had known more Turkish before his captivity in Constantinople.

Wingfield, who heard all despite Smith's efforts, sputtered and pushed aside the servant who was brushing off his doublet. Smith in charge of exploration? By whose orders? Why, this was mutiny! Insupportable, raw mutiny, and Smith would answer for it.

The trial was a mockery of English justice.

No jury, no defense other than the accused's own testimony which was used against him by the prosecution. Being the sole judge and citing his own evidence from his own observations, Wingfield made short work of the proceedings; neither Gosnold nor Ratcliffe, the two other ships' Captains, would have anything to do with it. Although the men on the *Susan Constant* were surprised to hear that Smith was a mutineer, no one dared cross Wingfield; he held too much power as patentee.

Few listening to the trial in the crowded bowels of that ship were convinced that Smith had mutiny in mind or that Wingfield held impartial views.

"I declare John Smith guilty of the crime of mutiny and sentence him to hang by the neck till dead."

Wingfield did not anticipate the riot that occurred with these words and was stunned to hear the roar and see the angry faces moving toward him.

The push of the throng was held back only by Admiral Newport's shouts as he came down the ladder.

"What the blazes are you doing? Back! Back! Every one of you hold your tongues or I'll have you all whipped!" The crowd parted to let him through. "Edward, did I hear you say you're going to hang Captain Smith?"

"That is what this court has decreed," Wingfield replied.

Newport, now standing in front of the portly Wingfield, raised his hand and his voice. "Now, gentlemen, let me assure you—let me assure you," he said more loudly, "that Captain Smith will not be hanged—not just yet anyway."

Wingfield's face lost some its smug satisfaction, and in its place small fear and uncertainty took root.

"As Admiral of this fleet, I have the authority to impose the death sentence when I will, and I do not, I repeat, I do not wish to impose it in any manner that might be taken as hasty or without the seriousness such a sentence deserves. Furthermore, I will not hang a passenger on board my ship nor on any in this tiny fleet. Therefore, be about the business of going ashore and do not fret about Captain Smith. He is now officially under my jurisdiction and will remain there until such time as I decide when – or if—to fulfill Master Wingfield's sentence."

Newport, his eyes steady on every man as he left the lower deck, maintained his position in front of Wingfield not knowing if he should just let the men at him.

Smith's feelings were equally ungenerous. What a fool! That old man, he thought, has earned the disdain of every man here and no amount of status or money will erase that from their memory. Not now and certainly not when they reached Virginia and were setting up the governing body as decreed by the Charter. How could a man hope to govern those who thought him foolish, shortsighted, and morally corrupt? For surely as Smith's father had been a farmer, Wingfield would be named to the Council. Money and privilege and patents secured much in this world.

Newport watched the last of the men depart, including Smith, and then steeled himself to speak with Wingfield who had sunk onto the barrel that had served as his judicial seat. Wingfield pulled his handkerchief from the silk lining of his doublet, dabbed his nostrils, and arched a supercilious eyebrow waiting for Newport to speak.

"Edward," Newport began, trying to control his own anger. "I serve the Company, as you well know, and I am bound to deliver this contingent of colonists to the shores of Virginia. I promised to deliver them all and, barring disease or an act of war or God that deprives us of men, I intend to do so. I do not intend to lose any colonists to dissention or to the unreasonable acts of any one passenger. You, sir, are a passenger on my ship and I will not permit you to hang anyone. Doing so will be taken as an act of mutiny against me, and I can assure you that you would receive the same sentence you have handed Smith."

Wingfield's mouth twitched and the thin line of his lips hardened as he considered Newport's words.

"I see." Wingfield's lips drew tighter. "Well, then. Is there any reason why he cannot be held in restraint? He is a nuisance, to say the least. Let us keep him under arrest, then, until we draw up our Council in Virginia as the Instructions tell us to, and let the Council decide whether to finish what we have started here."

"What you've started here. Don't put my name on the deed."

"So he will remain restrained then?"

"To the best we can under such conditions, yes, I suppose we can keep Smith under arrest. But no hanging. Are we agreed?" Newport held out his left hand. Wingfield took it in a gentleman's agreement.

When all but a skeleton crew, Smith and Newport had moved onto the island to partake in its delights, Newport offered Smith a flagon of wine, which he gladly took.

"You must have been born under a lucky star," Newport said.

"What do you mean? I am going to hang soon. And for something I did not do. I don't call that lucky." Smith drained his cup.

"No, my friend, you'll not be hanged. At least, not by Edward Wingfield or any time soon."

Smith let out a blast of breath and grinned, his mustache twitching. "Does he know that?"

"Yes, he does. I appealed to his obvious sense of justice by threatening to hang him for hanging you against my orders. But I could not convince him to set you free altogether, so I am afraid you must live under restraint until we settle in Virginia, and the Council decides what to do with you."

Smith stroked the underside of his wiry beard with the back of his hand.

Newport continued. "There is a way, of course, around that agreement without seeming to, if you are interested. We can appease Wingfield and still give you a certain amount of freedom."

"Freedom is a limited commodity on such a small ship. What sort of plan circumvents that?"

"While under sail, you keep to yourself in the brig we have fashioned, but you may visit and stretch and eat with the other passengers as needed. When we land to take on supplies and to rest as we do here in the Canaries, why, then you'll go ashore under guard but be free to move about as you please."

"I'll be under arrest in name only?"

"Yes. Things will work themselves out on land. Wingfield is feeling a little too crowded and is not used to such close proximity to the lesser sort."

Smith started to protest.

"I know," interrupted Newport, raising his hand. "I know. But in English society, he is the better sort; that you cannot deny. Here I warn you, John. Avoid confrontation with Wingfield. Tweaking his nose will do you no good. You keep to yourself and all will be right while we sail." Newport seemed satisfied with the whole idea.

"A most agreeable arrangement," said Smith, pleased that he would not be hanged and delighted to be separated from Wingfield's company even if it were on such dubious grounds. "I will need a guard, I suppose."

"That will contribute to the appearance of arrest."

"Who do you have in mind?"

"It matters not. Name your man."

"Master Stephen Halthrop."

With the Canary Islands behind them, the food stores replenished and the men refreshed, the three ships headed for the West Indies. The early March winds worked to their advantage and the quarreling quieted. Smith's trial and subsequent death sentence had jolted the Company men back to civility, at least for the present.

And so, at Nevis Island in the West Indies at the end of six days of rest in the tropical sun, Newport was surprised to come across three colonists building a gallows in haste and with language that would have raised the eyebrows of his saltiest sailors. He guessed who the gallows was for – it had to be Smith – but why now?

Had they been in England, a solid oak tree with heavy lower limbs would have been their choice for a makeshift gallows; here, with only palm trees to serve as Death's courier, the matter was more challenging. The colonists had produced a serviceable platform with a gallows and were throwing a noose over the top when Newport arrived.

Smith was not in sight, which Newport deemed an advantage. He cleared his throat as he approached the volatile men who, noting the Admiral's presence stopped both their work and the colorful descriptions of what they wanted to see done to Smith's body and soul.

"Explain yourselves," said Newport, waiting.

The men had the wit to look uncomfortable and, after a long pause, one stepped forward, hiding the hammer behind his back. A man with arms the size of small cannons, his hair was dark, stringy with sweat, and staining the collar of his white shirt. His large black eyes were deep-set, eyes that never looked directly at the Admiral, cool and elegant in the extreme.

"You see, sir," he started, "we was jus' finishin' what was started afore. We know you don't want no hangin' on your ships and we would never do that, knowin' how you feel, sir." He stopped, sure that this was explanation enough.

"What's your name, sirrah? I don't recognize you from the *Susan Constant*."

"James Read, sir."

"And what is your commission on this expedition, Read?"

"I am the blacksmith, sir," said Read raising his head slightly. "And I'm travelin' on the *Discovery*, sir, with Captain Ratcliffe."

"And these two men with you?"

"This here's Will Laxon and Edward Pising. They be carpenters." The two men nodded their respects to the Admiral.

"So I see. They do fine work. Now, tell me what the devil is going on. I can see you're working on a hanging—not on one of my ships, thank you." Newport suppressed a smile. "Just who will you be hanging today?"

Anger swept aside uncertainty on the three faces before him. Read let it burst from him. "That lousy knave, Smith, a-course. The one what calls himself Captain. Captain! — Damnable liar!—Beggin' your pardon, sir.— Why, he's no more a captain than I am. Not in His Majesty's service, I mean. Or for the Queen, God rest all Christian souls."

"But you can't hang a man for that, Read. Surely you have other reasons."

In truth he did, although Newport wasn't sure they were any better than the first. It wasn't until Wingfield's name crept into Read's rambling narrative that Newport began to understand. Read believed Smith required hanging because Wingfield and Kendall had convinced him it was so.

When Read had finished listing Smith's offenses, Newport asked where the convicted man was. Read moved his shoulders in a half-hearted shrug. Wingfield had sent two men to collect Smith a while back, and they had not returned. "We only just finished the gallows, sir, so it weren't much use to have him here afore, was it?"

Newport paused to consider this bit of smithy wisdom, then said, "There'll be no hanging today or any other day, Read. You three are to dismantle this contraption and report back to the ships. I'll see to Captain Smith."

Read wiped his face with a dirty hand, motioned to the others to do as the Admiral bid, and reluctantly joined them. Gone were the oaths, and in their place a sullen silence settled throughout the island vegetation.

Smith stumbled out of the palm trees, his shirt soiled with sweat and blood and hanging loose under his jerkin. His slops were torn from waist to knee on the right side, and his stockings had fallen for lack of garters. Breathing heavily, he slackened his jaw to allow more air in, and each hand gripped a pistol. His hair, usually pushed back, dangled over his forehead and in his eyes in wavy, sweat-soaked lines. Skidding on the sand and dropping to his knees, the sound of snapping branches and hurried footsteps behind him caused him to raise his pistols in anticipation, aiming at the sound and praying he aimed true.

Halthrop, emerging from the trees, limped to his friend's side. "You should have seen them run, Captain!" he gasped. "They won't come after you again! Ha!"

Relieved to see a friendly countenance, Smith withdrew the guns and said between breaths, "No. They won't. Try to hang me, will they?" Sweat dripped from his nose and ears. "Where are they now?"

"I don't know. Probably with the ships over yonder. They looked too scared to come after you any more." Halthrop whistled while catching his breath. "I've never seen a man take on two brutes like that and still live to talk about it. Where did you learn to do that? And you didn't even use a pistol!" He paused. "Sorry I was not more help."

Smith, his breathing returned to normal, put a hand on Halthrop's shoulder. "They were smart to tie you up while trying to capture me. I'd have done the same in their place. Why fight two when one is all you need to take with you?"

"Will you report this to the Admiral?"

"To what end? I'm still here. The problem is Wingfield, not his henchmen. And I cannot prove that Wingfield was behind this sudden invitation to swing from a rope, can you?"

Halthrop shook his head as much in amazement as in answer to the question. Smith's calm, rational demeanor in the face of death surprised him. Smith accepted everything, even threats to his person, as if someone had unwittingly brought him ale instead of wine.

Smiling at his hurt friend, Smith offered assistance in walking the sloped beach. "Wingfield may lay all the traps he pleases. In the end, he will be his own undoing, one way or the other, and I will be as ever I was. Now. Let us hie to the ships, lad. The next time we make land, it shall be in Virginia!"

Chapter Four

Meeting the Naturals

"Be still, Master Archer! Be still! You'll live. Men do not die from an arrow shot into their hand." Thomas Wooten coolly assessed the bloody hand with an arrow head clean through on one side and feathers on the other. The sight reminded the barber surgeon of a conjurer's trick he had once seen in London. He snapped off the feathered side, and then pulled the remaining shaft out the other.

Archer roared then grabbed a cup of beer to drown out the pain. Wooten cleaned the wound as best he could and wrapped it in linen. "There now. You see? That shall keep you, sir. No, sir, not a drop for me. Thank you just the same."

Gabriel Archer, solid and large with heavy eyebrows that merged into one line he wielded like a weapon, gulped the last of the brew, tossed aside the cup, and left. He was irked to be injured in what was a lame, grossly inadequate attack by five Naturals. He was even more disgusted that he alone had been hurt.

This, the Company's first day upon Virginia soil, had been a joy; the Atlantic coastline beckoned with unfettered sunshine, temperate April breezes, a pleasing, sandy landscape, and solitude everywhere.

Archer, George Percy, Newport and a handful of soldiers had dallied on shore till after sunset. In the light of the moon, full and gloriously uninhibited by clouds, Archer had heard the arrow before he saw it slice into his hand, not quite sure how it had appeared there. Five Naturals, naked scouts, had crept along the underbrush nearby and fired their arrows at the unwanted white men. Archer and his men had dropped to the ground, firing pistols without much regard for accuracy, sending the attackers scurrying off in a whooping frenzy.

Archer, thirty-two, gentleman lawyer, spat over the side of the *Godspeed*, trying to think of way to work this incident to his advantage in the narrative he would compose for the official record; the pain in his hand kept him from thinking clearly – but he was sure he would come up with an answer soon enough. He always did.

George Percy interrupted the thought. "Come now, Archer. The Admiral is about to open the boxes. You want to be there, do you not, when the names of the Council are read?"

"Of course," answered Archer aloud, thinking but you probably don't, you poor bastard.

Percy, eighth son of the eighth Earl of Northumberland, long of limb, with a sallow complexion and a face generously described as plain, had no reason to think his own name would be read – three older brothers were in the Tower for conspiring in the Gunpowder Plot two years ago and a cousin had been killed trying to enact it. Though he had played no part in the deed, his name was no more likely to appear on the list than King Phillip's. It probably didn't hurt that Wingfield was a distant cousin, but it wasn't enough to loosen the brotherly ties that bind. Catholic ties.

"To the *Susan Constant*, then," said Archer, resting his injured hand across his breast to ease the pain.

"Gosnold. Wingfield. Ratcliffe. Martin. Kendall. Smith."

Newport paused. A rolling murmur of the gathered Company, all one hundred and four of them, bubbled up and then receded. Smith was as surprised as anyone else that his name was called. Certainly Wingfield had not arranged it. John Ratcliffe, Captain of the *Discovery*, quiet and bland, had no connection with Smith at all. Martin was the sickly passenger with the pasty complexion. Never met him before we sailed, thought Smith, nor Kendall. No, the only possible benefactor could be Bartholomew Gosnold; he must have put in a kind word with the King's Council, as Smith could not account for any other source of such fortune. On the Virginia Council! Smith smiled in spite of himself and bounced on his heels.

Newport continued. "Our President, to be elected from this Council, will govern with the Council. Matters of moment are to be examined by a jury, but determined by the major part of the Council, in which the President has two votes. I am appointed to oversee the Council when I am in Virginia, and shall carry one vote as well on such occasions."

Newport paused again, waiting for Wingfield's undoubted objection. He was not disappointed.

"But, Admiral." Wingfield's voice was cloying. "Smith is under arrest, as you are well aware. He cannot possibly be permitted to serve on the Council under such conditions." He sniffed.

"The list was drawn up by the King's Council, with the King's blessing."

"But before Smith was arrested. They would be the first to agree that his disgrace is cause for removal." Wingfield saw a way to win while appearing to give a little. "At least, he should not be allowed to vote for President. Once that matter is concluded, let the Council decide what is to become of him."

Newport, hoping for the best, agreed that this course seemed most fair and looked apologetically at Smith. The Council members, now sworn in except for Smith, voted Edward Wingfield as their first President.

Smith held his tongue. It did not matter to him if he were Council or not; explorers did not need to be governmental leaders. "He invested the most money," Smith whispered to Halthrop during the applause, "so he is the best of the better sort here, if you believe that sort of thing. Money and rank speak loudly, even across an ocean."

After an oration by Archer who used all his lawyerly skills to argue against swearing in Smith—he was a madcap ruffian, a wanton mutineer who deserved arrest or worse—and an equally compelling speech by Bartholomew Gosnold who used his own legal training to argue for admitting Smith – there was no evidence of mutiny, Smith had been a model prisoner, on his best behavior, and the King's command must be obeyed—the votes were cast. Aye, it must have been Gosnold's influence, thought Smith.

With Wingfield's two votes guaranteed, only two Council members needed to agree with him to eliminate Smith from the Council. John Martin, preferring to be in a President's good graces, and George Kendall, still holding a grudge for Smith's interference in the Hunt matter, resolved the issue to Wingfield's satisfaction and Smith's pointed indifference.

"Well, you know who's for you, at least," Halthrop said later. "Captain Gosnold. And the Admiral. That's mighty good company, if you ask me."

Smith didn't answer right away. The two men had settled in for sleep, still crammed together in the bowels of the *Susan Constant*. No one was allowed off the ships after the evening's earlier attack. He stroked his beard, occupied with other thoughts. Never one to dwell on the past, even the immediate past, Smith had turned his mind to the matter of plantation.

"And Ratcliffe abstained. So I am not on the Council," he said. "That does not matter so much. I am amazed to find the King's Council named me to lead.

I am more interested in exploring than governing. But other matters must come first."

"Such as?"

"We need to find a place to build our fort; then we can proceed with the business of finding the South Sea Passage. That's where our glory lies."

"A fort? That's our big colony? A fort?" Halthrop hadn't pictured it quite that way.

"Yes, a fort. What did you expect? A city? A town? From nothing? Why, you saw what happened our first day here – the natives attacked! Surely you don't think that was the most they have to offer. Remember Roanoke. Remember that these Naturals live here and we are just visiting, at least for now. Today was a reminder that we need to be fortified before we do anything else. Self-protection should be our first concern. Everything else carries no weight because we could be dead before we take root."

"I had not thought of that."

"No, and you can wager your last pair of boots that Wingfield hasn't either. He's memorized the *Instructions*, and they say we're 'not to offend the Naturals,' and we're to create profit as soon as possible, which will lead us into a fool's paradise."

"Why? I think not making trouble is a good idea."

"Because, my friend, not offending is only part of the bargain – our part. What if they offend us first? Are we to stand by and not defend ourselves? This all comes from the problems we had in Roanoke, I can assure you. They all think that White's colonists – or the two groups before—somehow offended the Naturals and were massacred for it. Thus, by their great logic, if we don't offend them, they will leave us alone. Ha!"

"So we need to find a place to settle – to build a fort – and then we're off to explore. But you are still under arrest. What of that?" Halthrop raised an interesting point.

"I don't know," Smith admitted, "but, give me time; I'm sure I'll work out something. After all, as you say, I have the Admiral and Gosnold taking my part."

On May 13th, six months and a thousand lifetimes from London, the fractious Company claimed their new home on a tree-filled island and called it "Jamestown."

"Forty miles upriver, on an island, as directed, and with the convenience of tying our ships to trees on the island itself. What a boon!" Wingfield, giddy at such a choice, ordered the off-loading of all supplies and materials. "You, Smith! What are you doing?"

Smith, who had been counting paces parallel to the shoreline, stopped and turned. "Measuring for the front palisade of our fort."

"Stop at once. We are not building a fort."

All movement within earshot on ship and shore ceased.

"Not building a fort?" Smith could do nothing but repeat the phrase.

"We mustn't give the impression of hostility. And we have no need to fear. We are nowhere near a native village or settlement. These Naturals will not bother us here, and if they do, our guns and cannons will frighten them away. You shall see that I am quite right."

"Not building a fort?" Smith began to recover. "Are you mad? Exposed day and night without protection?"

Wingfield sniffed deeply. "I said no fort. I do not recall asking for your opinion."

Smith snapped his mouth shut and sought out Halthrop and Sam who were pitching tents a hundred feet down river.

"I confess I am amazed," he said as he helped with the canvas and ropes. "I had not thought Wingfield this sublimely stupid." Shaking his head and slapping his thigh, Smith lowered his voice. "Best keep your pistols handy and an ear cocked whilst you sleep. We will not be alone long."

A knot of red-dyed deer hair crowned the chief's head, the two feathers sticking out of the coronet like horns. A hundred nearly naked bowmen with dark drawings on their limbs surrounded him. Although a round copper plate covered the right side of the chief's head, Smith could easily see that the hair that should have been underneath it was shaved close to the scalp. And for all that the right side of his head was shorn, the left side was long, dark and oiled.

The leader's body, strong and lean, was painted crimson and a great chain of copper beads hung from his neck. Blue paint, sprinkled with a silvery ore, covered his face and caused his eyes to sink deep into his skull. From each regal ear dangled a large pearl bracelet with a copper-encrusted bird claw. A leather loincloth covered his privates, but the rest of his body was an artist's canvas of colors, swirls, textures, and tints. With a few words and motions he indicated his name was Wowinchopunk, king of the Pasbeheghs, and he expected the English to lay down their weapons.

"He's a werowance," Smith whispered to Halthrop.

"Wear a what?"

"Werowance. A native king."

"What does he want?" Halthrop asked.

"Probably testing to see why we are here. If he wanted to attack us, he'd have done it by now."

Ignoring the obvious attempt to disarm them, Admiral Newport and Wingfield stood before the werowance and signaled for him to join them at what was passing for a table: hickory logs hewn into rough planes with fresh tree stumps serving as chairs. Wowinchopunk, King of the Pasbeheghs, eyed the table and raised a powerful arm, saying something to one of his bowmen.

From the back of the hoard came two youths carrying a deer tied by its hooves to a tree branch which they dropped at Newport's feet and returned to the ranks behind Wowinchopunk. Newport and Wingfield smiled and nodded their thanks, but when it became clear that some forty of the werowance's braves were to spend the night at Jamestown, the pleasantries evaporated. When Wowinchopunk refused to accept the English denial of accommodations and started to have his braves settle in, Newport decided to act.

"Smith," Newport said evenly, without taking his eyes off Wowinchopunk, "take six men and fire your pistols at the trees over there, if you don't mind. Once will do. We need to show our guests what would happen if they try to stay uninvited."

While Smith and his men readied their pistols, a bowman who had become bored with the proceedings spied a hatchet protruding from a tree stump where a colonist had left it to take arms. Now the bowman pulled it out, tested the sharpness of the blade, and walked away with the prize.

The hatchet's owner, taking umbrage at such brazen thievery, strode over to the offender and with a loud "Oy, there!" grabbed the hatchet. With the back of his hand, he slapped the youth's upper arm in rebuff.

The entire contingent of white and native men turned to see another Pasbehegh youth unleash a wooden club and raise it over his head. Indignation and anger burned in his dark eyes as he swooped toward the colonist.

At the same moment, every colonist with a pistol or musket raised his weapon, cocked the hammer, and aimed at the attacking youth who had stopped, club in midair, at the unfamiliar sound of metal weaponry.

Nobody moved, nobody breathed. It was as if an artist had required them to hold a pose while sketching their likeness.

Finally, Newport, with steady voice said, "Now, Captain Smith. Fire your pistol at a tree."

Smith complied, moving slowly to show his good intentions. The lead musket ball slammed into a full-grown specimen, splintering the trunk and revealing fresh wood, leaving behind a strangely mixed odor of cedar and gunpowder. Smith stepped back behind Newport and was satisfied to see the visitors retreat to a neutral stance.

Wowinchopunk angrily waved his arm in a great arc signaling the end of the visit and stormed away, his features changing to purplish-red under the blue paint, the copper-dipped bird claws raking his neck.

"I reckon he knows what we're about now," observed Halthrop.

Drawing a collective breath of relief, the Company returned to the immediate tasks of felling oak trees for clapboard, clearing a field for planting, and building the storehouse for their victuals and supplies. Some were apprehensive about the visit, but Wingfield stressed that the kindness and restraint shown by the English would benefit them all in due course. Demonstrating the superiority of their weapons had proven persuasive testimony to the natives that the English were not to be interfered with, he reminded them. There was no cause to worry on any account and certainly no cause to erect fortifications that would imply hostility.

"I don't think that wer-o-wance was impressed with our 'kindness,' " Halthrop said to Smith as they hauled clapboard. "He looked mighty angry when he left. I think we need protection beyond a puny pile of sticks that wouldn't keep out a dog." Someone had managed to draw together several boughs into a crescent around part of the encampment. "Our tents are open to any sort of attack they would want to try!"

"You're certainly right, my boy," said Smith, "but you and I have no power to change the Council's mind – or should I say Wingfield's mind. As wrong as he is, he truly believes what he's saying. Just keep your pistol and daggers ready. I doubt we'll have much warning when they do attack."

A week into their settlement, Admiral Newport decided to take twenty-five men to explore upriver. The Company and the sailors were making progress on the storehouse and field and could continue with minimal supervision. Doubts, however, plagued Newport, and he conferred with Captain Gosnold.

Bartholomew Gosnold, second in command, stood with Newport on the deck of the *Susan Constant*. The late May evening was delightfully cool and

Gosnold closed his eyes and drew into his lungs the glorious fragrance of newly leafed forests and salty river air.

Gosnold, thirty-five, was a man of substantial means, modest fashion and exceptional teeth. Comely, kind, even tempered, with an intelligent air and a quick understanding of any situation. It was at his home in Suffolk that he had met with his cousin Wingfield, the sea captain Newport, and friend Smith to promote this Virginia Venture. He had invested most of his money, time, and heart into the enterprise; now that they were here, he would do everything in his power to make it a success. He trusted Newport as he trusted no other.

He turned toward Newport, smiled, and said, "Well, sir, I assume you asked me here for more than a breath of air, as pleasant as it is. I am at your service."

Newport wasted no time. "Let us call it a favor. As you know, we are required to explore upriver. We had planned on taking twenty-five men, including you, then dividing into two groups. One of us would continue on upriver, the other would put axes to earth in search of gold. The Company requires this to be done, and I am most eager to begin." He paused.

"And so am I, but you know that already."

"Yes. Well. What of Wingfield?"

The question startled Gosnold who had been expecting some other line of conversation. He deliberately looked up into the velvet sky at the North Star, then down at his hands draped over the ship's railing and said evenly, "I think we hold the same opinion, sir. As my cousin, Edward has always been loyal and kind to me, but he is a man with a foolish head and a small heart. I fear that he could not lead a fleet of paper boats down a gutter. Yet, for better or worse, he is our duly-elected President."

"And Smith?" Newport looked at Gosnold out of the corner of his eye.

Gosnold began to see where Newport's concerns lay. "He's a remarkably good sailor for a soldier, isn't he? Smith has borne his arrest admirably, and has been especially forbearing concerning the denial of his position on the Council. I would say he is a man who needs to be useful and hates to see waste. I rather like his willingness to act for what he knows to be right, even if he encounters trouble when he does so. But you know all this."

"And can you predict what the situation would be if we – you, Percy, Archer and I – left for several weeks with Wingfield in charge here and only Martin, Ratcliffe and Kendall to back him up? Martin who's sick, Ratcliffe who does not involve himself with anything, and Kendall who causes dissention at every opportunity? And Smith under arrest—at least on paper—but free to move about the settlement?"

"Death and destruction at our own hands. It wouldn't take the Spanish or the savages to ruin our Expedition." Gosnold rubbed the wooden railing and turned to face his friend and admiral.

"Precisely. Which is why I wanted to talk with you. What say you to having Smith take your place on the exploration and you stay here to lend reason to the unreasonable?"

"I should rather explore than be a nursemaid to boys in men's slops."

"But are you content to make it so?"

Gosnold gave the matter thought before saying, "You are my commander, sir, and I will gladly do your bidding for the good of the Company."

"Let it be done, then. We'll leave tomorrow. And many thanks, Bart, many thanks." Newport clapped his friend on the back and left him there to admire the stars on his own.

By mid-day, Newport and his twenty-odd men departed in the shallop that had been reassembled upon landing in Virginia. The shallop, a large, open boat equipped with seven pairs of oars and a single bow-mounted sail, could easily navigate the river when it became narrower and shallower. The original plan had been to spend two full months sailing upriver to determine the extent of the waterway, and to look for the coveted South Sea Passage and gold, but the late December start and the subsequent lolling in the English Channel had placed the Venture so far behind schedule that one week was all they could afford. Newport, along with the *Susan Constant* and *Godspeed*, would need to return to England with clapboard and gold in time to turn around yet again and bring fresh supplies to the Virginia colony before winter set in.

As the shallop sailed past the Pasbehegh village several miles north of Jamestown, the Naturals clustered on the shore to watch the white men in armor. Wowinchopunk was nowhere to be seen. While the Naturals did not wave or in any way signal they were happy to see the broad, flat boat filled with English, they did not shoot arrows or yell angrily either. They, in fact, stood in silence as Newport sailed on, ignoring the crowd and looking forward up the waterway the Council had dubbed the King's River.

After an uneventful night anchored near a low meadow, the explorers moved northward to an island where they stopped for a breakfast of wildfowl.

In the midst of their succulent feast, a canoe bearing four nearly naked braves pulled up on shore.

With a great show of welcome, Newport offered the natives a portion of the juicy, roasted flesh, which they gladly took. All was smiles and laughter while Newport tried to persuade his guests to tell them what lay up the river. From his bag he pulled a handful of small bells that tinkled prettily as they tumbled into open palms. From another bag, Newport grabbed copper beads and added those to the bells. Chuckles of delight told Newport that the baubles were well received.

"Admiral," Smith said quietly while the braves were entertaining themselves with the gifts. "You should be more careful, sir, about how many and how often you dole out these little trinkets. They will lose value if too many are spread about too quickly."

"What? Oh, I see. Yes. Well. Can't be helped now."

One of the Naturals, a youth of twenty years or so, with eyes that were calm and observant, stood up and brushed aside debris that covered the dirt at his feet. Using his big toe, he began to make marks on the dirt, every now and again looking up at Newport or Smith for signs of recognition. At first, neither knew what to make of the dirt designs, but gradually, with much hand gesturing and toe drawing, they realized that their young visitor was describing what the river and land were like further north.

Archer, seizing the moment, brought forth a paper and pen with ink. The brave watched attentively as Archer recreated the river as far as the white man knew it. Within minutes the native, understanding completely, continued drawing with his toe the river and its landmarks as far as he knew it. There seemed to be a great waterfall near another island, but, more profoundly, only two kingdoms and a mountain range were all that separated the English from what they were looking for—the South Sea!

The Englishmen could hardly believe their good fortune. The South Sea!

"Let us pack up our lot, men, and be quick about it. Thank you, sir," said Newport, shaking the young man's arm in a very English manner that puzzled him. "Thank you! No, we cannot stay any longer. No, you keep your corn."

The youth with the talented toe and one of his comrades climbed into the canoe, watching the excited white men eagerly clearing their gear, while their remaining friends stayed on shore. When the English shallop shoved off and made its way up river, the natives followed patiently both on land and by canoe. Occasionally, the map-drawer would shout an offer of food in exchange for more bells or one of his friends would ask for beads, but Newport and his men ignored the requests and pushed on.

By mid-day, their escorts had divided up and only the canoeists continued in attendance. The river had narrowed considerably, and the land on either side had gradually changed from even meadowland to slight rolling hills and small bluffs. The mountain range the map-drawer had told them about was certainly growing nearer.

The canoes pulled up alongside the shallop and, with a round of high-pitched whoops, the followers called to their tribesmen and women.

The Arrohattocs had prepared a feast for the white visitors. The entire village had gathered to greet the English with great ceremony. They were nearly naked, as all the Naturals were, wearing only a leather skin for an apron, and had either painted their bodies or had tattooed rectangles, squares, and borders on their limbs. The men had no beards, wore their hair long on the left side as the Pasbeheghs did and were lean and well muscled. The women were equally unclothed, to the sailors' delight, and not in the least ashamed of it. Bedecked in copper, the werowance raised both hands and spoke for what seemed an hour before he ultimately led the group to the feast where a special mat had been laid for the white werowance, Newport.

Before the food was brought forward, the werowance and his selected leaders carefully washed and dried their hands and expected their visitors to do likewise.

"I would say this is damned pleasant company, almost civilized!" said Percy to Archer who was seated beside him. "I don't know if we will find such a fine reception in London when we return. But I am confused. This werowance is not the same one who came to Jamestown. Just how many kings does a country need?"

Percy accepted the smoked fish and flat bread made of cornmeal offered to him by his Arrohattoc neighbor and rearranged his long legs for comfort. The brave momentarily held Percy's hand to observe closely the stub of his left middle finger, a souvenir of a battle years before. Percy didn't mind, really. He usually forgot that his hand was not normal. Most of the Company's gentlemen had battle scars; some were just more visible than others.

Seated around Archer, Percy and his inquisitive friend, interspersed with Arrohattocs were the Admiral, Smith, and the surgeon Wooten. Smith answered for Archer.

"I am beginning to think that 'werowance' doesn't mean king or sovereign in the way we are used to it. From what I understood of the speech we just heard, there are many werowances, and they are leaders for their tribes. But there is one Great Chief whose name is Powhatan and he is chief of the chiefs. He was mentioned several times and I think we would do well to note whatever we could about him. He seems to be respected and feared."

During the long feast, which included many courses of meat, fish, beans, corn and baked breads that sometimes resembled English cooking but more often did not, the men watched as native women and men danced around them, the beat of the drums steady and strong for an hour. When the meal was finally finished, the Arrohattocs offered pipes of tobacco and were delighted when the English produced their own clay pipes to share. Smith and his friends willingly shared what they had knowing a barrel full of pipes was waiting back at Jamestown.

All but Smith partook of the Arrohattoc's tobacco – much more powerful and intense than the tobacco the English had from the West Indies. Newport, Percy and Archer coughed and swallowed hard on first puffing, but soon grew accustomed to the potency. Smith, like King James, found smoking to be a vile, filthy habit, and declined graciously, then stared into the fire as they all enjoyed the respite from trying to communicate verbally. Here was communication that needed no words.

The peacefulness of the moment was broken, however, when a youth burst from the crowd. "The Great Powatah! He comes!"

As Powatah, a man of thirty-odd years, tall, powerful in appearance, with the sun blazing over his head, proceeded, the crowd parted, hushed and reverent and eager to please. The Arrohattocs jumped to their feet and then fell to their knees in respect.

The English did not. They waited in silence for the Great Powatah to seat himself on a mat and speak to them. When he did, he was commanding, not belligerent. Newport signaled for Archer to bring forth a bag of gifts.

The same bells and beads used earlier that day brought appreciative murmurs from the crowd, but Archer also laid two dozen solid English penny knives and shears in the great chief's hands. Smith tried, by coughing discreetly, to prevent so many gifts in such a short time, but no one heeded him. Newport and Archer shot him irritated looks.

Powatah, delighted with the gifts, returned the gesture by assigning five of his youthful braves to accompany Newport up river, to serve as guides. He would meet at his royal residence with the white werowance. The English, bellies full, hearts content, and eager to see the South Sea, accepted and departed for the shallop.

As the broad boat made its way up river, clusters of natives whooped and yelled in happy enthusiasm for them on from the riverbank.

"We seem to have made great friends, wouldn't you say, Smith?" asked Percy.

"It's possible."

"Don't you trust them?"

"More or less," said Smith. "I trust them more when I can see them, less when I cannot."

Percy laughed. "I don't think we have too much to worry about right now. They damned well could have tried to kill us back there, but they didn't."

"Never trust anyone unless you have reason to. So far, we have no reason to think these Naturals will not murder us in our sleep. They have done nothing but feast with us and talk gibberish. They have not had to prove their loyalty to us in any way. That is when you figure out who your real friends are."

Percy shook his head with a rueful smile and turned to look where the guides had begun to point in silence. A high hill by the water flanked a plain some twelve paces beyond where grew fields of corn, beans, peas, tobacco, pumpkins, gourds, hemp, flax and more. It was a magnificent sight. Richly textured, fresh and well ordered. Such bounty signified wealth and power and intelligence on Powatah's part. He was great indeed.

Waiting for Newport and his four companions were both the werowance of the Arrohattocs and Powatah, sitting in silent splendor, calm and patient. Newport and Powatah, through hand signals and broken words learned from Hakluyt, managed to communicate several important ideas.

"Cheisk," Powatah repeated several times while casting his arm in a wide circle. "Cheisk." Newport took this to mean that all the Naturals in the area were under this man's power and protection.

Powatah further demonstrated that the Chesapeakes were not friendly at which Archer stepped forward and showed his hand.

"Chesapeakes did this to me! See? I'm barely healed." He traced the wound with a finger from the opposite hand, making sure to show both sides of the hurt hand. "I will take my revenge when I can!"

No one was sure if Powatah understood the spoken words, but they could see from the look on his face that he recognized an arrow injury and that this particular Englishman could be an ally. Looking over the group of white men, he then proposed that they and the Powatah people be united in friendship against all enemies.

Newport, without conferring with his own men, took the great black woolen cape from his own shoulders, placed it around Powatah's large torso and signified that this made the treaty legal by saying what he thought were words for the greatest friendship, "Wingapo chemuze!"

Powatah then reached forward, took Newport's right hand and hooked the white man's forefinger with his own in a sign that all readily recognized as union. He refused, however, to escort the party any further, nor would he allow them to go on alone.

Newport, after conferring with Archer, Percy and Smith, concluded, "With the South Sea route so nearby, we can afford to indulge the chief now and come back later for access when such blatant disregard of his wishes might not be noticed. That is the best path."

Sailing back toward Jamestown with the moon hung low enough to touch, Percy leaned over to Smith and said in a low voice, "What more could the King ask for? We have made alliance with the great chief of all the savages and found the river that connects us to the South Sea! And we've only been here a few weeks!"

Smith nodded and remained silent. Four more days and the little expedition would be back at Jamestown—if it still existed—with unparalleled good news to share. It has all been too easy, he thought, too remarkably, irresistibly easy. And that's what bothered him.

Chapter Five

Defending the Company

Four boys, drawn by the rhythmic slapping of the river on small rocks and longing to swim, escaped the confines of the tent-town on a bright Tuesday morning just after Common Prayer. The Admiral and his exploring men had been absent five days and nothing had occurred save the sporadic comings and goings of one or two Naturals who seemed interested in the English way of life. The boys, weary of routine both dull and heavy, sought to refresh themselves on the banks of the King's River, within easy reach of the camp.

The oldest was Smith's page, Sam, tall for his age, sinewy, with feet and hands that promised he would be as broad and sturdy as any as wrestler once he was fully grown. His straight, coarse hair was black as printer's ink and his eyes, keen and sensitive, were the color of honey, fringed with the thick, dark lashes that young maids coveted for themselves.

In challenge Sam elbowed Nathaniel, a year younger and a hand's breadth shorter, and the two broke into a run, laughter free and joyful bubbling from their lips as they galloped to the river's edge, kicking off their shoes, pulling off hose and doublets as they went. They charged into the icy spring water with gasps and splashes, urging the two younger boys, Richard and James, to do the same. The ten-year-olds—one all freckles and curly hair, the other brown as a berry—ever eager to imitate the older boys, grinned in anticipation and obliged them.

From the bow of the *Susan Constant*, one of the sailors on duty watched enviously as the boys jumped and dove, kicked and paddled, spewing water and mild epithets at each other.

"Oy – take care out there, lads!" said the sailor. "The current's strong and dangerous."

Intending to make the ship a diving platform, the boys swam as one toward the vessel. Up the side ropes they clambered as easily as spiders on a curtain. Wiping the river water from their eyes, they pushed and shoved and sloshed their way to the bow then leapt in merry succession into the brackish bath.

Three figures climbed the ropes. Sam, Nathaniel and James squinted into the early morning sun bouncing off the water, and draped themselves over *Susan Constant*'s port side waiting for Richard's curly head to bob up the ladder.

"*Arm! Arm! Arm!*"

For one long moment, the world stood still as men and boys took in the meaning of the frantic cry. Suddenly the deck of the *Susan Constant* was confusion and shouting as the sailors on board repeated the frantic cry from the shore and ran for their weapons. The boys found themselves pushed to the stern of the ship, as far away from land as possible. Nathaniel and James looked to Sam, and all three began shouting.

"Richard!" The name was drowned out by the running footsteps and bellowed orders of the sailors. "Richard!" The boys scanned the river, screaming the lost boy's name.

"You two wait here. Don't move, don't do anything till I return." Sam was firm. The younger boys nodded in stunned silence and watched him creep along the ship's railing.

Arrows, straight and furious, surged overhead, some hitting the mast, some the ship's side and some missing the ship entirely and landing in the King's River.

Sam cautiously peered over the railing and saw to his horror scores of natives in canoes and on shore loading bow after bow and shooting arrows with rapid skill into the camp and at the ships tied nearby. He had just made it back to the other boys when they felt strong arms gather them together and force them to run for the open hatch that led 'tween decks. They tumbled in, heaped together in a jumble of limbs, wet clothing and tears and only just dodged sailors pouring in to man the ship's artillery.

Nathaniel wiped his nose on his soggy sleeve while blinking back tears.

He shuddered and huddled with James as far from the agitated seamen as they could. Both boys fought off fear for themselves by replacing it with fear for poor Richard left in the water. With stifled tears and tense bodies, they watched as sailors and colonists stuffed ordnance and powder into the cannon and prepared to fire upon the approaching enemy.

Sam began strewing straw and broken crates with the men in the rush to arm. All the Company arms and artillery lay pristinely in dry vats aboard the ships, just as Wingfield had commanded. Naval artillery had to be moved into position for firing onto land and not into the river from whence the Spanish, if they ever came, would attack. Four men strained to move two of the cannon into position while four others searched and found ordnance, gunpowder and fuses. Sam heard the arrows crashing into the wooden ships with thumps and thuds and prayed that Richard had had the sense to duck under the ship and stay there as long as breath allowed.

Men streamed from tents and the field, some loading pistols, some gathering lead balls for muskets, each trying to shoot at the attackers without hitting any comrades. A few managed to don breastplates and helmets, but because of the hour most of the colonists wore no armor as they fired over the half-moon twig and brush barrier that separated them from their attackers.

Gosnold, positioned behind a barrel for protection while loading pistols, cursed to himself that the Company should be caught so unaware, so unguarded. He had known better but had, in the name of following the *Instructions*, allowed himself to be persuaded that any kind of true armament would offend. Now it appeared that their offense was not in arming but in merely being present. The Instructors had not considered that a possibility.

As arrows tore into canvas tents, Gosnold shouted orders to anyone who could hear and motioned for Ratcliffe to go north, Kendall west, and Wingfield to defend from the east section of the camp. The four Council members aligned themselves accordingly, taking any men and arms that could be had with them, stepping over wounded and moaning colonists as they went.

Gosnold was reloading his weapons when thunder rolled over his head. He saw smoke rising from the gunwales of the *Susan Constant*. Cautiously raising his head to see where the cannonballs would strike, Gosnold watched as one landed heavily in the tall grass just outside the perimeters of the camp, but a second round splintered and toppled a sturdy young oak, sending natives first to the ground for cover and then off the island for fear. God bless the men who had managed that!

The attack was over as quickly as it had begun. An eerie calm and the smell of blood and smoke hovered over the camp as sunlight, clear and hot, enveloped the stunned company. Posting four men to stand watch, the Council members gathered together to take account of losses. Eleven men lay on the ground, most with injuries that would heal well enough with time and the proper salve. Gosnold bent over one unfortunate soul with stone-sharpened arrows lodged in his abdomen and side, his grey doublet stained with a trio of dark red circlets. Roger Cooke, a gentleman who had till this moment successfully avoided drawing notice, lay unconscious and dying at Gosnold's feet, commanding all of the Captain's attention.

Orders to move the wounded into one tent were promptly obeyed and William Wilkinson, the physician, followed in close pursuit, wiping the sweat from his lean face with the back of his linen shirtsleeve and mentally taking inventory of the medicines he had in stock to tend the wounded. All arrows would have to be removed first, of course, and that would take steady nerves and a second or even third pair of hands. Wilkinson looked about for Nathaniel and Sam.

"Be a good man, Read," said Wilkinson to the blacksmith passing by, "and fetch Nate and Sam for me. I saw them trotting off for a swim just before we were attacked. I need their help in the surgery tent." Read obliged with a nod and a grunt, wondering what good two gawky youths could do in surgery, and lumbered toward the river.

The boys were standing side by side with James, all three motionless, looking down at the water's edge when he approached. He called out as he neared but they did not answer. He was about to drop a large friendly paw on each of the older boys' shoulders when his eyes were drawn to what riveted their attention.

There, on the bank, half in the water lay Richard, the ten-year-old page. Read pushed apart the boys, saying, "Well, now, lads. Why are you standing there like three little statues? Go to, go to. Help him to dry land." When they didn't stir, Read clucked his tongue disapprovingly and planted one foot on each side of the prone boy to hook his hands under the Richard's armpits and drag him up. Richard's eyes were closed, his mouth parted as if he were about to speak, and his freckles stood starkly against the pallor of his cheeks.

"I think he's dead," said Sam quietly. Nate and James, eyes wide with fear and uncertainty, sniffled and rubbed their noses.

"Aw, I don't think so, lad," said Read. "He's jus' had the wind knocked out of him, that's all. We'll set him to rights quicker than—"

Read broke off as he carefully laid Richard on the grass and knelt beside him. A puzzled look crossed his face as he leaned an ear over the boy's mouth trying to catch signs of breath. Raising his head, he rested a meaty hand on the thin chest.

He gulped, then whispered, "The poor lad *is* dead." And Read, as gently as if he were handling a newborn babe, turned Richard over where they could all see from the open, raw wound between his shoulder blades that some savage's primitive arrow had taken down a sapling among a forest of mature trees.

Sam, a quiver of emotion in his beardless jaw and honey-colored eyes, swallowed twice before allowing himself to speak. "We'd best bring him to Captain Gosnold. He'll know what to do now." With that, Sam wordlessly guided the shocked Nate and James to follow Read who had scooped up the ten-year-old casualty, cradling the damp, curly head upon his burly chest, and was trudging back to camp.

A fortnight had passed since the attack, and while President Wingfield had grudgingly agreed to a true fortification, anger and resentment stirred the hot, summer air and rumbled in the stomachs of those who had survived and were now building a triangular structure with bulwarks on each point. Oh, how much good it would have done Richard or Roger Cooke, thought Hunt as he dodged post-carrying men on their way to the eastern palisade line, but will we finish any part or whole before we are assaulted again?

Hunt stood outside the eastern bulwark, facing toward the Chesapeake. He squinted as the morning sun glinted off the waters of the broad river before him. He thought of young Richard and of Roger Cooke, and said a quick prayer for their souls and for the families in England who would never see them again. He thought of the quarreling, of the disquiet of the Council and wordlessly prayed that the discord would soon end and they could all live in peace amongst themselves, regardless of what the Naturals had in mind. And then, in a most uncharacteristic move, he decided to act.

Hunt found himself on board the *Susan Constant* and facing Admiral Newport without quite knowing how he'd arrived. His soft hands were folded neatly in his ample lap as he sat in the trim, elegant cabin.

"I have heard a great many things these last two weeks, Admiral, and under different circumstances I would not bother you with any of them." He paused, looking about the cabin for inspiration. "I mean to say, sir, that certain parties question certain situations and have asked me to bring them to you, on their behalf. And on mine, if I may so say." Hunt coughed into a doughy, ecclesiastic fist.

"Go on, sir. I am not without my own ears and anything you have to say can only be kindly meant. You may speak freely, sir," Newport said, hoping the priest would get on with it.

Hunt relaxed. "Thank you, Admiral. It's about Captain Smith and the preposterous proceedings we endured at sea that have left him in a kind of purgatory—he is under restraint, but lives at large. He is a Councilor, but not yet sworn in. His manner and daily discourse are exemplary, and he has proven himself worthy in every respect. Why, the Captain has turned the other cheek, as Our Lord would have, neither provoking nor retaliating, as others would have, given so ridiculous a circumstance.

"I have heard many say, sir, that if Smith had been on the Council, he would have made certain that a suitable fort would have been in place in a timely fashion and the unfortunate attack on our camp would have been avoided. And, without pointing the finger of blame elsewhere, I must say I agree. In short, sir, I would wish—and so would most of the gentlemen of the Colony who do not sit on the Council—a reformation of the Council whereby we admit Captain Smith to his rightful place."

These last words exploded from the man as if from a cannon and ended with a deep sigh. He sat back in his chair, having discharged his ordinance, pleased that he had made his petition without naming names or revealing too much.

"I see your point, sir," said Newport, "I have heard much the same and I think we may encourage the President to listen to reason this time."

"Captain Smith has the following of a good number of the men – he has natural leadership qualities that certain others do not possess. He is the kind of man—"

"Yes, yes. I see what you mean," Newport interrupted. "I shall call a meeting of the Council this evening and invite you to be present, as always. You need not say anything, unless it pleases you. I will direct the proceedings and, with God's good graces, the Council will for once be reasonable and in agreement."

"If I may, Admiral, there is, perhaps, one more thing you should know."

The Admiral, appealing to the loyalty and affection the Council had for him, implored them to confirm a faithful love to one another and to subscribe in obedience to the wishes of their superiors in England. It did not take long for the Council to be reconciled, although it may be said that President Wingfield did so most reluctantly.

Hunt did not say anything but afterwards shook Smith's hand with such boldness, duration and warmth that the Captain knew well who had instigated this pleasant turn of events and was profoundly grateful.

"But how, sir, did you work this miracle?" asked Smith, pulling Hunt aside, and searching the soft brown eyes for some hint of steel.

"God works miracles, Captain, not I."

"Then God be praised. But surely He had earthly help."

"Did you not wonder at the ease with which Captain Gosnold and the Admiral persuaded the rest of the Council to change their minds?" Hunt smiled.

"I did, but dared not ask. Was this your doing?"

"It was the President's doing—or, rather, his undoing. The recent attack that killed our poor Richard and Roger Cooke left many injured as well, though not as many as could have been. Let us say, when 'twas done and the costs totaled, all the Council save one were injured in battle. Captain Gosnold can say for certain that our President was there, but no one, not even Gosnold, can say he saw the man fighting."

"Are you saying that Wingfield deliberately hid from his duty?" Smith was shocked. This was more than he had expected from the man.

"There is no proof, of course. But is it not odd that of the five Council members defending the Company, only Wingfield escaped even a scratch? Cowardice is a strong repellent, especially in our leaders."

Hunt's face revealed surprisingly little sympathy.

Admiral Newport, who had heard this exchange, stepped in and added, "Foolishness can be overlooked; self-preservation when the colony is in peril cannot. Welcome to the Council, Captain."

Chapter Six

Mischiefs Within

A lone figure stumbled toward the *Godspeed*, darkness tripping him and pulling a growl from his slackened lips. At the gangplank, he called up in a voice slurred with ale, "Pssst! You! Pssst!"

He was hardly quiet.

A sailor on watch signaled to his comrade that he would tend this one; how many more colonists would find their way to the ships to barter before they left for England?

He made his way down the gangplank. "Oy there. What do you want this time of night? You should be abed." The sailor stepped close to the man who had bent over to pull up a boot.

"More ale, sirrah, before you set off. God knows when this Company will see ale again." He belched air so vile the sailor had to avert his face. "Let me pass," said the drunk, this time loud enough to wake the Pasbeheghs six miles upriver.

"We have no more to sell." Grabbing the man by the shoulders and ignoring the potent breath, the sailor lifted him so that they were face to face. The man's knees buckled so that the sailor had to hold him up by the shoulders while the besotted man grasped at the sailor's coat pockets to steady himself.

"Aw, now go to, you drunken lout," said the sailor pushing him away. "Go back to your bed and leave us be. You are a disgrace to the Company."

The dark figure reeled on one foot and jerked the other foot forward toward the tent-city, his head rolling, arms swaying.

The sailor returned to his post and only when he was alone much later did he reach into his pocket. The papers were compact but still too large. Removing the heel of his boot, he folded the papers into a wad and stuffed them into the hollow. Zúñiga would have to smooth them out as best he could.

Everywhere Smith looked men languished in the oppression and clamminess of the July heat. Fear of another attack had forced them to cut nearly a thousand trees and put up a fort in record time. Two weeks of frantic labor had exacted its toll, and all but six men were too sick to work or even rise from bed. Over thirty colonists had died since June. Newport, upon returning to England for supplies and colonists, had left the pinnace *Discovery* for their use and comfort, but it lay idle without any hope of exploration, certainly not before September.

No, we will not be sailing up river or anywhere for some time, thought Smith bitterly. He had been sick himself, but had rallied with unnatural ease. Now he and the five other healthy colonists had to figure out how to feed the rest of the Company.

And yet Wingfield has enough in his personal store to feed us all for a month, thought Smith. Wine, ale, pork and pease to put us on our feet and back to work in a fortnight. How anyone could enjoy his meals or think that no one noticed him enjoying his store while others went in need was something Smith could not understand. Wingfield did not offer his personal goods and no one dared ask, but every colonist knew what was going on. Smith found it deplorable.

And so July passed in hunger, sickness and death until late one night, the report of a musket followed by an anguished cry caused him to bolt from his cot, nearly colliding with the Sam at the flap of his tent.

"An accident, Captain! Come quickly!"

Smith ran with Sam to the top of the east bulwark where Stephen Halthrop lay on the ground, blood gushing from his left leg. Halthrop's face was white, his body rocking in pain. Beads of sweat stood out on his ashen brow.

"What the devil happened?" demanded Smith.

Halthrop lost consciousness before he could answer. Wooten tried to staunch the bleeding, but nothing he did could change the amount of blood Halthrop had already lost. Smith turned to the men who had come forward at the alarm. Not many were present; not many would be, in their present states. Wooten, himself, Sam and Read were the only men standing at the bulwark.

"Read, were you here? Were you nearby when the gun went off?" asked Smith.

"Aye, sir, I was over yonder." Read waved a thick hand in the general direction of the Church tent.

"Well? What did you see? Halthrop was alone on watch, this much we know. Did he accidentally shoot himself?"

Wooten broke in. "He couldn't have, Captain. The wound is behind the knee. He was shot from behind." The surgeon looked down. "I'm afraid he's not going to live long enough to tell us much more. Jesus, he's gone. God pardon all sinners." Wooten bowed his head.

"Amen," whispered Read, Smith and Sam as one. Smith picked up Halthrop's musket.

"It's not been fired," he observed, feeling the cold barrel and sniffing the hammerhead.

"Then what happened?" asked Sam. "Did someone try to kill him on purpose? Why?"

Wooten and Smith exchanged somber glances.

"No one *tried* to kill him, Sam," said Smith. "Someone *did* kill him."

"But in the knee? What kind of murderer is that?" Sam almost laughed, but the sight of poor Halthrop lying lifeless on the ground, his mouth twisted in pain no longer felt, stopped him.

Read was edging away until he felt Smith's eyes bore into him.

"Read, what did you see?"

"Nothin'!" Read insisted, raising his chin.

"What did you hear, then?" asked Smith impatiently.

"I heard the gun fire and that was that. I was tendin' my own matters I was, havin' a little pipeful before bed. It helps me sleep. I been sleepin' fitful ever since the bloody flux. Not enough food around here to fill a man's stomach. Might as well have a little somethin' to take my mind off it. Besides, I heard only the gun, just like everybody else." Read was calming down.

"But you should have heard more—someone running away? Or moving? You heard nothing like that?"

"Nothin'," Read said flatly.

Smith sensed that Read was hiding something, but questions now weren't bringing many answers. "Go to, then. Back to your tobacco. We will make it right here. And keep to yourself all you have seen and heard here, do you understand?"

Wooten and Smith carried Halthrop to the Church tent, laid him on a cot that Sam procured, and made their way to Gosnold's tent.

"Do you think Read knows anything else?" Wooten asked Smith.

"I think he does, but he's such a simple fool. Fear has been living with us since we were attacked in June. He may just be afraid."

"Of what?" Wooten asked, puzzled. "The savages did not do anything here tonight."

"Exactly. It is unnerving enough to have Naturals skulking about the woods and to worry that the Spanish may sail up the King's River any day and battle for the land. Halthrop did not shoot himself, certainly. Now we have enemies in our own fort, or so it appears. And nobody knows who it is. That is enough to frighten us all."

Gosnold, propped by pillows, patted the perspiration from his sunken cheek as he listened to Smith recount the evening's disaster. Two weeks of fever and chills and the bloody flux had taken their toll on Gosnold; he could concentrate but a little. He forced himself to focus on Smith's words and face.

"So we have laid him by the Church altar, and come directly to you. You have the facts as we know them, few though they are." Smith felt sorry for Gosnold's pain, but knew that Wooten had distributed the last of the laudanum yesterday. "We have no witnesses, at least no helpful ones."

"But could it have been an accident?" inquired Gosnold.

"If so, why run away? Would not the natural course be to rush to the lad's side and call for help or at least apologize?"

"Perhaps. But if the shooter was afraid of punishment—and well he could expect some—then he might very well run away. Do you know of any reason someone would want to deliberately shoot Stephen Halthrop? Had he quarreled lately? Has anyone? I have been too ill to take note." Gosnold's breath grew shorter as he wheezed out the last words.

"Few of the Company have been able to stand, sir. We have not had more than six to stand watch at any one time. No one dares leave the fort for fear of savage arrows taking them down," said Wooten, watching Gosnold's pasty countenance for signs of distress.

"Mischief beyond and mischief within," murmured the sick man.

"Many are the mischiefs, Captain, that plague our Company," said Smith, looking directly at Gosnold. "Since the beginning of July we have lost nearly thirty men to arrows and sickness—one per day, sometimes more! We cannot give decent burials because so many of the living are unable to lift themselves from their beds. The Company store is practically empty except for some barley and though we may fish for crab and sturgeon, a handful of healthy men cannot feed dozens per day. And Wingfield! He feasts on his own store and does not care that his men suffer! And now we are under attack from within our own Company! Mischiefs indeed! Mischiefs and miseries." Smith slapped his thigh as he sat down.

"But we are not certain yet, are we, that Halthrop's death was intentional?" Gosnold tried to soothe his friend.

"It matters not, Captain, for you know as well as I that men in their present state of fear, illness and lethargy will not let the facts or lack of them stand in the way of their own determination. Mark me, every man jack in the fort will assume we are lying if we say it was an accident but cannot provide the proof. Fearful minds have wicked imaginations, and once they trundle down a path, rarely do they stop for the truth. We are in a dangerous place, gentlemen, a dangerous place."

"The Council should be told, of course," said Gosnold. "Smith, I leave that to you." He lay back, dropping his head on his damp pillows. "I suggest we simply do nothing, say nothing, but bury the poor boy quickly within the fort this very night. Forgo the usual instruction of burying the dead in the woods. Best be done safely and while the fort does sleep."

"Or at least," replied Smith, "while all are preoccupied with their own suffering. It is difficult to pay heed to others' pain when your own is so great. Thank you, Captain. Wooten. Find Hunt and fetch Read to help you dig the grave. I'll to the Council."

Wingfield's pudgy frame filled the tent entrance, the inevitable handkerchief clutched in his sweaty palm. His face, round and red with exertion, puffed at the sight of Smith in Gosnold's tent.

Gosnold answered the question in his eyes. "He was about to come see you, Edward, concerning the death of young Halthrop. A most unfortunate accident has occurred. Shot by some unknown person and then dead in minutes. Most regrettable."

"Died?" Wingfield, usually so pompous and arrogant, shrunk in fear.

"Aye. Died. By some hand yet unknown."

"I heard a shot earlier. I thought the sentry was shooting at savages," said Wingfield, stunned. "Halthrop was shot *inside*?"

"That is what happened. We will probably never know who the culprit is. There are no witnesses, no one knows anything, except Halthrop, and he is dead." Gosnold sighed and closed his eyes.

"This is Smith's fault, of course." Wingfield's voice was suddenly firm.

Smith's mouth dropped before he could compose himself. "My fault? *My* fault?"

"Aye, for you started trouble on the passage here and young Halthrop followed you in every aspect. Someone here has merely meted out justice for his part in the crime."

Smith's chest heaved with the effort it cost him to hold back angry words. Wingfield, back in form, waved him aside.

"But this Company does not hand out justice in such an infamous manner," Gosnold said wearily. "If the man is caught who would do such a thing, he shall face Justice in the proper order and time. We cannot tolerate murder, Edward, if that is what this is. Order and rule of law must prevail or no man is safe."

"And a man who feasts himself while the rest of the Company starves will not long be protected unless order is maintained," Smith couldn't resist pointing out.

"I do not know what you mean," retorted Wingfield, sounding as if he knew exactly what Smith meant.

"That you, sir, enjoy a bounty of your own—pork!—while the rest of us suck on barley soaked in river water. That you have not had one moment's sickness while the rest of us have suffered fevers, swellings, and fluxes."

"Is that true, Edward? The rest of us gave up our private stores weeks ago," said Gosnold.

"No! I have not been feasting! I…I did boil some pease with a piece of pork, but I gave it to old Edward Short, my servant who has since died. Christian charity bade me offer the pork from my own store. If Smith says that this came from the Company's store or that it was for myself, why, he lies!" Wingfield's disdain overtook him. "Furthermore, I have proof –proof!—that he begged in Ireland like a rogue! Without a license! To such as this I would not want my name to be a companion! And I do not understand you would want such for yourself."

Gosnold closed his eyes again. "The matter at hand, Edward, is Company survival. Whether Captain Smith begged in Ireland or not is of little consequence here. The Captain has never given me cause to doubt his word or his integrity, and until he does so I shall continue to hold him in high esteem. Now, if you please, I need rest."

Wingfield departed with a flourish.

Wooten and Smith, both dazed by the President's venom, moved to notify the Council and bury poor Stephen.

Fingering his tiny jet crucifix, Captain Kendall sat in a dark corner of the *Discovery's* brig, a prisoner of Archer's making. Disgust flooded his being. The straw beneath his breeches itched, and the moldy air made his head ache. Pressing Archer, however subtle he thought he'd been, was not his best idea. Archer had understood the nuances and promptly arrested him for what? Annoyance? He had not heard exactly what the charges were.

Still, he had managed two victories, as underhanded as any could conceive. The map and letters were on their way to Spain, and Halthrop, instead of being merely injured, was dead and no one knew who the murderer was. Kendall laughed to himself. No one ever will, he thought. Now the general fear that had held the colonists together against the evil outside had turned to blind terror of each other inside.

Chapter Seven

Catching a Spy

A week later, Gosnold lay dead.

Smith, Ratcliffe, Martin, Percy, Archer and Wingfield, shuffled uncomfortably shoulder-to-shoulder in Gosnold's tent as Hunt prayed over their friend and closed the unseeing eyes. Dawn was breaking, and the August air hung immovable around them.

"Lord, what's to become of us without the Captain?" whispered Hunt.

"Need I remind you that I am still here," snapped Wingfield, stepping to put his face close to Hunt's, "and that I am President?"

"I need no reminder, sir," said Hunt.

The other gentlemen exchanged quick glances behind Wingfield's back. Within the hour, they had gathered in unspoken understanding in the Church tent.

Martin, agitated and nervous, breathed hard and heavy.

"I am sorry about Will," Smith said as they all sat down. "He was as fine a lad as ever I knew." A murmur of agreement passed round the tent.

Martin's body shook. "He did not have to die! Not when there is food to be had but not shared! And Wingfield" – Martin spat the name—"who has food stores to keep himself fed and well! Should he not have made his stores open, as we all have, to the Company when all about us are sick and wanting? Should he not have the decency to stock the common pot or starve with the rest of us? And now my Will is as dead as Captain Gosnold."

"And nearly fifty others," added Percy.

"How can such a man live in conscience? How can he think nothing of tolerating misery and anguish when he has the means to stop it?"

"He believes only that he owes nothing to anybody and that his own comfort and welfare come first. It is not an admirable quality," Smith said.

"I have a proposal," said Archer, his eyebrows forming a deep V as he spoke. "The Company has given us means to discharge Council members – or Presidents – in the *Articles of Instruction*. It only requires a warrant and unanimous consent of the remaining Council members. We do not even need to be specific about the charges, only saying that he is unworthy. We may discharge him from both the Presidency and the Council or merely the Presidency, if we choose."

The men considered this revelation in silence for several minutes.

"And this is legal? The Company cannot charge us in turn for insubordination or disrespect?" asked Percy, puffing on a small pipe.

"Or mutiny?" asked Ratcliffe, aware of greater dangers.

"It is all sanctioned, legally, morally and otherwise, and I have it here in writing." Archer waved a sheaf of papers over his head, then handed them over to Percy.

Percy read aloud the pertinent article, adding, "With Kendall imprisoned, we have three voting members of the Council: Ratcliffe and Martin, and Smith. It must be one of those three, and we must be careful about our choice. The Company cannot afford a weak President."

"I want none of it," said Martin tonelessly. "And I do not care who is elected—so long as Wingfield is out."

"That leaves myself and Ratcliffe," said Smith.

"I will not join in your scheme," said Ratcliffe boldly. Ratcliffe who had until this moment been more shadow than man. "Unless I take Wingfield's place. Smith has had too much dissention associated with him. I have not had one spot of trouble, and my name is untainted. This will show that we mean the Company well. There are those among us who would see Smith's Presidency as a conspiracy of some sort. I will be President." He paused to clear his throat, his receding chin peeking from a mass of starched ruff. "Or I will not comply and you will have no deposition of Edward Wingfield."

News of Gosnold's death did not sit idle. The funeral was set for the next day and his body was laid in the Church tent for all to pay respects. Any man who could drag himself upright and lean on a comrade or tree limb made his way to the open grave to see Gosnold lowered into a beautifully made gabled coffin. No one else so far had been buried in a coffin at all, let alone one so well crafted.

Wingfield, impeccably dressed in embroidered black silk, his ruff starched and rolled to perfection despite the humid air, stood piously at the head of the open grave, intoning words of praise that no man really heard.

Smith waited for Hunt to finish the Psalms and Prayers for the Dead, then he stepped forward and placed into the open grave the leading staff Gosnold had kept with him since his early sailing days. From each corner of the triangular fort sounded the report of artillery, precious munitions used to honor the most honorable man of the Company.

Salvation and salvos, thought Smith. No man deserves them more.

At the close of the evening, Archer, in the company of Smith, Ratcliffe, the grieving Martin, and a Sergeant at Arms, entered Wingfield's tent.

"What's all this?" asked Wingfield, stroking the nape of the mastiff at his feet. Phaeton, sensing danger, rose and stiffened by his master's side. His brother, Phoenix, followed suit and soon rumbling noises reverberated from their hefty throats.

"We charge you yield in King James' name to the warrant now before you," said the Sergeant, staring blankly over Wingfield's head and holding forth a paper.

Wingfield stood up, snatched the paper and looked from man to man in the crowded tent before he read the contents.

"You lie! You have not the power." Wingfield trembled and threw the offending warrant to the ground. "Out of my tent! Sergeant, take these, these...festering usurpers from my sight before I faint from the smell."

No one responded. The Sergeant blocked the doorway, his musket heavy across his chest, his match fuse lighted and gripped tightly between his fingers.

"Out! Out, I say! I will not tolerate your insolent behavior!" His Mastiffs bared their teeth and growled, waiting for the command to attack.

Wingfield, seeing his words had no effect, stared for several minutes, then sat down hard and fumbled for his handkerchief, hoping to stall the inevitable. Minutes dragged by and finally Wingfield said stiffly, "It would appear I am at your pleasure. Dispose of me as you will. But I want it written down, Archer, in the record, that I am greatly wronged, greatly wronged indeed."

"If they do you wrong, sir, they must answer for it, to be sure," replied the Sergeant, taking the former President to the pinnace and leaving the others to reform and reconstitute the Council into something respectable.

George Kendall and Edward Wingfield were an odd pair to share the close, damp quarters of the *Discovery*'s brig.

"God damn this place, and all the whoreson dogs who live here!" cried Wingfield. "Why did I ever leave England? This fetid hole they call a jail! A man like Smith would find it hospitable, to be sure, but for a gentleman?" He kicked the straw and was instantly repulsed by the pungent odors left by months of stagnation. "Uncivilized, that's what this is, completely uncivilized."

Kendall listened with his head in his hands, unmoved.

"Being confined to such as this," continued Wingfield, "is more insulting than all the rest. The humiliation!" The rotund man squatted down and wrinkled his nose as he finally plopped onto the floor. "Oof!" He searched for his handkerchief and, finding it, applied it to his nostrils and looked woefully at his fellow inmate for some sign of agreement.

Kendall stared back blankly at Wingfield, who soon realized his sputtering fell on unreceptive ears and fell silent.

A fortnight later, two soldiers arrived at the brig and removed Kendall leaving Wingfield to fume at the injustice of it all. "And what of *me*?" he wailed through the open hatch.

Kendall squinted in the late summer sun. Archer had retracted his grievance and released him; no word of explanation, no apology. Kendall, sure now that his arrest had been part of the ploy to depose Wingfield, was at liberty to put into motion his plan to abandon Virginia. Time in the brig had given him opportunity to consider his choices. With the proper attitude and persuasions, he could now gather the men and the means to leave. If Wingfield were on the ship, so much the better, but his presence or absence would have no effect on Kendall's plans. Yes, he would be delighted to leave this plagued and pitiful island. Four months had proven an eternity.

Ratcliffe, happily installed as President, appointed Smith as Supply Officer who in turn announced that the Company had but eighteen days of food remaining in the stores. What was left of the Company, some forty men and three boys, were easier now that Death had ceased to be a visitor, and the survivors' health had mended. And God bless the Pasbehegh women who had brought baskets of food twice daily at Smith's behest and payment. Stability at the fort meant Smith could venture out again.

The hopeful murmured of Newport's imminent return with wine and ale and other good things; the disheartened moaned that the Admiral was not coming back at all and the colony was forgotten. Smith wanted to believe that Newport's ships would soon be spotted, but practicality told him there was no proof that this was so. No, it was better to assume a later arrival and prepare for the winter without the cherished supplies Newport would eventually bring. Whenever Newport did arrive, Smith wanted the Admiral to find order and the jubilant welcome of the well fed, not chaos and the desperate clawing of starving men. Besides, it was not in his nature to gamble lives on maybes.

Cooler autumn days prompted Supply Officer Smith to set sail downriver with the idea of trading beads and copper for a portion of the fresh harvest and to try the river for fish, an idea that invigorated and satisfied his restless mind. Thus, the rest of September and all of October were spent in gaining as many bushels of corn as could be had from willing natives. Upriver, downriver, wherever the Naturals were open for trade, Smith many times over sailed the barge and returned with corn, fish, oysters, bread and venison, to the satisfaction of English and native alike, for both sides profited by the exchange.

Smith had never been more content. He was at last active in a productive manner, and his spirits rose with each deposit of edible treasure brought back to Jamestown. His dealings with the natives had boosted not only the Company stores but his reputation as well. Pasbehegh, Chickahominy, Kecoughtan and other tribes surrounding Jamestown respected the burly, bushy-bearded Captain for he showed no fear, no cowardice in any situation. They were delighted to trade their extra food for novel baubles and for iron hatchets, shears and the like. Smith reveled in the travels, the new faces, and the challenge of supplying the needy Company with victuals to last through the winter. Everywhere he went, he noted in his journals the topography, villages, and waterways. He was exploring and documenting England's New World while providing sustenance for his comrades. He had no opposition to bear, no complainers interfering. And, as Supply Officer, he had freedom to sail and explore, so long as the company store was full. Could life be grander?

If his thoughts strayed to his lost friends, Halthrop, Gosnold and Will Martin, he promptly said a prayer for their souls, which invariably strengthened his resolve to make a success of the Colony. They shall not have died in vain, promised Smith to himself and his Creator.

Whenever he returned to Jamestown, however, Smith's contentment and resolution dropped into frustration as he saw no useful activity: no building, no drilling at arms, no clapboard in the making, nothing. Ratcliffe spent his days reading or playing chess with Archer or Percy. Martin was never well enough to come out of his tent. Kendall lurked and loitered, sometimes conversing, most times not. The remaining Company men, now fed and healthy, did little more than play, eat and sleep. Games of chance and betting bridged the gaps between Common Prayer, meals and slumber. No order, no discipline. No goal other than living through another day until Newport arrived. Boredom would soon spoil any happy attitudes; certainly the winter would do so but no one seemed to regard that idea with any sense of import.

"John Ratcliffe," Smith noted to Sam one day as they were sailing upriver, "is no more a leader than Edward Wingfield."

Read, whose blacksmith's forge had lain idle for months, was sitting quietly one day by the church-tent, as he was fond of doing, smoking and watching the men imitate the rough stick game taught to them by the Pasbeheghs in September. The sticks they carried had webbing at the top to throw, catch and hold the small, stuffed deerskin pouch that flew between men in the attempt to hit a log at either end of the fort.

"Looks more like a beating than a game, doesn't it, friend?" asked a voice at his elbow.

Read turned in surprise to see Kendall on the bench next to him.

"Why, indeed, sir, it do." Read puffed on his pipe. "It do seem like they enjoy hittin' each other about the head and legs with them sticks."

"Tis quite the trick to run and keep the ball in the webbing, isn't it?"

"Aye. I ain't never seen such a game. And you won't see me playin' it. My mother didn't raise no fool. It might do damage to my pretty face." He chuckled at his own joke.

Kendall laughed the hollow laugh of an appeaser. They sat in silent observation as the dozen or so players constantly reversed direction while using the sticks to gain control of the ball, inflicting bruises and worse on all players in the process. That the Naturals sometimes used this game to settle disputes between tribes seemed appropriate: a savage answer to a savage's problems. But Kendall had his own problem right now.

"What a weariness!" sighed Kendall.

"What?" asked Read, startled. He thought the game was anything but wearying, at least for an observer.

"A weariness. All this waiting. Waiting for Newport. Waiting for Smith. Waiting for what? To do what?" Kendall looked at his comrade, searching the broad face for signs of agreement.

"We're doin' what we was told, that's what. What should we be doin'?"

"What a shambles this is. We've lost half—more than half!—of our Company in ways that would make other men cry. And what do we have after six months? Barely enough food, tents instead of houses, natives who are friends one day, murderers the next, and, worst of all, no gold—no profit! Let us go back to London and be done with it."

"How? We signed contracts," asked the stunned Read.

"Easy enough, my friend. You see the pinnace is ready to meet Smith upriver on his supply voyage. We will merely take her out to sea instead of upriver. It is properly loaded with supplies and all the things needed to reach Bermuda at least. Ratcliffe was her Captain on the voyage here and so knows the way back; the crew is still with us."

"I don't know," said Read, rubbing his jaw.

"We leave tomorrow. You don't wish to stay here, do you? Sleep on it and the wisdom of the notion will settle on you soon enough. Anybody not on board at the morning tide will be left behind."

"Left?"

"Aye."

They sat in heavy silence, Kendall sure of his persuasive talents in securing the only blacksmith the Company had, Read confused about what to believe and what to do.

Certainly if this departure was legitimate, the President would make a formal pronouncement. Surely he would do so when the full complement of Company men was present, not when Captain Smith and an assorted group of sentries and laborers were out on a supply mission. And most assuredly all men would be on the ship, with none left behind for any reason. No, if the colony were to be permanently disbanded, the powers that made up the Council would take swift and clear action to that end.

But these thoughts did not cross the blacksmith's troubled mind. All he could envision was the sight of the *Discovery* sailing toward the Chesapeake without him, and that thought stirred his brain and blood into such a boil that what little reason God had given him disappeared at that moment.

The stick game was coming to a close. Men filed past the two spectators in a profusion of sweat and heavy footsteps as they flung their webbed sticks into a pile by the tent and headed toward supper.

Kendall rose, patted the blacksmith reassuringly and left him. On his way to the common table, Kendall's heart warmed to the thought of the feat he had orchestrated. It had taken months of plotting, planning, good fortune and a few random horrors, but the deed was almost done. Jamestown, King James' First Colony in the New World, was about to fail.

The blacksmith rose from the bench, his brain swimming with the possibilities lain before him. Leaving had not occurred to him. He had heard comrades suggest it, of course, but it had always been said with a whine, never with such clarity of purpose or direction, and never by one of the Company's gentlemen.

Read followed the men towards supper, his head cast down in such a way he did not see President Ratcliffe on a similar path. Had either man been paying attention, they might have dodged both each other and calamity.

Neither Read nor Ratcliffe was attentive, however; the former's mind churned with Kendall's proposition, and the latter's eyes were focused on the Mastiffs at his side, prizes won of Wingfield's disgrace and deposition. The force of the collision caused the President, lighter by three stone than the sturdy blacksmith, to reel as if drunk and to deliver two hard if unintentional kicks into the sides of the dogs before landing on the ground in a most undignified manner.

Read's mouth hung open as he watched two men pull the yelping dogs away and try to help the President to his feet. Ratcliffe, his teeth clenched and bared, needed no assistance. He jumped up, grabbed a handful of Read's doublet and shot a hard fist to the gaping man's chin.

"You, you good for nothing bastard! What in hell are you doing?"

Read staggered backwards at the blow. Then, faster than his bulky physique would normally allow, he lunged forward to let loose a series of cannon-arm punches upon his assailant. Ratcliffe, doubled over in pain and gasping for breath, spat out a tooth and the words that mattered.

"Arrest that man! Arrest him, I say!"

Read, the fire of anger quelled as quickly as it had ignited, did not resist. Eyes widening in horror at Ratcliffe's bloodied ruff and the dogs' howling, he consigned himself with regret and confusion to the Sergeant at Arms.

A jury of Ratcliffe, Martin, Archer and Percy required but little time to convict the hapless blacksmith of gross insubordination.

"To be hanged at dawn," was the pronouncement.

Ratcliffe commanded the entire Company to witness the execution. He addressed them, his voice as hard and icy as the Thames in January.

"English law abides in Virginia. The Council was appointed by His Majesty King James and I as President here in Virginia represent our Sovereign. When Master Read struck me, he struck at the very Crown itself. He must and shall be an example, a reminder that all men here best hold their tongues and tempers in check lest they earn the same punishment as he. Any man who promotes insubordination or mutiny will forfeit his life."

A drum rolled low and steady and Read lumbered forth, hands tied behind his back, Hunt at his side reciting the twenty-third Psalm. A ladder leaned against an oak tree, an old specimen half dressed in golden leaves that dropped gracefully to the ground when the wind blew. The thick brown bark stood out against the pale November sky. Dangling over a hefty limb, the hangman's noose gaped in anticipation. As Read approached, he desperately searched the faces around him for some sign of reprieve, some signal of forgiveness.

With none forthcoming and his guards shoving him up the ladder, Read began to babble. "Wait, wait! I beg you! I am sorry, sorry indeed! I meant no harm! Set me free and I will tell you of a worse crime. Mutiny! Mutiny! I will tell all if you but let me down. Hang me now and you will never know till it is too late." His face was gray with fear and he closed his eyes and gulped several times.

Ratcliffe signaled for the drum to cease. With Martin and Archer, he conferred at a distance some minutes before returning to the scene of execution and said, "Let him down, but do not untie him just yet. Come, sirrah, what is this mutiny?"

With weak legs and weaker voice, Read said, "I can tell you that yon Captain Kendall is not all that you believe him to be."

"Go on," demanded Ratcliffe impatiently.

"He wanted me, sir, to join him aboard the *Discovery* and to return to England with all he had collected. He has bought the crew, and means to take himself and Wingfield back. He...he sails today. Even now, I reckon."

At this revelation, Ratcliffe's head spun about, looking for Captain Kendall in the crowd. There were not many in the throng who seemed as surprised as he was. In fact, the faces in the throng before him held more caution than surprise.

Kendall was nowhere to be seen. Nor could anyone see the ship for the execution was taking place in the woods to the northeast of the fort in a spot where the eye could not take in the part of the river where the *Discovery* lay anchored.

"To the ship!" cried Ratcliffe, pushing aside anyone in his way.

Panic seized the President and his Company as every man scrambled to see if the pinnace had indeed departed without them.

Upon reaching the bank and seeing the *Discovery* as she ever was, the group stopped as one and stared at the sight before them. Captain Smith stood on the bank, sword drawn, and shouting something towards the deck of the ship. Beside him his men were readying the artillery on the demi-lunes of the eastern and western bulwarks, six cannon now pointed at their own ship, the only possible means of returning to England for any of them.

"Stop!" bellowed Smith. "Or I will fire, by God, I will, and sink her where she lies!"

Kendall, now in view on the upper deck, ignored the commotion on shore and continued to instruct the small crew he had paid so well.

"Fire!" cried Smith, every sinew of his body ready to charge the vessel if necessary.

The fuse in the cannon nearest the ship crackled and spit. A heavy shot rang out and crossed the bow of the pinnace. Kendall froze in shock as the men on shore began roaring, and ten of them plunged into the cold river water. They crawled up the side of the ship on ropes dropped to them by a sympathetic partner on board. Before any more shots could be fired, angry Company men surrounded the sullen Kendall, pushed him roughly across the deck and threw him overboard as the men on shore cheered.

Ratcliffe, who had not quite believed Read's near-death revelation, now saw the earnestness of the blacksmith's tale and ordered him released. Kendall, contempt glowing in his small, dark eyes, staggered up the bank and dropped to the ground in defeat.

At the second trial in as many days, Read acted as witness rather than prisoner. His testimony was damning, his relief palpable. Kendall watched all in morose silence, and then had his say.

"I have no wish to deny the charges before me. Indeed, I am relieved to acknowledge them aloud. I did intend to sail today." He caught the eye of several colonists.

"You drooling, mindless wretches! I was sailing, aye – but not to England. England? A cesspool of heresy! No, I was sailing to Spain where the one true religion still reigns. Did you think the Pope would allow your vain, blasphemous, false religion to take root in the New World? No, no, not here. Not with Spanish and French plantations blooming to the north and south. My charge was to put you down, to do what needs must be done to prevent your success. I did what I could. More than you could guess at! Look at you! You are but half in number, with no housing, little food and winter pushes at your tent flaps. Fools you did elect for your presidents, and they have served you thus. Your greatest asset is arrogance, thinking you could plant yourselves on King Phillip's land. I would have given King Phillip a full report on the colony here, and it would have pleased him well to hear the pitiable estate that dwells here."

He drew breath. "I would say, 'Damn you all to hell' but that, you see, has already happened."

With this last Kendall exhaled a dry, brittle laugh and sat down. The Company stared at him with mouths open, like a giant school of fish. Never before had Captain Kendall uttered so many syllables side by side. And what syllables they were! They branded him a traitor – no, worse—a spy. A *Catholic* spy!

A collective shudder rippled through the assembly as the prisoner was led to execution.

"He is a gentleman, regardless of his actions and backward religious ideas," Ratcliffe said at the end. "Let him die by firing squad."

For the second time that day, Ratcliffe warned the Company of the price for mutiny. Every gentleman, soldier and laborer felt rattled to his core. Those who had followed Kendall were flogged. Everyone was confined to quarters for the duration of the day.

Later, Hunt, though not required to for a Catholic, prayed over the condemned man's lead-filled body in silent Anglican prayer as it was buried in the woods.

Chapter Eight

Captivity

Smith gladly spent the next day unloading the food stores his travels had yielded: pumpkins, round and golden; cornbread, flat and flavorful; grass green Virginia beans; ripe kernels of sweet corn. To that bounty he and his men daily added fat geese and ducks, and fresh fish of diverse kinds, providing enough to feed the Company until every man groaned with the pleasure of a full belly and soon forgot that he had ever been wanting at all or that anyone had ever desired to return to England.

"But, sir, you have not yet discovered the head of the Chickahominy River. With all your travels for food, could you not have also managed to gain that knowledge?" asked Martin of Smith several days after Kendall's demise, licking the grease off his fingers after a fine feast of roasted goose.

"Truly," added Ratcliffe, similarly engaged with his hands, "I cannot imagine that any one of us would not have done so by now, food gathering or no. You spend an inordinate amount of time with the savages."

Archer, seated between Martin and Ratcliffe, joined in. "Surely Admiral Newport will be arriving any day and we should at least have new territory mapped for him."

That Smith had mapped and documented almost every square inch of the King's River, a good deal of the Chickahominy that lay just off to the north of the larger river, and every village that existed therein, did not impress them. The Council had seen his notes and maps, but still they were not satisfied. Newport himself had traveled there. It would be an embarrassment not to have more. They had no gold, and they must offer something besides sixty-plus burial plots in account for their time in Virginia. The financial backers in London would have a fit of apoplexy and disband the colony if Newport had nothing of value to take back.

Smith, eager to be away from the oppressive confines of the fort, agreed to take the barge as far as it would go this time, and pledged not to stop till he had made good his promise to find the head of the Chickahominy. With the common pot now near to overflowing, Smith felt no need to tarry anywhere in order to secure food. This would be a discovery trip, pure and simple, and that pleased him.

Jehu Robinson, a Derbyshire gentleman with a pinched face and pointed nose, asked to go with Smith and was granted the request easily enough. Smith also selected carpenter Thomas Emry, a young man of twenty with bright red hair and freckles; laborer George Cassen, a ruddy-faced man with straw-colored hair that stood out like a brush; and six robust men to row. Within two days they set off to find the source of the Chickahominy.

Seventeen miles up river they traveled, the wide Chickahominy becoming narrower with each passing mile until at last, some twenty-seven miles from Jamestown, the river became a stream too narrow, too shallow and bounded by too much sand to be navigable on a barge.

"We will not go a jot further, Captain," noted Emry as the oars struck bottom. "We best turn back."

"Let us return to the last Chickahominy village we saw some miles back— Apokant, and tie up for the night. I can hire a canoe to take me up further. If I return to Jamestown without finding the source, they will say that I dared not to go on. This I must prove false. You and the rest of our men can stay at Apokant till I return."

"I would like to go with you," Emry answered quickly.

"I, too," said Robinson. "There's nothing but boredom here for those who stay."

"You both are welcome," said Smith. "We shall hire a canoe and possibly a guide or two. We shall say we want them to take us hunting for fowl. They need not know what we are truly about."

At Apokant, they found two worthy youths who accepted payment for their services and the use of their canoe, and soon they were but a fast-fading dot to the men left on the barge.

Cassen and his comrades on the barge, having fallen back asleep, were awakened by the sound of a high-pitched cooing coming from the shore. As Cassen pushed back his hat and leaned up on one elbow to see what was making the row, his eyes fell upon the maker, a smiling young woman who beckoned to him. Cassen, surprised but pleased, raised his eyebrows and pointed to himself in the universal sign for "Me?"

The girl, who looked hardly more than sixteen, was signaling to him in a coy way. Her black hair, shaped in the fashion of a bowl, bobbed with the nodding of her head. Black eyes, sparkling and wide, told him to leave the barge and step on shore. Her smile promised more than a few pleasures waited for him if he only would come over.

Cassen grinned back and immediately jumped into the shallow water by the shore's edge to follow her wherever she wished. The cold water squelched any passion temporarily but did not impede his progress toward the beautiful, shapely young thing that had on naught but an apron around her privates and a deerskin over her shoulders.

His fellow travelers heard the splash and saw their friend's destination. Alert to the possibility of more pretty wantons, they were disappointed to see she was alone.

"Cassen!" his friends shouted in good humor, "you'd best come back! Remember that the Captain said to stay on the barge till he returned!"

"Bah! I'll be finished before he is," scoffed Cassen.

The others laughed and settled down to sleep some more, sure that he was right.

Cassen waded to shore and then waddled with open arms toward the pretty girl who started to run lightly into the sparse forest, leaving a delightful giggle lingering in her place.

Cassen called out, "Wait!" and trotted after her in sport.

He tripped over something and landed on his knees and palms.

"Come back!" he called, laughing.

Cold, hard hands pulled him to standing. Cassen stopped laughing as they pushed him toward the trunk of a cedar tree.

"Oy! You! What the devil do you think you're doing?"

Five Naturals held him while two others prepared their tethers.

Struggling did no good. Breathing hard and trying to communicate with heathens who did not know the King's English, Cassen begged to be let loose, offering food and trinkets from the barge, but the captors did not understand or did not want to understand.

Cassen felt his hands and legs forced behind the tree and tied with ropes. In horror, he watched the silent men build a fire and pull shells from a sack on the ground. He started to shout for his comrades; if they could but hear him they would come to his aid.

The biggest captor, taller and thicker than any Englishman Cassen had ever known, picked up a mussel shell, sharp-edged as any English knife, and walked over to where Cassen was tied. Circling the tree several times, the brave held the shell for Cassen to see, testing the sharpness of the edge with his finger. On the last circle, the brave paused behind the tree, and Cassen thought with relief that the ropes would be cut soon and he would be set free, that this was some strange sort of game the savages liked to play. He knew he had done nothing to antagonize them; he had not shot at them, nor fought with them in any way. The Naturals they knew from Jamestown were friendly, had brought food to them when they were starving, had nursed them with herbs and potions till the Company was well again.

But these were not the Pasbeheghs. Tense and unblinking, taut in body and mind, these men did not have healing or kindly countenances.

Cassen felt the warmth of the brave's body on his bound hands and then a stinging, excruciating pain shot up first his right arm and then his left. Warm, sticky liquid oozed over his hands. The brave came triumphantly around the tree carrying two of Cassen's fingers and threw them into the fire to the guttural whoops of his brothers.

Cassen, his screams now full, wild and terrified, struggled desperately to escape. The natives took turns sawing off his fingers and toes, until all were cast into the fire. Thus they continued till every scrap of skin on Cassen had been removed from his person and used as fuel for the fire. They then set fire to the tree and what was left of poor Cassen, dancing around it in fitful, barbaric glory.

On the barge, Cassen's mates awoke abruptly to sound of his anguished cries and saw smoke rise from the woods nearby. The smell of burning human flesh, putrid and nauseating, left no doubt of George Cassen's fate.

With one accord, the six oarsmen frantically pulled up the ties that held them to shore and paddled in terror toward Jamestown, leaving Smith, Emry and Robinson to make it back however they saw fit. If they ever returned. If these unholy creatures had captured Cassen, then Smith and his men would surely be next.

Captain Smith, as he departed in the canoe with Emry and Robinson and their two guides, enjoyed the ride upriver to the place where they had turned around last night. The morning was crisp and clean and fresh, the December sun shining but not blazing. The air was cold, to be sure, but not so icy that that it hurt to breathe or be without gloves. Lincolnshire Decembers, he remembered, were bitter, frosty and filled with sleet that bit your cheeks if you were fool enough to go out without a wrap across your face. Yes, Virginia's weather is far superior to England's, thought Smith, so long as it isn't summer.

The little party glided twelve miles past the previous night's stopping place into a thick marsh, and by noon Smith spied solid ground.

"We shall stop here for our dinner. Emry, Robinson, start a fire and begin cooking. I'll take this youth with me." Here he signaled to the guide closest to him. "To see if I can discover the nature of the soil. Keep your wits about you, and your muskets ready—aye, and the fuses to light them. If you should even see but one Natural, fire a shot, and I shall return immediately."

Smith and his guide slopped through the marshy land and had not been gone fifteen minutes when brutal cries pierced the cool air and pulled the hairs on the back of his neck on end. No shot of warning, thought Smith.

His eyes absorbed everything, measuring distances to land, between him and his comrade, and the distance of the screams. Seeing nothing but judging danger to be close, he grabbed his guide, pushing his French pistol into the guide's back, and snarled, "Go to."

Undoing one of his garters, Smith then tied the Natural to himself, arm to arm, using him as a shield. The guide showed little fear, but followed Smith's every instruction without resistance.

The whooping drew nearer.

Adrenaline surged through Smith; his eyes and ears picked up every nuance of the surrounding woods. A small crack to his left gave away their position. Two braves were nocking arrows into their bows. Smith's shot pierced the shoulder of one brave, which sent both bowmen running. Smith, tethered as he was, still managed to reload his pistol, grateful the Natural did not seem to understand that process which would have given him time to wrestle free and flee without fear of being shot.

Ready again, Smith stood still, listening for sounds of approach. Before he could fire another shot, two hundred braves surrounded him with nocked bows raised to their cheeks.

The guide began to talk in a rush of sounds that Smith could fathom readily enough from his experience with other tribes encountered in the past six months of excursions.

"This man is Smit, werowance of the English," said the guide in his native tongue.

"Ah! Smit!" Those near enough to hear repeated the name in admiration.

One of the two hundred stepped forward. He towered over Smith and the tethered guide and shot a questioning look in Smith's direction. Still he recognized the name. He then addressed Smith, speaking slowly as if to a child.

"Your friends are slain," said the leader, with a jerk of his head in the direction of the canoe. "Werowance we will reserve. Lay down your weapon and come with us."

Instead of complying, Smith started to back away, still using the guide as a shield and the gun as the trump.

His eyes were on the leader, wary of any sudden move that would indicate the use of force. With four hundred eyes watching in patient, armed silence, Smith stepped backward and felt the earth beneath his feet turn to mush. Instinctively, he tried to raise his legs and find stable ground, but with every effort to pull away the marsh tugged back.

With a heart sinking as fast as his feet, Smith realized he had backed himself and the guide into a bog that refused to let go.

The two were knee-deep in icy ooze and sinking; slowly, to be sure, but sinking indeed. Death by suffocation threatened to overtake both of them in minutes.

Smith sighed.

Tossing his pistol to dry ground, he untied his companion, and surrendered.

Smith tramped after his captors to the fire Emry and Robinson had made. He forgot his numb legs and stiff arms when he saw the grisly scene before him. So heavily were their corpses stuffed with arrows that he barely recognized Emry or Robinson as human.

Once seated by the fire, two braves started to chafe and rub his legs till the blood flowed freely and the tingling ceased. Staring into the fire, Smith considered his situation in full view of Emry and Robinson and his several hundred captors.

What was to be his fate? Clearly his captors could have killed him had they wished. He had surrendered his arms, Emry and Robinson were slain, the barge's passengers were—alive? Probably not, but possibly. Would they have the sense to seek help from the Fort when he did not return within the day? Would aid be forthcoming?

In truth, he could not—nay, did not – expect that anyone at the fort would attempt a rescue if the others had returned safely to tell them of it. Who would order it? Martin and Ratcliffe were not inclined to action, if Martin were able to participate at all. And Ratcliffe—that man did wear no eyes or ears on his head but Archer's.

Archer. Hungry for power and eager to take it at any cost. What was it Archer and Martin had said before he left? Go as deeply as you can, make more discoveries, take your time. What mischiefs were now being planned? What a fool he had been to think they were concerned about the Company!

Smith, warmed by the fire and hot to be moving again, asked to be taken to their chief, whoever he was. They said they were Chickahominy Naturals and not beholding to Powhatan. I was sold into slavery once and lived to return to England, thought Smith. I shall do whatever necessary to return to Jamestown.

The group trudged through the frigid forest an hour before a village came into view. It looked like so many other villages Smith had seen he wasn't sure which one it was. The same matted frame houses, the same fires inside and out. The smell of food cooking made his stomach growl. The children and women in the middle of daily chores or play stopped what they were doing to watch the little man in dark cape and enormous boots go by, his head lifted, his stride confident. Show no fear.

At the center of the village, they brought him to their werowance's hut. Curiosity pushed the entire village to gather behind him, waiting to see or hear what their chief would do with the odd-looking stranger. Smith stepped in, adjusted his breeches, and stood up to his full height to gain as much advantage as possible.

The chief identified himself as Opechancanough, the great Powhatan's brother, and werowance of the Pamunkeys. Pamunkeys, not Chickahominies. Are they going to bargain for me? Am I a hostage?

Smith, noting a steely quality in the middle-aged chief's face, breathed deeply to steady his mind and racing pulse, his right hand unconsciously smoothing his doublet. Something hard in the pocket interrupted the gesture. Ah! Perhaps I can conjure for them, he thought, and they will think I have great magic. It worked with the Turks.

Careful not to give the idea that he was belligerent, Smith drew forth an ivory double compass, a sparkling half-sphere in a box, placed it flat in his palm and, like Balthazar on Twelfth Night, offered it to the chief. The chief handled the little box with due care and a puzzled eye. He shook it, put it to his nose and then his ear and handed it back to Smith with a questioning gaze.

Smith smiled, raised a hand to the crowd and then beckoned the chief closer.

"Turn the compass and the needle always points north. You try," said Smith, encouraged at the reception he had received. He restored the compass to the chief's hand.

Opechancanough imitated Smith's rotations and smiled to see that the needle performed for him as it had for Smith. He poked at the half-globe with a thick index finger, expecting to touch the dial, and was surprised that the clear covering could not be penetrated. Still, the elder man delighted in dipping and turning the box, watching the needle always point to the same intriguing direction.

Pointing to the gleaming compass, Smith demonstrated the movement of the sun, the earth, the moon and planets; he continued by describing the races that populated the world, England, King James and virtually anything else he could think of that sounded important. The Pamunkeys did not understand much of what he said, but oh! how he said it! No courtier, no peddler in all of Britain could have pontificated longer or better than John Smith did in that hour. Drawing upon every dramatic skill he possessed, he waved his arms; he stooped closer to the children; he roared then whispered; he imitated crones, children, thunder and rain, cannon and musket fire, trumpets and drums.

The patience of the braves who had brought him to Opechancanough had expired, however, and while the werowance was examining the compass again, they pulled the little actor toward the nearest tree. He held no magical spell for them; he was their prize.

They lashed Smith's arms and legs to an oak, and he saw the captors nocking their bows, some twenty or thirty young men ready for blood. His performance had gone unheeded, and now he prayed for absolution and salvation. Through my fault, my fault, my most grievous fault.

Opechancanough looked up from the entrancing bauble, noticed that Smith was about to be skewered, and barked an order; the multitude parted for him to pass. Holding the compass over Smith's head, the chief looked expectantly at his people. Bows and arrows clattered to the ground and when Opechancanough waved his arm in a giant circle, a great roar rose to the heavens and Smith felt his bindings loosen and fall away.

Relieved, Smith stretched his arms and shoulders. "Thank you. I am grateful."

Within minutes, Smith was marching through the forest in a procession that included six armed guards on either side of him plus two great natives holding him fast by each arm. Perhaps my death was but postponed, he thought. Opechancanough and his sentinels marched first, followed by Smith and finally every man, woman and child in the tribe in single file behind him.

Winter had seized the air and land with frigid winds and hardened ground. The temperatures had plummeted so that ice crackled on the trees and grass. The natives paid no heed to the temperature, but Smith shivered and stamped to keep his blood warm.

Arriving in a town made of thirty mat frame houses, the Pamunkeys stripped him of his cloak, garters, boots, leather satchels and pockets, and even the points that fastened his slops to his doublet. Left with a linen shirt that reached to his knees and breeches that succumbed to gravity unless clutched, Smith tried to think of a way to win back the clothing that would keep him both sane and warm.

The braves finally escorted Smith to a long hut and left him there guarded by forty tall, iron-armed braves with bows and arrows. Smith, determined to keep moving rather than die from exposure, trotted round and round the hut, waving his arms and blowing hot breath onto his stiff fingers while holding onto his breeches.

The aroma of freshly roasted venison and warm bread made his head swim, and he realized how long it had been since he had eaten. Five Pamunkey women stood at his door with baskets and bowls full of the most glorious-smelling dinner.

From the bounty laid before him, Smith expected to be joined by Opechancanough or at least the guards. Surely they do not want me to eat all this by myself!

Since the women left, some with shy looks, some not daring to meet his eyes, and the guards paid him no notice, Smith made himself comfortable on a mat and scooped stew and bread into his mouth with relish. The thought that he was being fattened for some tribal feast at which he was to be the main serving crossed his mind, but, as before in his lifetime, he decided that he'd best eat while he could and leave the questions for later.

When his belly was full, Smith signaled that he needed to perform nature's necessities. Upon returning, a distraught villager, gray and weathered, jumped to block the doorway, a wobbling bow and arrow at his chest, aimed at Smith's heart. One of the guards stepped forward and snatched the weapon. The angry old man shouted at Smith while jabbing a crooked finger in the direction of a nearby house.

His son is dying, thought Smith, able to grasp the pertinent point and his breeches at the same time. And he thinks I killed him.

The guards led Smith to the dying man, who was unconscious on the earthen floor. It was the Natural hit by musket fire during his capture. Smith could barely see the man drawing any breath, but a great heat radiated from his body despite the freezing air. From his left shoulder a gunshot wound, raw and blood-crusted, gaped; Smith's shot had been true and did not graze as he had thought.

Briefly Smith examined the man's burning body and fevered visage. This man will not last till sunset, thought Smith. But they don't know that.

Through sign language Smith told the family that he had water that would heal, but it was back at Jamestown. Smith moved to go, but the guards grabbed him again.

The guard threw a skeptical look at the little white man and grunted.

"Very well, then. Let me write——write," said Smith, motioning in the air, "and send a message so they will know I am well. They will then give you the water and some other things I require. I will need my personal belongings, please."

The guard believed some magic was conjured by the waving motion. He led Smith back to the prison-hut and waited while the strange man first laced his clothing together and then pulled a page from a notebook in his leather bag, scribbling black marks upon the white sheet with liquid from a bottle and bird's quill.

"Here," said Smith to the guard and the three chosen messengers, pantomiming as he spoke, "when you first approach, they will shoot at you, I promise. Return to the woods and wait, then put this paper on a tree branch, like so. They will send out a boy to fetch the paper. Let him take it without harm. They will stop shooting when they see the paper, I promise, and they will invite you into the Fort while they gather what I ask for. You will then be allowed to return safely. Now let me dress."

Three braves ran off in the cold December gloom, one carrying a neatly folded square of paper in his moccasin. Smith smiled to himself, confident for the first time since his capture that his life was worth more to these Naturals than he had thought possible.

When the messengers returned in three days' time, they were eager to tell how all that the little Captain had predicted had come true. Wondrous magic. Either that or the strange paper with the dark markings could speak.

God is good, thought Smith as the villagers beamed at him. And since the wounded son died before the water was brought, I have no need to prove its worth. I will surely be allowed to return to Jamestown soon where they know

now that I am safe and what happened to Emry and Robinson. Though he was guarded almost every moment, his captors, especially the women, had begun to smile and relax around him.

Thus they traveled, from village to village over what Smith calculated to be an area equal to Lincolnshire. Tappahannock, Rappahannock, Potomac— rivers aplenty to sketch and enter into his notebook. Tribe after tribe he met, all under the rule and benevolence of the great leader, Powhatah, whom he had met in June with Admiral Newport.

At each stop, the captors made a show of Smith, with Opechancanough standing next to the captive at the center of each dance and feast, entertaining him lavishly and with great delight. Eventually he was given relative freedom to roam amid the tribe, so long as he did not try to escape. He hardly felt a prisoner now. Everywhere he went, the women smiled and offered food, the children chased him and turned cartwheels for his amusement, the men respected him and gave him space. Smith, never one inclined to fear of anything or anyone, found he liked his position and reputation and used them gladly to make his life more comfortable and easy, all the while thinking of how to escape or leave with the good grace of Opechancanough.

After two weeks of parades, feasts, and moving from one village to another, Smith found himself being marched toward a much larger village than he had yet seen in Virginia. As they approached, he saw hundreds of houses in various sizes. The people were much as he had seen before—barely dressed and glistening with bear oil– but here were ten times as many in one place as he'd ever encountered. Chanco, his servant boy, a gift from Opechancanough once Smith's powers had been recognized, told him where he was.

"This is Werowocomoco, home of the Great Powhatan, wise and just ruler of all our tribes."

"I have met him before," said Smith to the boy's surprise. "I met Powhatah two seasons ago, in a village on the King's River."

"Powhatah? No. Powhatan," replied Chanco.

"Powhatah, Powhatan, they are the same, are they not?"

The boy bit his lip to keep from laughing. "No, Smit, they are not."

Smith, taken aback by the revelation that Newport had given a cape and a solemn pact of friendship to the wrong man, marched forward with his captor hosts, ready to meet the Great Powhatan.

When they entered Werowocomoco, two hundred tall, well-muscled men draped in copper beads stood in straight lines and watched closely the solid, English form that strode confidently toward the largest house in the village.

An impressive assembly waited for him. Powhatan, whom Smith judged to be near sixty years old, much older than the Powhatah he had met in June, lay on a platform stacked with mats that set him at a considerable height over his courtiers. He looked weathered and stately and wore a thin gray beard, even though every other Natural male plucked out his beard. A cape of raccoon skins covered his long torso and arms, with striped tails hanging from the folds like flags in James's court on a windless day. Two exquisitely beautiful young women, no more than eighteen surely, posed nearby, one at his moccasined feet and one at his regal head.

Beautiful, thought Smith, but for the tattoos.

Ten braves and ten women lined up on either side of the werowance, every head painted red and decorated with the white down of some bird or fowl, and every neck draped with ropes of great white beads. Masks of resolute patience stared at Smith as he came forward.

Admiring the portrait of gravity and majesty before him, Smith stood respectfully before the assembly and waited to be addressed.

"I welcome you, Captain Smit, and invite you to eat with me. Sit and we shall be friends." Powhatan spoke in his native tongue but the meaning was clear.

"I thank you, sir," answered Smith respectfully in Algonkian and sat down on the matted floor in front of the greatest array of victuals he'd yet been offered. Venison, oysters, clams, mussels, fowl, beans, squash, corn, dried fish, warm cornbreads – nothing was wanting. While they ate, the two men, the tall and the small, each tried to fully understand the character of the other while not giving away too much of the truth.

After asking to hear the same discourse given to his brother Opechancanough regarding the moon and sun and then plying Smith with questions about his magical powers, Powhatan arrived at the core of his curiosity.

"Why have white men come here?" asked the great leader, looking directly into Smith's eyes.

Smith, having expected this question from someone, had a ready answer.

"Our great enemy, Spain, attacked us on the great eastern sea. We retreated when we saw that we were overpowered. Then bad weather caused us to put to shore where the Chesapeake shot at us but the Kecoughtan treated us kindly." Pantomime helped greatly.

Powhatan nodded at this, for he knew the Chesapeake and Kecoughtan well and this matched the behavior he was familiar with.

"By signs we demanded fresh water," continued Smith, "whereby the Kecoughtan told us that fresh water was up river. About the time we were next to the island, our boat started to leak and we were forced to stay and mend her, all the while waiting for my father Admiral Newport to come back and carry us away."

Smith looked intently at Powhatan. He had not yet said to anyone that Newport was his father. Surely this information would carry weight.

"You took a smaller boat even further upriver. Why?" asked Powhatan, ignoring the remark about lineage.

Smith switched tactics. "We had heard about the black sea. We were curious to see such a great water."

After a pause, Powhatan said, "You will tell your father when he comes for you that you were welcome here. How many ships will your father bring to carry you home?"

"My father will bring two ships this time, but our greatest werowance, James, has many, many more ships. Bigger, faster and with more guns—BOOM! And a thousand trumpets!" cried Smith, doing his best imitation of a cannon and a brass instrument.

"How many? This many?" asked Powhatan, unshaken, taking from a servant's waist a rope with ten knots worked into the sinew.

"More."

Powhatan pulled an identical rope from another servant. "More?"

"Yes, more. Your village cannot make enough knots to equal our Great Father's ships."

Powhatan handed back the ropes to his servants and sat rigid and silent for several minutes, his face dark and unmoved.

Finally he spoke. "I will give you corn, venison, all good things to feed you and your English friends. You make hatchets and copper for us. No one will disturb you and you will not disturb us. We shall live in peace until your father comes to take you home."

"This I can promise for my father and my friends," replied Smith. "I shall return today with this good news."

"You stay here four days, then you will be free. Tell your father Newport we treated you well. He will be happy to know this," said Powhatan.

"Upon my honor, sir," replied Smith, wondering when Newport would be coming back, if he had not returned already, and why he himself must wait another four days before leaving.

Two days passed in relative ease, everything much as it had been. On the third day after the conference, Powhatan summoned Smith to his longhouse where the burly Captain sat alone in front of a fire for a good while before anything happened or anyone entered.

Patience, Smith, patience. They will tell you all you need to know in their own time. Remember the Turks.

Suddenly, from behind a mat hanging midway in the hut, Smith heard a doleful wail, sustained, starting low in pitch and rising till it hurt his ears.

The mat rose, revealing Powhatan himself painted all over in black, hideous paint, looking more like a devil than a man. Two hundred braves, all painted in the same greasy ebony as their leader, followed. The effect was meant to be horrifying, but Smith sat serene and still, intrigued and unafraid. Intimidation was a familiar tactic. He had not been frightened by the Turks, either.

Several braves pulled him to the door and tied him to a tree. A dozen or so black-painted warriors danced around him to the beat of deep drums for half an hour.

Could they really mean to kill me after all? Smith wondered, his heart pounding in his ears.

The dancing and drums stopped as suddenly as they had begun and Smith's bindings were cut loose. The villagers had all gathered to watch as the little Captain was pushed to a large stone altar situated at the end of the town.

His head they forced to the table.

The black-painted dancers approached, this time carrying clubs.

Smith prayed in earnest for redemption and everlasting glory, repenting all his known sins and any he may have forgotten. He did not, however, close his eyes or flinch as the clubs were raised. They will not have the satisfaction of seeing me quake in fear, for I am not afraid to die. Let it be thus.

From the gathered throng a small voice cried out and the people parted to let the owner pass.

"Oh, Father. Let him live!"

A child, no more than ten or eleven years old, climbed onto the altar and laid her shining black head upon Smith's, her tiny arms draped across his shoulders.

"Amonute! Come here." Powhatan's voice was firm but not displeased. "He is a fearless man, more Powhatan than English. He shall be our son and your brother. Come here, Smit."

The Captain, now upright, looked Powhatan directly in the eye and saw that the gray-haired leader meant what he'd said.

"Captain Smit, let the English and Powhatan be friends. You have a Powhatan heart and courage. You are to be my beloved son, Nantaquaus, and I give you Capahowasicke to rule as werowance. You are free to move among our tribes and your people. We will welcome your return and mourn your leaving. You will take with you as guides and servants these twelve braves. In return, send them back to me with two great guns and a grindstone in respect for your new father."

Smith, astounded at the rapid turn of events, simply said, "Upon my honor, I shall give them to your servants to carry back to you." He then patted the little girl Amonute on the head and smiled at his new sister, who beamed back.

Chapter Nine

New Arrivals

Cheers and shouts of joy from behind the palisade walls and atop the bulwarks blessed Captain Smith's ears as he approached the fort for the first time since early December. Smith, if he had calculated aright, knew this morning to be the second day of 1608, and that he had been gone for three weeks. What a triumph to return whole and escorted by a dozen worthy Powhatans who wanted nothing more than to hand over baskets of food and to return to their master with promised prizes!

The gates swung open and every able-bodied man and boy in the Company met Smith with such a rush of glad tidings and merriment that his heart beat hard and fast. He could not help but laugh and smile till his cheeks ached and his hand was sore from being pressed and pumped in delight.

He noted that Archer did not join in whole-heartedly, but that was to be expected. Now that he had come to an understanding of how the game was being played, he felt a sense of control where before he had not. There would be time for Archer later.

First, the guns and millstone promised to Powhatan. Smith put up his hand to quiet the crowd and directed his escorts to the demiculverins positioned outside the bulwarks.

Patting the cold iron bellies, Smith said, "Here, my friends, take them and use them as you may," to the astonishment of his Company comrades. Young Sam started to object but Smith laid a finger to his lips and stopped him short with a frown. Two of the braves had made their way to the cannon and had tried to push one. They called for the help of their brother escorts so that soon all twelve men were leaning and grunting trying to move one cannon even one inch. It could not be done.

"I am sorry, friends. The cannon must stay here," said Smith sympathetically. Then, seeing they were considering bringing assistance from Powhatan to move the two-ton artillery pieces, he quickly added, "Let me show you how they work. Gunners, let loose a shot. No, not a cannonball – why waste it? A glut of stones will do. Now, fire into the river, if you will."

The tremendous roar of the cannon and the subsequent shattering of ice-frosted river sent the escorts running in fear. In good humor, Smith gathered his nervous Powhatan brethren, gave them baskets of beads and copper, a few hatchets for good measure, as well as his thanks for their watchful care of him over the last week, and finally sent them on their nervous way back to Powhatan.

Rubbing his hands together, Smith followed Sam to his tent where he turned and asked to be apprised of all that had taken place in his absence.

"Why, sir, we all thought you dead, like the others, at first. The barge you left escaped, with only George Cassen lost." Here Sam paused before saying in a voice barely audible, "The savages flayed him alive, Captain. The rowers heard it. They made haste with all speed, thinking you were dead as well."

"They could not have known I was alive, Sam. They did right in returning. Think of how many more men might have been lost if they had not."

Sam gave Captain Smith all the particulars of the cold weather, the rather tame Christmas celebration the Council had decreed as fair in this time of need, and the news that somehow Captain Archer had been appointed to the Council.

"How could such a thing happen?" asked Smith, more of himself than of Sam who could not have possibly been privy to the goings on of the Council.

Archer appeared at the tent entrance. "By vote, of course."

"Whose?" demanded Smith.

"The Council's. President Ratcliffe and Captain Martin, as the only members present and accountable, held a vote. Now I am a Councilor."

"But I did not vote. I am on the Council."

"Aye, but we had no guarantees of your safe return, had we? Were we to wait indefinitely for a possible return? No, we voted and that was proper."

"Impossible! *The Articles of Instruction* clearly states all Council members must be present for a vote. You knew I was unharmed and in the company of Powhatan—you had my written word! I demand an immediate meeting of the Council to set this matter aright."

Archer, his lawyerly brain churning, stared at the pugnacious face. "Very well. Let us have a Council meeting in one hour. We shall meet in the Church tent."

Smith sought out Hunt for his clear and impartial opinion on just what had occurred to bring Archer into power. Apparently, said the good priest, Ratcliffe had used his two votes as President to override Martin who had objected, rightly so, on the grounds that they knew Smith to be alive and well treated by the Pamunkeys and that they had to assume he would be restored soon enough. And they could not vote in any new Councilors, not until Admiral Newport's return with new instructions, which was expected any day.

"So Captain Archer used his influence on the President to push forward a vote that was sure to fulfill his ambition," mused Smith. "This cannot stand. Will you speak on my behalf, sir, when we meet shortly? I know you do not have a vote, but you have a reasonable voice."

"Gladly, Captain, if you think it would do any good. I'm afraid you do not have much of a chance. On paper it is legal enough, and that is what will carry weight for the Company."

Together the two men made their way into the Church-tent, a sorrier house for God than ever Smith had beheld. Rotting, moth-eaten sails covered a few sapling posts and damp logs stood for pews. Waiting for him were Martin, Ratcliffe and of course Archer, all seated on a hewn log bench in front of a table set up for this purpose.

Smith, expecting a seat for himself, was startled to see there was none. He stood expectantly in front of the three men and it struck him just as Ratcliffe began to speak that the scene he was about to play had him in the role of defendant and the others as judge and jury.

"Captain Smith, I understand you have objections to Captain Archer's appointment to the Council. As President, I assure you all proper procedures were followed and Captain Archer is here to stay."

"But—"

"Do not interrupt me. We have other, more urgent business for the Council. You are under arrest, Captain Smith, for murder."

The Sergeant at Arms stepped into the tent with two guards.

"You will stand trial immediately for the deaths of Jehu Robinson and Thomas Emry, men under your charge who were cruelly murdered while you went hunting. The law you are accused under is called"—here Ratcliffe leaned over to hear whispered the correct wording from Archer—"the Leviticus Law."

Smith, noting that Hunt's face was a changing palette of purple surprise and red anger, said nothing and merely waited to see what happened next.

"But you can't do this!" blurted the astonished priest. "The Captain did not murder his men, surely you know this!"

"An eye for an eye, sir," answered Archer smoothly. "It is a law you should well know."

"'Breach for breach, tooth for tooth.' Leviticus chapter 24, verse 20. But not here! Not in Virginia!"

"English law is Virginia law. We keep it here as we would in England."

With a swiftness born of ambition and hate, the Council arrived at its predictable verdict, leaving Smith to spend his last earthly night in prison with none other than Edward Wingfield. The sentence, death by hanging, would be carried out at dawn. Hunt tugged at Archer's sleeve as they left the Church-tent. "But can you not use the firing squad, if this must be done at all? It is a swifter end, to be sure."

Archer looked over Hunt in a derisive glance. "Firing squads are for gentlemen."

Smith requested and received his leather bags with notebooks, letters and maps, as well as the small wooden desk he had brought from England. He would need to make haste if he wanted everything presentable by tomorrow morning.

Wingfield's physical appearance, after months in the ship's brig, shocked Smith as he entered the small confines of the jail. Once portly and arrogant, the ex-President had a wan face and defeated air, his flesh hanging loosely from his jowls. He barely looked up from his reading as Smith arranged some straw for his bedding. Wingfield did not need to ask why the rough, bristly upstart was here; he had heard everything from the guard who brought him dinner at noon. A certain satisfaction filled his small heart as he continued to read, ignoring everything Smith did.

Although he could not say exactly why, Smith was not particularly aggrieved at his present situation. He had faced death so many times it was like a heartburn: occasionally annoying but application of the proper tonic made it go away. In the past the tonic had been combat or a duel or old-fashioned fisticuffs or, in the most recent case, magic, showmanship and a little girl's protest. And he was still here. His faith in his ability to escape Death's clawing grasp wavered only slightly now—the Council had managed to fulfill the last death sentence they had imposed – but ultimately he was not afraid of dying. He may or may not end up in Heaven, but he trusted in his Lord to sort it all out for the best.

Shortly before dark, a great commotion from the riverbank set the fort abuzz. A canoe approached, carrying two Company men from the lookout post downriver who whooped and hollered and whistled in such a fashion that soon the entire complement of men came running from the Fort. The words were lost in the dusky twilight, but as the canoe drew closer to the fort and the *Discovery*, Smith could discern the best parts of the raucous message.

Newport was sailing up the river!

Slamming the notebook shut, he called for the guard to come let him on deck to see for himself. The guard, not having been told not to, let both Smith and Wingfield up onto the main deck where they could see the red cross of St. George on a white field flying boldly in the cold air. The evening tide was bringing supplies, colonists, news, and relief at last.

Smith roared a deep-throated laugh and slapped Wingfield on the back. Archer and Ratcliffe would have to answer to the Admiral, that was certain, and only good things could come of that. And though Powhatan had no way of knowing I was to be sentenced to die, Smith thought, he must have seen Newport's ships on the coast and timed my return to join with his. The strategy filled Smith with admiration. He is a force we should not take lightly.

Indeed, that evening, when the Admiral heard the whole sordid affair over supper with the Council on board the *John and Francis*, he ordered both Smith and Wingfield brought to the dining table immediately. Archer, Ratcliffe and Martin shifted uncomfortably but did not try to dissuade him.

"I will think on this…interesting entanglement…overnight, gentlemen," said Newport deliberately, "and give you my verdict on the morrow. All new colonists will stay aboard ship until you have set up housing to accommodate them. Tomorrow being the Lord's Day, this all should be done on Monday. No one, I repeat, no one is to hang Captain Smith until I so say. Is that clear?"

"Aye, sir," was all Newport heard and that satisfied him for the moment.

"Edward, you are no longer confined to the pinnace. Sleep in your own bed this evening. Take your ease and comfort but nothing else until I so say. Is that clear?"

"Aye, Admiral. And thank you," said the now-humble Wingfield.

With that, all retired for the night: Newport amazed at the state of affairs he'd sailed into, Smith dazed at the perpetually shifting landscape of his life, Wingfield pleased to be free from the brig, and Councilors Ratcliffe and Archer dismayed at the prospect of losing the advantage for which they had so long connived.

True to his word, Newport put his sailors to work Monday immediately after breakfast and Common Prayer, making housing for his newly arrived colonists and replacing tents that had been taken down for lost comrades. Seeing that all were working as swiftly as the frigid air would permit,

Newport gathered the Council, as it stood at the moment, plus Percy, Master Hunt, and a stranger, young and straight as an arrow, in his cabin.

"First, let me say that I am most grieved at the loss of Captain Gosnold and the other honorable men who died here during my absence. It will be a hardship to convey such sad news in London. As for Kendall, he found his just desserts, no more, no less, though I had not thought so ill of him as all that. A traitor and spy!

"Second, the situation you have presented me is most unusual, to be sure, but I have thought deeply upon the matter and have resolved it as follows. Please note that I shall brook no arguments; my decision is final. As Admiral and highest-ranking member of the Council present dictated by our Company in England, my word shall be the last we hear or speak of it from this day forward.

"Edward, you have free and uninhibited access to all the fort offers. Your deposition stands as legal and authoritative, but you have your personal freedom once again. You shall return with me to London at such time as I deem proper for sailing. If you do not accept these conditions, you shall remain in the *Discovery*'s brig until I set sail for London. What say you?"

Wingfield, happy to hear he was to leave as soon as Newport was ready, quickly said, "By all that's Holy, I accept."

"The choice does you credit, Edward," said Newport. "Captain Smith, you are free again, by God's grace and the good wind that blew us here. No justice was served in your trial and sentence; you are not responsible for the deaths of Robinson or Emry or any other man who lost his life that day you were captured."

"You have my deepest gratitude, Admiral," answered Smith with all sincerity.

Newport turned to face Archer and Ratcliffe.

Archer's eyebrows had knitted themselves into a knot. Ratcliffe's narrow chin had sunk even deeper into the folds of his ruff. Truculent schoolboys never looked so unrepentant. The Admiral's voice shook with emotion, though he did his best to control it.

"As for you two. How dare you circumvent the Council's direct instructions? You had no authority to vote without all current Councilors present and yet you did so. I void these unauthorized actions. Archer, you shall retain the office of Recorder, but nothing else. Ratcliffe, you shall retain the office of President for the year to which you were elected. Council membership is restored to the duly elected—Ratcliffe, Martin, and Smith."

95

Newport paused for a moment, pulling together in his mind the last of his announcements.

"In truth, the Council is larger. You have not met our newest Councilor, appointed in London, Master Matthew Scrivener." With this, the stranger stood up and bowed, smiled congenially to all present and sat down again.

Every face in the tiny cabin turned to appraise the Councilor who had been, from a corner, quietly observing the entire proceeding. They had forgotten that anybody else was present and now had the grace to be deeply embarrassed at having a total stranger, a new Councilor at that, see the Company at its worst.

A reprimand, a reversal of leadership decisions, and a near-hanging of one of their own could hardly be construed as the most favorable of introductions, and yet the young man stood unfazed by any of the untoward revelations laid before him in the last hour. His manner was composed, his jaw strongly set, his mouth well formed and relaxed. His smile was guileless and genuine, and a natural playfulness bounced in his clear blue eyes when he saw how his arrival had surprised some and nonplussed others, showing him to be a quick study of human nature. Smith immediately suspected that this young Councilor and he would be great friends.

The rest of the day was spent making ready for the unloading of eighty new colonists, none of whom had been allowed to disembark until accommodations were satisfactory. An orderly arrival and controlled settling in would show any natives watching that this Company could not be taken by surprise in the confusion of the day. By Tuesday, the new colonists were permitted to enter the fort and engage themselves in any manner agreeable after so long a voyage, and by Thursday all were happily situated in what would be their new home. Newport declared a holiday and finally opened the coffers for a belated New Year's celebration.

Ale and wine flowed freely and were matched cup for cup with mouthfuls of food supplied by Powhatan, for the Great Werowance had made a point of sending messengers daily with bushels of venison, smoked fish and oysters, corn, beans, squash and more. Powhatan's munificence was not lost on Newport, and the fact that every delivery was laid at Smith's feet was not lost on Archer and Ratcliffe.

"They are quite envious," remarked Scrivener to Smith as they enjoyed the holiday supper around the central fire.

"Green is not a becoming color," said Smith, between bites of roasted corn and beans.

"They certainly do not try to hide their distaste for you."

"No, you have seen us at our worst, I'm afraid."

"Surely the men are grateful for the supplies your connections have elicited. Why, then, are Archer and Ratcliffe so eager to have you out of the way?"

"I promised to fulfill my obligations with regard to the Company, and I have stopped anyone who thought to abandon or delay the Colony, for doing so would be a disgrace. In simple terms, we came here to forge a new Colony and, by God, I will not let it fail. We owe it to King and Company. There are those among us who think differently." Smith shrugged his compact shoulders.

"This Company here has had a devil of a time," said Scrivener simply. "Six months ago you had one hundred and four men, now you number thirty-eight. And you yourself were thought lost to savagery not so long ago. I see many of you are sickly and weak. The weather is biting and your houses are only tents, no strong buttress against the howling winter wind. 'Tis no wonder they want to go back to England."

"Aye, but a contract is a contract, and we all knew what we were about when we signed the agreement. We who are left should be even more determined to succeed, if not for ourselves then for the lost souls buried here so that they might not have died in vain. I cannot stomach the thought of telling Bartholomew Gosnold's wife and children that his dream died here with him."

"And Archer and Ratcliffe do not think beyond their own comfort, is that it?"

"You have ably grasped the point, young Matthew. And therefore I am an enemy in their eyes, though I do not believe it is as personal as you might perceive. They would squawk at anyone who stood against their wishes. And I, a yeoman's son with little education, am doubly offensive."

Scrivener threw back his head and laughed. "Squawk? They damn near hanged you, Captain – twice, you tell me – and you call it squawking?"

Smith smiled back affably and thought once again that this wine merchant's son from London would prove a fine companion in the coming months.

"Tell me about the savages, Smith. You lived with them for three weeks. You must have seen plenty."

Smith thought about his answer a long time. "They are much the same as any people I have encountered: loving and harsh, intelligent and slow witted, cheerful and morose. Some cook better than others; some make better hunters. They fear and respect their leaders and put great store by their children. The most interesting thing is their custom of going to the river at dawn, every day, and bathing. Astounding!"

"They bathe every day? Even in freezing water? Don't they know that frequent washing leads to disease?"

"No, on the contrary, they even wash the babes from birth. Every day. And throw bits of tobacco into the river in prayer to some god or another. They tried to persuade me to join them, but I was allowed to decline."

"They do not seem to understand that clothing is needed to ward off disease as well. How do they keep their health, I wonder?" Scrivener was perplexed. "Everyone knows that disease enters through our skin so it is best to keep covered at all times. The Naturals must suffer extraordinarily. Maybe that is why there are so few of them."

Smith had no answer for that.

"But stranger than that, Powhatan, the great and mighty, was ready to kill me—I swear, the clubs hovered over my head and I was praying for a swift end—when his little daughter ran up and told him not to do it. Can you imagine an English girl, even a princess, telling a king what to do with a prisoner? Unthinkable!"

Scrivener thought for a moment. "Maybe he never intended to kill you at all. Maybe it was a staged event, like a play or something."

"To what end? I was either a prisoner or guest, at Powhatan's mercy."

"Having a child rescue you makes him look beneficent, does it not? He appears merciful without losing respect or seeming weak. Is it possible, then, that Powhatan planned it? He made you a son and gave you chief's rights immediately after. No, I think it was not an accident that—what was her name? A-man-u-tay?—saved you."

"Her name was Amonute but I heard Powhatan call her Poca-hon-tas later. One must be a pet name."

"Whatever they call her, she was not as spontaneous as you might think. That's what I say." Scrivener sounded convinced.

Smith, full of good food and friendship, yawned and stretched, thinking how good it was to be with his own kind again. "'Tis late."

Music arose from the ranks somewhere, a fiddle and a recorder, followed by laughter and slurred voices. Someone started to dance but fell to the great enjoyment of his companions. Torches burned brightly in the crisp January night, warming old and new colonists who could not worm their way through the throng to the main brazier pit. Newly arrived wine and ale filled the stomachs and the spirits of all, and soon the singular afterglow of a party well done had crept into everyone. Men fell asleep where they were, some in solitary heaps, some draped over kegs, cannons or each other.

Smith bade his new friend good night and picked his way around the drunken bodies at his feet back to his tent. He did not begrudge the men their celebration, but he knew that overindulgence this night would make tomorrow's workers irritable and slow at the least. Well, he sighed to himself, tomorrow will come soon enough. Saluting a sentry, he left the Company behind and made ready for bed.

Hardly had he sat down when he felt the hair rise on the back of his neck. Every sinew was attuned to his surroundings.

Yet, nothing was out of place. No noise reached his ears other than the bass snoring and treble whistling of colonists sleeping off too much drink. No reason to fear, but there it was. He knew something was wrong. He stepped to the entry of his tent and looked around outside. Nothing was different from what it had been two minutes before.

Then, the unmistakable odor of burning cloth and damp wood stung his nose.

Looking up, he saw red and yellow flames leaping up from a tent on the far side of the fort; two sentries began beating their drums in a fevered frenzy, followed by the word Smith had been about to shout out himself: *"Fire!"*

Chapter Ten

Golden Dreams and Retribution

Smith dashed from his tent, found Scrivener scrambling from his own, and the two men ran as one toward the flames.

The sentry beat out the alarm on drums, Sam blasted the same on his trumpet, Smith and Scrivener shouted for aid. Someone managed to open the massive front gates, and from the *John and Francis* a sleepy Admiral Newport squinted toward the Fort, thinking how strange it was that the sun was rising from the northern horizon.

The cook's tent was consumed in flames, with sparks flying upward and dying against the velvety night sky like fireflies on a summer's evening. The two men stood in stunned silence for a minute then started shaking their sleeping comrades who were too stupefied by ale to heed the unrelenting drum and trumpet.

"Come to, man! Stand! Stand, I say!" shouted Scrivener at Read. "We need your help!"

"What the devil?" cried Read, struggling to his feet. "Can't a man sleep in peace?"

"Fire! We need water—fetch as many men as you can and make a line to the river with buckets. Do you understand me?" asked Scrivener, shaking Read's shoulders and looking straight into the cloudy eyes of the blacksmith.

"Aye. I do." Read belched and staggered toward the main gate.

Smith, having tried unsuccessfully to rouse the nearest men, resorted to dragging them to safety outside the fort. As a few men managed to stumble through the gates without assistance, Smith surveyed the scene before him.

Too many men were incapacitated. Sparks and flames danced wickedly over the cook's tent. No other tent or building was afire—yet.

Smith ran for the river, catching up with Read as he wobbled on the bank, hoping to at least bring a bucketful of river water. His felt his feet give way, and suddenly both men were sprawled on the ice that had formed a protective skin on the King's River, ice that stretched outward at least a hundred feet.

Smith slid his way back to the embankment, hoisted himself aright on land, and ran back to the fort.

Men stood or sat in a drunken stupor all around the fort's perimeter, their breath smoking in fitful bursts from their gaping mouths. Scrivener met Smith inside the gate.

"Where are the water buckets?" gasped Scrivener.

"Too much ice on the river and not enough sober men to form a line. We have only five sober men among us. The best that we can do now is—"

He stopped when he saw several adjacent tents alight and spitting flame.

"By God, we're lost! Quickly, man, fetch what you can from your tent. Quickly!"

Here Smith grabbed the men on watch, sober by default, and with them dragged forth as many munitions as they could before these, too, caught fire. Smith then returned to his own tent to gather what he must save: his papers, maps, and notes. Smoke choked him as he instinctively moved toward the gate.

Newport, wrapped in a great woolen cape, arrived outside the gate in time to meet Smith and Scrivener exiting with their belongings. Words were not necessary. All around them huddled colonists both old and new, blinking in slack-jawed, foggy horror at the sight before them.

Within minutes the fort and all its contents were ablaze. A loud crack and then the frozen earth rocked under the colonists' feet. Men turned to shield their eyes and persons from raining debris. Whatever munitions had remained in the fort were now obliterated. Phaeton and Phoenix howled the sorrow of every man there.

Still coughing up smoke and gasping, Smith bent over his knees to pull in more air.

As he recovered himself, he turned to look upon the giant bonfire that was once their bastion of safety, their home, their place of worship. Hot emotion churned in his belly and his hands shook as he pushed his hat more firmly on his head. What was left to be done but watch? Tears of anger made it difficult to do even that.

How stupid could they have been to leave themselves open to such needless waste? Had half the Company been sober, the loss would have been contained to one cook's tent, surely. Why had he not thought to guarantee the safety of the Company? And who was responsible for the blaze itself?

"How did it start?" asked Newport.

"We don't know, Admiral. We went to bed and minutes later the cook's tent was on fire and no one about to speak to," answered Smith. "It must have been an accident, surely."

"What else could it be?" asked Scrivener, blowing his nose into a handkerchief smeared with soot.

"Sabotage," Smith said.

"Sabotage! The Naturals?"

"No, I don't think so. They have been more than friendly since I returned to the fort. And Powhatan made me his son. I don't think he's in a temper to do us harm – not right now, that is. Someday, perhaps, but not now. No, if this fire was not an accident, then someone here set the fire and is pretending to be shocked or drunk or both. The question is can we discover him?"

"Does it matter?" asked Scrivener bitterly. "The fort is destroyed, our lodgings, gear, food and munitions reduced to ashes. What more can he do to cause suffering or ruination?"

"He can do the same again, once the new fort is built. We must be a vigilant and sober Company from now forward. No more revelries that end in drunkenness. Had enough men been clear-headed, we could have limited this loss to one tent, maybe no fire at all. Admiral, would you not agree?"

Admiral Newport did not reply, but pursed his lips in concentration. The conflagration was all-consuming, roaring and crackling in front of him. He turned his back on the sight and stomped back to his ship.

Within the hour the fort, once a sturdy, reassuring triangle of timbered protection, was reduced to a pile of pungent ashes cooling in the frosty night air.

Weeks of hard labor in freezing temperatures partly restored the fort, not as it had been but with a substantial expansion to more comfortably house the new colonists and those expected to arrive with a Captain Nelson at any time. Sabotage now seemed remote, and all agreed that the official record would only show that a terrible accident had occurred in which the whole fort had been lost to fire. Nothing more. No explanations. Losing the fort was embarrassment enough; no need to add humiliation by admitting it was human folly and drunkenness that had caused it.

More labor during the early spring thaw had produced a plot of land, cleared and turned, ready for planting corn at the Pasbeheghs' instruction.

"Gentlemen, it is time to fill our ship with saleable goods," said Newport at a Council meeting on board the *John and Francis* not long after the first of March.

Sam came running up the gangplank and interrupted the thought.

"Naturals, sir," said Sam to Admiral Newport. "Coming with food! We need Captain Smith, sir, right away."

"Go to, Captain, and offer our thanks," said Newport without enthusiasm. The generosity of Powhatan was clouded only by the practice of first laying half of everything at Smith's feet.

Soon Smith and several Naturals approached the ship, bearing baskets of fish, bread and corn and several deer tied to poles, which Newport accepted gratefully and solemnly, his earlier pique not evident.

"By God, Smith, you have made yourself useful," declared Newport to the Council, as he motioned for the foodstuffs to be taken below decks for Cook.

Ratcliffe and Martin struggled to maintain neutral faces but it was clear to Scrivener, deeply engrossed in brushing lint off his breeches, that they were physically pained to hear Newport's praise of Smith.

Newport returned to the topic at hand. "I suffered sore embarrassment in London when our cargo was deemed nothing but dirt, and I have sworn to bring back gold this time. Anything less would be a disgrace and could cause not just embarrassment but ruination."

Martin sputtered and coughed at these words.

Newport gave him an odd look, but continued. "Here, then, are Masters William Dawson and Abraham Ransack. They are refiners who will help us locate and ship our gold to London."

Two men stepped from out of nowhere to bow and smile at the Council.

The former, a lean, gaunt man of thirty years who the Council only knew minimally as a gentleman colonist and enthusiastic assistant in rebuilding the fort, intuitively moved closer to the Admiral, said, "I am pleased to begin my assignment."

His companion, shorter and darker in every respect, said nothing but remained attentive. Black eyes peered over spectacles and his beard was grizzled and bushy. He waited patiently for the Admiral to continue.

"They have two goldsmiths and a jeweler between them and the hope is to return to London with true gold this time. Captain Martin will do all in his power to ensure success."

"I have already discovered a place, Admiral," answered Martin, "rich in gold. Just along the north shore."

Smith almost gasped out loud at the blatant lie, but held his breath and his tongue. In his dealings with the natives, he had seen plenty of copper and victuals, which were the Naturals' main status symbols. Gold? Not a glimmer of it anywhere, certainly not on or near Powhatan who would be the most likely to have it displayed on his person. If Powhatan did not have it, no one did. No, gold was not to be had in Virginia, not, at least, in Powhatan's realm.

"You have? Well, why did you not say so earlier?" exclaimed Newport.

"I only found it recently, and with the soil being so hard-packed in winter, it hardly seemed worthwhile to mention it. We could hardly do anything about it till now anyway," answered Martin smoothly.

Smith rolled his eyes at Scrivener who discreetly looked away before he was forced to laugh out loud. If Martin had found gold, then, he, Smith, was the next in line for the throne of England! But the gleam in Ratcliffe's eyes, the smug smile on Martin, and the joyful patting of Newport's singular hand on his breast put to rest any notion that steadier heads might prevail.

Within the hour, the entire Company had heard that Martin had found gold nearby and that they, the men, were going to begin digging immediately. Men who had barely completed the daunting task of palisading a larger fort and erecting buildings within fought each other to earn the first shift and from that moment on, gold was the only subject worth speaking of.

"Gold is a seductive mistress," Smith commented to Scrivener as they watched the men crowd each other out to sign up for digging shifts.

"Order! Order! Back off and stand apace!" barked the foreman. "No man touches a speck of dirt until we have the work shifts in tolerable sequence and properly filled."

"Even gold that's not there?" inquired Scrivener.

"Aye, that's the worst kind for she promises and promises without ever actually giving up her prize."

"But this is part of our mission, is it not? And if he has truly found gold, then we are blessed indeed."

"If indeed. I will concede it is possible that Martin has found gold, but not likely. No one, no Natural within a hundred miles of the ocean wears or displays gold in any form. Isn't that odd if gold is to be had?"

"Perhaps they do not recognize gold as valuable," answered Scrivener, trying to be fair.

"True. In faith, I do not know for fact that this Virginia earth is barren. I only say that what I have observed leads me to conclude that barren it is. Of gold, at least."

The mad dash for digging at last quieted when the first workers departed, but the air crackled with anticipation and expectation, and Smith finally had to remove himself to his tent for refuge against the barrage of gold-related activities. Dig gold, wash gold, refine gold, load gold. There was no talk, no work, no hope but gold. By the end of fourteen weeks, the *John and Francis* was filled to the beams with chunks of glittering Virginia dirt.

"You shall see, Smith, that we are right," said Martin on the day before sailing. "You will be judged for the simpleton you are when the King sees all the gold we are bringing back! And I will earn four fifths of the profit, as promised by the Charter!"

"Four fifths of naught is still naught, Councilor. The King's assayers will quickly pronounce your 'gold' worthless. You have not carried out sound testing here and when they do so in London, you will pay the price. And," here Smith seethed, "all necessary business neglected in the meantime. What are we to live on if the Naturals do not continue to feed us? We must be self-sufficient! We must be self-reliant! And I have watched these past months as the ship's crew devoured all our cheese, butter, beer, beef – such that we have nothing! Nothing of the supplies originally brought for us! They leave us as they found us – pitifully unable to feed ourselves, and waiting for their return! Is this any way to run a Colony?"

"Oh, be gone, Smith. No one needs you here." Martin turned his back.

Smith left in disgust, leaving Martin to watch in childish glee the final preparations for departure. Dawson and Ransack, the refiners, congratulated themselves on the bounty they had collected and spent the afternoon assuring anyone who asked that they would protect the shipment with their lives, if necessary, and return for more whenever Newport sailed again for Virginia.

"You have Captain Martin's word, then? The elder Martin will pay?" Dawson whispered to Ransack.

"When the Company spurns the shipment, Martin's father has promised a fair price for the 'gold.' All we need to do is make sure it finds its way to him after the Company rejects it. The zinc in the soil will produce brass. He will happily take it." Ransack's eyes glittered behind his spectacles as he laid a finger along his lips. It was best not to speak of the matter. Not here.

Eventually Smith stopped agitating the situation in his mind. He had no power to change anything here, and his energy would be better spent actively pursuing food and exploring where he could. Newport would find out soon enough that looking for gold in Virginia was like looking for generosity in a miser's heart; it just wasn't there.

Smith's humor improved also as he recalled that not all the cargo aboard the *John and Francis* was a disappointment. Edward Maria Wingfield, who had spent the last months in a gentlemanly purgatory as neither a true prisoner nor a member of the Council would be on board, as well as Gabriel Archer, who had decided he had had enough and wished to return to England, relieving not only themselves but the colonists as well.

"So we waited out the winter on a pleasant West Indies island." Captain Francis Nelson of the *Phoenix* was explaining the details of his journey. It was April 20th.

"'Tis a pity, sir, you did not meet with the Admiral. He has been gone but ten days," replied Ratcliffe, signaling for his steward to pour more wine into the glasses of the men seated around his table.

Captain Nelson, a solid, weathered man of forty years, blew air through his lips and waved a hand. He was here; the ship, crew and forty new colonists were unharmed by their delay and in fact were all the stronger for having spent the cold Virginia months in West Indian sunshine and sand. Now it was nearly May and all was right.

"And we thank you for your generosity, sir. Our common pot was never so full nor so varied," added Martin, wiping his mouth and clearing the phlegm from his throat.

"He's grateful because he pockets the profits himself, don't he now?" said the steward into Smith's ear as he poured.

Smith gave the man a warning look. It was no secret that both Ratcliffe and Martin had helped themselves to company store profits, though this move was not sanctioned anywhere but in their own minds. Nelson, unlike Newport, had been quick to empty his hold of the oatmeal, aqua vitae, salted pork and other hogsheads of victuals intended for the Company. Smith, seeing the supplies coming off the *Phoenix*, had already allotted proportions and put an end to personal profit. The Supply Officer's mandate could not be crossed, not lawfully anyway. The matter was closed.

"What was that exercise this morning, Captain Smith?" inquired Nelson. "I have never seen such chaotic military maneuvers."

"Having seen savage warfare, we are drilling in a new fashion. To best the Naturals, we must fight as they do."

"Lying about on the ground? Hiding behind trees? Never seen anything like it!"

"I suppose it is odd-looking from a distance, but I can assure you it is most effective, especially in small numbers. We have been practicing a week and my men are ready."

"Ready? Ready for what?"

"To fight Powhatan's whole force, if necessary! When I was captive, I told him that Newport was coming soon to take us all back to England. He surely knows that did not happen, and he will be angry."

"So you are worried about war?"

"Any sane man would be; but more likely we need to be ready to take seventy colonists and mariners up river to find mines, if they exist, and to see what lies beyond the Falls. The South Sea Passage is waiting for us to find her."

"Exploring without consulting Newport? You overstep your bounds, Captain," warned Ratcliffe from his end of the table.

Nelson listened to the objections of not only President Ratcliffe, but Martin as well, and then said, "I was hired to bring supplies and colonists here and back to England and that I have done, gladly and with goodly pay. If you wish to contract us for anything more, the Company must recompense me for my ship and time lost due to your expedition. Moreover, my sailors must receive extra pay."

Smith shook his head. "I'm afraid we cannot afford that, Captain. Maybe another time."

Ratcliffe suddenly changed his mind. "Smith, you could go without Captain Nelson's sailors, couldn't you? Take Scrivener and a few men on the barge. We could manage without you all well enough, and we wouldn't have to pay anyone extra."

"No," said Smith slowly, "no. We shall stay here, at least till the *Phoenix* sails for England. I shall take that offer later this summer, if you don't mind. There is much to be done right now and the Supply Officer should be here to oversee it."

Ratcliffe buried his chin into his ruff and glared into his cup; Martin clapped his mouth shut.

Nelson, puzzled by this strange discussion, mentally shrugged his shoulders and changed the subject.

Smith, faced with the forty newest colonists to house and feed, put his efforts into building living quarters and planting the field with corn, with weekly drilling in both traditional arms and native warfare. His instructions kept the Company working smoothly and, thanks to his allotment decree and Nelson's fine contributions, eating well and often. Great physical exertion followed by good food in substantial quantities and a restful night's sleep was as near to Heaven as any man might wish. If any man missed women, he had only to visit a nearby village where willing young women were plentiful and friendly enough now that Powhatan had embraced Smith as a son.

Within days of Nelson's arrival, a small group of messengers appeared at the fort's gate with twenty dead turkeys in tow, each as big as a schoolboy, asking for Smith and refusing to speak to anyone else.

Smith came out and stood in the bright sunshine, his hand on the pistol at his side. Scrivener joined him, musket and match in his hands.

"Powhatan sends Smit twenty turkeys as gift. He asks for twenty swords in return," said the foremost Natural with confidence.

Smith, startled but with enough presence of mind not to show it, surveyed the fowl at his feet and took his time in answering. "No. Tell Powhatan we will not give swords for turkeys."

Confusion crossed the messenger's face for an instant. He tried again. "Great White Father gave Powhatan swords for turkeys. Smit do the same as his Father."

"No, I will not. Tell Powhatan we will not trade swords for turkeys ever again." With that, Smith left the messengers to pick up the poultry in baffled resignation.

"Turkeys for swords! What possessed the Admiral to give away weapons to our enemy—for anything?" Smith asked Scrivener inside the palisade.

"Who knows? Maybe he thought a few swords would not do any harm. Maybe he does not think of Powhatan as an enemy, seeing as he made you his son."

"Perhaps you are right. Since the rebuilding of the fort we have not had cause for alarm from our neighbors. They come to Jamestown without fear, and we welcome them with their food and women. Perhaps the Admiral was acting in true friendship. But to give so much for so little! A few copper pieces would have paid for twenty turkeys. Mark me, we will now have to pay out much, much more to buy a basket of corn." Smith sighed. "It cannot be helped now. Let us hope it will not bankrupt us before the next supply ship comes in."

Naturals indeed ventured daily to the fort, some to give food, some to cook food, some to play, and some merely to gain a close look at the strange men with shiny armor, heavy clothing, and hairy chins. Close contact seemed natural and pleased the members of the Council who lived by the letter of their *Instructions*: do nothing to offend the Naturals, which applied even when the Naturals started helping themselves to tools and swords left within their reach.

"We cannot allow them to take whatever they like!" said Smith to the Council one day not long after he refused to give swords for turkeys. "It is thievery and were we in London the thief would have his hand cut off or lose his life!"

"But we cannot reproach them. They are our guests. Let them have the trifles and be done with it," Ratcliffe said. "They harm no one and we have plenty of tools and swords."

"They have harmed no one *here* or *yet*. Today it is trifles – but tomorrow it will be anything that's moveable for what schoolboy does not know the lesson herein? That a child may do as much as his elders allow him to do. If we do not teach our savage friends that thievery is wrong, they will not only steal trifles but grow bolder and take our guns, our clothes, our anything. Who, then, will have respect from the Naturals or anyone else? How may we garner respect when we do not have any for ourselves and our own property?"

Smith, back in the fields outside the fort, fumed as he recalled the debate. It had been a fruitless effort on his part for only Scrivener, loyal, sane Scrivener, believed as he did. The Council as well as Percy and Hunt all thought more of the *Instructions* than they did of the higher purpose before them. That no one could see the necessity of commanding rather than waiting for respect frustrated Smith to his very core. No one had ever waited his way to respect, of that he was certain.

So when, an hour later, five Chickahominies approached him as he planted corn, his temper was foul and his hand ready. With barely a greeting in passing, one of the five moved to take Smith's sword that rested on the basket he was using to haul kernels.

Eyes dark with anger, Smith growled and clenched his fist, darting toward the culprit. The thief, seeing Smith charging him, grabbed his tomahawk, but Smith's fist drove into the brave's face before the tomahawk was half-raised. He fell back with a force that pushed his companions into a tumbled heap.

Smith roared and pulled his flintlock pistols from his gear. The Chickahominies who had fallen like pins in a game of skittles managed to stand in amazement for half a second before recognizing the danger pointed in their direction. They sped away, leaving their friend unconscious on the ground where Smith's right jab had left him.

Smith, running and shouting damnations in their wake, chased them to the far end of the island where they had jumped into their canoe and paddled away. Running back to the field, Smith dragged the groggy thief to his feet and pushed him into the fort.

Ratcliffe and the rest of the Council were apoplectic over the incident reported to them by the sentries on watch at the North bulwark.

"I want this man arrested," panted Smith, shoving the culprit forward. "I want him in jail for stealing my sword."

"You cannot mean that," answered Ratcliffe, horrified. "We do not arrest our guests."

"Oh, but I do." Smith drew a deep breath. "He is a thief and not a guest. Arrest him. I want Powhatan to know he cannot steal from John Smith. I cannot speak for the rest of you."

Smith, mollified at last that action had been taken, resumed his field duties the next day, this time with both Scrivener and a brace of pistols at his side. Morning turned to noon and in the last of the daylight hours, Smith and Scrivener felt rather than heard danger approach.

The hair on Smith's neck prickled, but he remained bent over the row he was sowing.

Giving a low whistle, Smith slowly put his hands on the grips of his pistols. Scrivener followed suit, looking for all the world as if sowing corn was the only thing on their minds.

"Now!"

At Smith's command, the two men stood erect, back-to-back, pistols poised and ready. Coming at them from the far woods were five Naturals wearing black face paint and carrying clubs.

Smith fired one of his pistols. The intruders dropped to the ground.

"Run! To the gate!" Smith did not have to repeat the cry for Scrivener followed close enough to trip him.

The gate swung open just enough to let the two men in before the uninvited warriors arrived, shouting and gesticulating angrily at the closed palisade.

"We no harm Smit! We want to talk to the prisoner! Let us in!"

Smith, thinking they would be mad to attempt to harm him with a cadre of musketeers surrounding him, agreed to open the gate.

"Bring the prisoner here, Scrivener, if you would please. Let us see what can be gained by this enterprise."

Within minutes the thief, nose and eye sockets bruised and swollen in purple majesty, straggled forth and met his comrades a few feet inside the gate.

Without anyone speaking a word, the painted braves drew their clubs and began pounding the prisoner who stood stoically while the first blows fell but sank to the ground thereafter. Smith rushed forward in disgust and began prying the beaters off the beaten. As the angry mob turned to apply their clubs to Smith, he recoiled and drew his sword.

"Shut the gate! Arrest these men! Now!"

The musketeers rushed in, using their weapons as batons, and parted the belligerent Naturals. Shackles and chains bound their hands to each other, and they soon found themselves in the church. They could not be trusted alone with the first prisoner, and there was no where else to put them that would keep them both under watch and away from the Company for most of the day. Pinioned as they are, thought Smith, sitting through two Common Prayer services each day will either convert them totally or frighten them into good behavior.

The next afternoon, in the fresh twilight, two more Chickahominies arrived at the fort gate, one tall and slender, the other shorter by a head and thickset, carrying bows and hatchets in both hands, and bearing quivers packed with arrows.

They asked for Smith who eventually came out with five men, armed with muskets and matches ready for firing and aimed at the petitioners, who had come to negotiate the release of the captives.

Smith stared hard at the two braves before speaking.

"We will not release them until you prove yourselves good and true. Every hatchet, every sword, every tool taken from our men and fort which was not given honestly and in faith by our own good graces must be returned to me by dawn tomorrow."

"If this does not happen?" asked the shorter brave.

"If not, then all captives will hang when the sun reaches the top of the sky."

"Powhatan has two English. Let us trade."

"Who are they?" Smith said, narrowing his eyes and lifting his chin. They were counterfeiting, surely.

"Both named Fit-ee-plus."

Phittiplace! Two brothers, gentlemen from the *Phoenix*. Young they were and new enough to the colony to be foolish in their actions. Smith did not doubt the truth of the message now, for the name was too new, too queerly English for the natives to have contrived it. How the brothers were captured would have to be sorted out later, but their rescue was not in question.

"Go then," said Smith. "Bring them to me and we will talk about a trade."

"We talk trade now," insisted the short Natural. The taller one continued to stand by in strong silence.

"You bring them here tomorrow, unharmed, and we will talk then. I cannot promise anything until I see them unharmed."

"Easy there, lad," said Smith to Sam. "Steady. It is not ourselves we want to set afire."

Sam, a burning torch in one hand, stepped carefully onto the barge but when the small craft dipped under his weight, he had to reach with his free hand for assistance from the Captain. Wedging his thin frame into position next to the pile of lightweight logs with knobs of sherry-soaked linen wrapped around the tops, he smiled at Scrivener who was already in position and clutched the torch tighter.

"I reckon 'tis dark enough now," Scrivener said from his station. "Let us be off, shall we?"

The small party rowed toward the Chickahominy village that lay twelve miles or so upriver. The sound of crickets and other nightlife stirring were the only sounds they marked. Naturals, Smith had learned, did not travel at night and so the colonists safely assumed they were free to move about the river without fear.

"Ready, Sam?" Smith asked. "Do you know what you are to do?"

"Aye, sir. Light the logs and hand them to you or Master Scrivener when you call for them, one at a time."

"Good lad. That's right. We shall be calling for them directly."

Directing the barge to the river's edge and the six musketeers on board to load and be ready to fire should any Naturals try to stop them in their mission, Smith stood at the helm and peered into the darkness, looking for the first signs of a longhouse.

"There! Pull closer! Sam, hand me a firebrand!"

Sam dutifully lighted the first log with the torch. The whoosh of the ignition caused him to turn his head. Smith hefted the newly lit log, then threw it landward as easily as discarding a chicken leg at dinner.

In quick succession Smith and Scrivener hurled firebrand upon firebrand into the village, some hitting the bare ground but some striking huts as dry and brittle as a grandmother's bones.

The sleeping town awoke in a panic. Silence shrouded the little craft while all aboard watched the effect.

Sam, turning to Smith, asked, "No one will die, will they?"

Smith's face softened. "Not if they have their wits about them, lad. See how they have already gathered over there? No, they have time to be safe enough. But the point has been made. We shall see what they think of it tomorrow, I should say."

With that, Smith ordered the barge back to Jamestown.

Shortly after supper the next day, a cry went up from the sentry. Several Chickahominies were approaching with the hapless Phittiplace brothers in tow, followed by a group carrying the missing tools and weapons required by Smith the day before.

When they reached the gate, they dumped the metal tools with a clang at the base of the palisade and called for Smith.

Michael Phittiplace, the older of the brothers, at nineteen had been out in the world long enough to be stoic under difficult circumstances and thus stood among his captors with feigned disregard, but William Phittiplace, only just sixteen, had a pale, ashen face and dark-circled eyes that spoke of nights sleepless with terror. Smith noted the pair's condition – rumpled and dirty but unharmed—as he met them at the gate.

"I see you have returned all that is rightly ours. Master Scrivener, bring out two of our thieves. We shall exchange two for two."

The Chickahominy leader heard this and started to protest that all six prisoners should be released but caught himself.

Smith directed several men to gather the returned tools and weapons and take them to their owners. The Naturals waited patiently and when their comrades appeared they all marched off to their canoes without a word. Smith watched them until they had paddled out of view.

Sam called to him from across the interior of the fort.

"Captain, come look at this. These tools are not just from the Chickahominies. Look! This shovel belongs to Read—see where he burned his name on the handle—and he told me that it disappeared weeks ago when some Nansemonds were here. Nansemond! They are fifty miles away, sir!" Sam whistled and caressed the handle in awe.

"Nansemond, you say?" Smith said. "I told you so, Sam. Respect. You have to earn it."

The Council – Ratcliffe, Martin, Smith, and Scrivener—convened shortly thereafter to discuss the matter of their neighbors' insolence. With surprising alacrity and unusual agreement, they charged Smith to find out what was going on by interrogating the prisoners.

"But whatever you do, Smith," Ratcliffe admonished, "please be civilized about it."

Within the hour, Smith was waiting below deck on the *Phoenix*, six musketeers by his side. He heard the heavy boots of Scrivener and the barefoot padding of a prisoner come down the ladder and stop as their eyes adjusted to the gloom below.

The prisoner's black eyes grew wide when he saw Smith and the muskets. He did not resist when Scrivener shoved him over to the mast and bound him to it, back to the wood and hands pulled around the circumference.

In front of him, not six feet away, six matches glowed in the murky depths as six musketeers raised their weapons, prepared to fire the moment Smith gave the order.

"Speak, if you want to live, man," barked Smith in the prisoner's native tongue. "Why are you stealing and harassing us? What is the plan?"

The thief did not answer. Smith moved out of the line of fire.

"If you do not tell me, I will give the order to fire. You know me. I will not hesitate."

"I do not know," blurted the man, shutting his eyes.

"Who does know?"

Opening one eye, the prisoner said, "Macanoe," and squeezed it shut again.

Minutes later, Macanoe found himself in much the same situation as his predecessor. While the first had been clearly afraid, Macanoe was breathing heavily, sweat beading on his forehead, obviously not inclined to die for the cause, whatever it proved to be.

Smith signaled his men to raise their muskets.

"If you want to live, you will tell me what you know about the plan to steal from us. Who ordered it?"

The pungent smell of lighted matches soaked in salt peter, the close air of narrow quarters, and the stink of the white men so near with weapons looming in the shadowy hold overcame the captive, and he told all he knew in a rush of words.

"Powhatan! Powhatan gave orders. All tribes in his realm are to bring him your swords and to cut many English throats."

Smith signaled his men to relax and put out their matches.

"Thank you, Macanoe. That is what we wanted to know. You may live."

Just as Macanoe alighted on the riverbank after his ordeal, a cry from the sentry made him and his guards turn to look down river. Coming up from the east was a fleet of canoes, one in the lead and two following side by side.

Smith and Scrivener stood on shore with the firing squad musketeers near enough to be of use, should the occasion arise, but Smith doubted any shots need be directed at this entourage. In the first canoe, straight backed and resting her tiny hands on the rim, sat Amonute.

She had made countless visits in the past six months bringing gifts of food from her father, Powhatan, and turning cartwheels in front of the gate. Her playful laughter and quick intelligence had been a balm to nearly every man in the fort who either had children of his own in England waiting for his return or was young enough to miss a sibling or cousin of the same age. Shining black hair, sparkling eyes and a dimple in her chin made her the darling of the fort.

Behind her sat a brave, tall and deeply muscled, with a face disfigured by the claws of some wild animal. The scars, though light with age, traveled the entire length of his broad face, leaving not one square inch unscathed. These were nothing compared to the fierce and uncompromising stare of his eyes, altogether giving Smith the impression of being face to face with a murderer peering through prison bars.

Smith helped her out of the canoe, beaming in spite of himself for she was a joy to behold—despite being the daughter of the man who had ordered theft and murder upon his people. The other canoes pulled up and tied off, four braves unloading a freshly slain deer and a massive loaf of bread.

The disfigured brave stood by her side, nodded his greeting and followed closely as Smith and Pocahontas, as she preferred to be called, entered the fort, chattering and laughing as old friends do.

Once inside, Pocahontas, in a voice high and sweet, delivered her message. "My father sends his love and respect, Captain Smith. He has heard that some of his werowances have been troubling you. Please take this deer and bread as a sign of our deepest respect. He also sends Rawhunt with another message."

With this, her bodyguard stepped forward, stripped off his hunting glove and wrist guard and dropped them at Smith's feet, never taking his steely eyes from Smith's.

"We submit to your will, Captain Smith. We ask you to release our brothers now that we have peace."

Smith, having just heard the near-death confession of Macanoe, would not have been willing to believe this statement except for Pocahontas' presence. She was only a child, true, but Powhatan's child and as such a worthy emissary. She did not petition for the prisoners, he noted, as Powhatan could hardly afford to be seen begging for common captives.

Nor could Smith afford to be seen asking the Council for permission to release prisoners, though he should if he followed the letter of the law here. No, he would take action now and ask forgiveness later, should that be necessary. He had been the original apprehender, had he not? And Powhatan – and hence, all the local Naturals—recognized no other English leader, except Newport who was on his way to England at this moment and little use here.

"The great Powhatan was merciful to me. I shall be merciful to his people. Scrivener, bring the rest of the Naturals from the church and let them rejoin their families."

Smith glanced over to Pocahontas who dimpled her delight at the Captain.

Now The *Phoenix* was awash in the fragrance of the freshly hewn cedar stacked in her hold, the end of May 1608 was drawing near, and Nelson was advocating an early June departure. This cargo would have no need of assayers in London and would be profit guaranteed. The Virginia Company would be pleased at the effort of its fledgling colony.

The Council, aghast at Smith's heavy-handed dealings with the Chickahominies, nonetheless liked the calm that followed. The crops were growing, even though the rains were few; fish and game were plentiful; Nelson's supplies still filled the coffers; the Naturals were respectful and helpful once again. And although a number of the new colonists had taken ill recently, most were hale and eager to work on erecting housing. And no one was accosted by Naturals, ever. All seemed right with Virginia and thus the world.

Smith, ready to accept Ratcliffe's earlier offer of exploration, gathered the goods and gear needed to sail up the unknown path of the Chesapeake Bay. He and fourteen men would take the barge, follow Nelson out as far as the Bay, and continue north to experience and document what lay ahead. As always, his heart sped at the thought of exploration, a chance to be free of chastisement, of politics, and of personal grievances brought to bear in frequent, unhappy surprises.

Martin, long suffering and never fully in health, pleaded with the Council to be allowed to return to England on the *Phoenix*. The granting of his request left only three governing men at the fort—Ratcliffe, Smith and Scrivener— and the thought of Ratcliffe in utter and complete control of the fort while they were away instantly determined in Smith's mind who was going where and when.

Scrivener, eager to explore with the energetic Smith, agreed to stay behind and attempt to dissuade Ratcliffe, who could outvote him at any time, against any rash or untoward actions. Percy and Hunt, though not officially on the Council, might lend their voices in guiding the President if another Council member was there to lead their opposition. It was all supposition, but Ratcliffe's self-serving record was more than a hint that Scrivener's presence was justified.

And so on the morning tide of June 2, 1608, under a steady wind, the barge carrying Smith and his explorers followed the *Phoenix* out to the great Chesapeake Bay. Just before Nelson sailed onto the Atlantic, Smith climbed aboard for one last conference with the captain.

"Take these, please, Captain Nelson, and treat them as your own." Smith handed over a leather bag.

"Of course, Captain. What are they, may I ask?"

"They are my most prized possessions. Maps, in particular, but also an account of the past year and letters to friends and family. You are welcome to read what you fancy in the account, and look over the maps, but leave the letters be, if you do not mind. I have copies here, of course, but I trust you to deliver all in good condition and to the proper authorities."

Nelson agreed and, after a warm farewell, the two parted.

Filled with the satisfaction of releasing a finished work, confident that new maps would be drawn up shortly, Smith ordered the sails be tacked, so the barge would head north into the vast uncharted Chesapeake Bay.

Seven weeks later, Smith returned, wounded, with a strange, fully bearded Potomac Natural in company.

Chapter Eleven

Beyond Powhatan's Realm

Smith, his right arm extended on the table so Bagnall could assess the wound, related the parts of the exploration worth telling to the Council, Percy, Sam, and anyone else who wished to hear it.

"We did not find the passage to the South Sea, regrettably. But we did reach the Bolus River, which should please Newport when he hears. And we found furs such as would make a man rich in a day. Otter, beaver, marten, lynx and mink—enough to fill the *Susan Constant*. I mapped all we saw, traveling above Powhatan's realm. The northern natives are smaller, ruder. They have not the great agricultural knowledge Powhatan's people have, but they are cunning in their own way and eager to dispense with our barge, and us if they could. We did not let them, of course."

"But your arm! You are swollen from finger to neck!" cried Sam. "What happened to your arm?"

"A stingray, one of the vilest creatures God ever created, stabbed my wrist with its tail, and the poison he gave me caused swelling ten times what you see here. So gorged and in dread pain was I that I pointed to a plot of land— with my good hand, mind you—and asked to be buried there for I was certain to die within the hour."

Sam, forgetting what his own eyes did see, asked in awe, "And did you?"

Laughter from the men around him brought him back to his senses and he blushed at his mistake.

"Not yet, lad, not yet!" answered Smith. "Not only did I not die, I ate the foul creature for my dinner!" He patted his stomach with his good hand, rolled his eyes and smacked his lips.

"And who is this savage you have with you?" asked Ratcliffe.

"My name is Mosco," answered the bearded Natural, in heavily French-accented English. "I am from Potomac."

Ratcliffe was startled to hear him speak so easily in English; his clothing and manners were native. Mosco's skin was brown; his hair shaved except for a long lock on the top. He wore nothing except the ubiquitous breechcloth. In every respect he appeared native, except for the bushy black hair that grew untamed about his face and on his chest and legs.

"And, pray, how do you know English so well?"

"I do not know it well. I am only remembering. The Iroquois captured my family when I was twelve. We lived in the French colony. My mother was English. My father was French."

No one said a word at this unusual match.

"The Iroquois separated us soon after we were captured. They sent me to the Potomac. I do not know where my parents or sisters are. A Potomac brave and his family adopted me and I quickly learned their ways. That was eleven…years ago."

"So you remember English well enough. Do you speak French, too?"

"It is hard to say. I only just remembered English! Give me a Frenchman to talk with, and I will see."

"And so you wish to come and live as an Englishman again?"

If the question repulsed Mosco, he did not show it. He merely answered with more emphasis than seemed necessary, "No, thank you."

Once tended by Bagnall, Smith was free to walk the perimeter of the fort with Scrivener, who was agitated and eager to speak with Smith alone.

As they rounded the north bulwark, Smith stopped. Before him a crew of fifteen men was diligently framing an enormous structure, one Smith did not recall seeing the plans for. He turned a quizzical eye to Scrivener.

"It's a palace," Scrivener said unhappily.

"A palace?"

"Ratcliffe has ordered it made to his specifications and for himself as President. He thought it would be completed before you returned."

"And well it might have been, had I not been injured."

"There is more. The Company men are dissatisfied with his freehanded ways. He helps himself to the Store and serves himself and his gentlemen friends the choice bits. Your decree of proportions has been forgotten."

"What of the corn fields? They look overgrown and untended."

"They are indeed. All work has ceased except to build the President's house. The gentlemen of our Company have been granted pardon from labor of any kind. And the men you see here are the only ones fit to work. Every new colonist that did not go with you has been stricken with the bloody flux or the ague. We are half a force at best. In truth, they have collectively asked me— begged me—to depose him and install you."

Hunt, who had been bustling to catch up, arrived in time to hear the last and join in.

"It is imperative, Captain Smith," huffed Hunt, his round face reddening. "Ratcliffe has gone too far, and no man dare challenge him to his face. We need a new President. Master Scrivener, though as worthy and hard working as any could want, is too young and too new to take the job. He says so himself. And so, with no other Council members to turn to, it must be you, sir."

"But why now, why not wait the eight weeks or so until his term is up and we must choose among ourselves anyway?" asked Smith, trying to avoid anything that even resembled mutiny. If Ratcliffe had the friendship of the gentlemen of the colony, they could easily come to his defense and charge Smith with mutiny. The situation was volatile, one that Smith had seen too often before.

"We could, I suppose," said Scrivener haltingly.

"We should. Here is my proposal: I will leave to finish the exploration of the Chesapeake and return as close to September 10th as I may. Then we shall choose our new President. Since Ratcliffe is barred from succeeding himself and you, my friend, feel you are not yet seasoned enough in the ways of the colony and the world to be a reasonable alternative, it follows that I will be elected."

"But the men are agitated," protested Hunt, "and ready to flay Ratcliffe and his friends. That is, they would be ready if they were not ailing so. They entreat me daily for assistance that I cannot give. I fear that when enough of them recover, we will have a mutiny on our hands. Who will curb them if you are not here?"

"Let me think on it this evening and we shall meet in the morning to determine our best course. For now, say no more. If any man importunes you again, tell him we have taken the matter in hand and all will be revealed."

With that, Smith threw a disgusted look to the half-done framing and returned to the confines of the fort and his tent.

The pain in his arm has lessened considerably since the stingray had first sunk its tail into his wrist two days ago. Lying here on his bed was helpful, giving the blood and fluids in his arm and shoulder a place to settle besides his bloated hand.

Yet his head ached; his arm and shoulder throbbed. Despite his efforts to think, he soon fell asleep and did not awaken until it was dark and the fort hushed. Refreshed, he poured a cup of wine, sat at his makeshift desk in the dark and listened to the night noises of the fort: the sentry plodding the parapet just outside his tent, the crackling torches lighting the bulwarks, the river lapping the shore, the wind playing with the summer leaves.

Such quietude! Why did turmoil breed as quickly as the ague here? Why could they not come together as men with a purpose? The colony would fail, the business venture would fail, they would all fail.

Smith knew that factious rivalry among the Council was death to the men who had come here with glorious expectations of profit. Wingfield had been a disaster; no man argued that point. He had been the Council member with the most money, the best family, and the most influence and as such had been elected the first President, but he had not the leadership nor the cunning nor the sympathy to lead men who were not bred as he was. He could not see how he offended at every turn. His disregard for his men and his constant concern for his own position and comfort had led to his ruin.

Now Ratcliffe followed suit. The lure of prestige, of the vestiges of power had obliterated what concern for the Company Ratcliffe brought with him last year. Smith swallowed another mouthful of wine. Waiting for the elections was not going to help the volatile situation upon which they were sitting. But deposition now? Could it be cleanly done? And could he still then leave to finish his discovery of the Chesapeake?

No, once he was President, he could not leave for discovery, not now, not for a year. And he clearly must become President whether he willed it or no. There was no one else in a position to lead, not immediately. Newport could be bringing more Councilors on his next supply but no one knew when that supply would arrive; it might be Christmas! They could wait till September, perhaps, but not beyond.

But the Presidency was too confining, too unvarying for his nature. He would rather be a mere Councilor and continue excursions with handfuls of men filled with the same desire for adventure.

Despite his own intentions, despite his distaste for politics, his duty now lay in taking on political power, tenuous and brittle.

But how to effect the change and still finish his Chesapeake explorations? How to depose Ratcliffe and yet not become President himself until September? Smith's brain cleared.

The first rays of sunlight illuminated the tent's canvas as Smith finished his wine and pulled together the finer points of his plan.

The next day, over a supper of roasted fish, corn, peas and oysters, Smith met with Scrivener, Percy, Hunt and President Ratcliffe at the foremost table in the dining hall. As expected, Ratcliffe was loath to give up his privileged position.

"You must resign, sir. There can be no other opinion on the subject," said Smith to Ratcliffe who had just finished the last of the oysters.

"Can there not?" Ratcliffe looked about for another delectable bite within his reach. His hand hovered over the fish platter before landing on the meatiest hunk. "I will not resign, Captain. Not for you. Not for any man."

"Not even for yourself? The company is sorely angered at seeing you appropriate for your own pleasure, at your leisure, from the company stores. The house you are building for yourself—"

"For the President, sir, the President!"

"It is not the best use of the men's time and strength. It is an unnecessary luxury that points out their own lowly accommodations and burdens them when they most need to regain their health. They may be sick now, but they shall recover soon enough. I cannot promise your safety if I am not here. No, I could not promise your safety even if I am here."

Ratcliffe stopped chewing. "Is that a threat, Captain?" he said with his mouth full.

"No, sir, not a threat. An observation. I am only one man. I have not the talent to halt a mob incited to revenge. I only speak the truth of the matter. Discipline and the rule of law do not survive long when deprivation and servitude eat at the heart and soul of most men here."

"You must see the necessity of resigning, sir," prompted Hunt quietly. "Only two months remain of your term as it is. What is that? Eight weeks? Let Captain Smith assume the Presidency two months early, to save your dignity and restore the men's good favor. You would be kindly and favorably thought of. The man who recognizes his faults in public is more admired than the man who pretends his faults do not exist."

Ratcliffe considered the choice lain before him: Resign and maintain a modicum of the respect he deserved or stay as he was with constant bickering and the threat of mutiny on his hands. Yet, he thought, there was a third path, one the men surrounding him had not thought of.

"Very well." He belched. "I will concede—given one condition, if it pleases you. I will resign, but it will be Master Scrivener, not Smith, who takes my place until the elections in September when, as you have so graciously point out, Smith is the only man who could be elected. Scrivener shall be Acting President and Smith may continue his exploration of the Chesapeake. Does that suit?"

Surprise replaced the thoughtful concern that had embedded itself on the surrounding faces.

"Ah! Well! That could be the answer. What say you, Captain? Can this be agreeable to you?" asked Hunt.

"Indeed, sir, it can be and is. I wish I had thought of it," replied Smith, forgetting that one of the reasons he would be elected in September was that Scrivener was not qualified to be President, acting or not. "What say the rest of you?"

Percy and Scrivener nodded in baffled, silent agreement and that settled the matter. Scrivener would take command, Smith would take leave, and Ratcliffe would take the mantle of Councilor.

Smith, grinning, left his comrades to hasten the resupply of the barge so as to set sail as quickly as possible. He would need to hurry in order to make it to the head of the Chesapeake Bay and back again in time for elections. Ratcliffe, usually so self-concerned, had acquiesced rather easily, Smith thought. I must return in time for the elections.

The mood of the fort shifted perceptibly after the change of command ceremony held in front of company members well enough to stand in the heat and humidity of that late July afternoon. Spirits soared when Smith ordered Ratcliffe's ill-gotten hoard be reclaimed for the Company and work on the house outside the palisade be halted. Ratcliffe did not object.

Three days later, as the last of the gear was loaded on the barge and the last minute duties were being tended to, Smith looked about for Scrivener who had promised to see them off.

When his friend did not appear and the time to sail drew close, Smith marched inside the fort expecting to find Scrivener delayed by a petitioner or perhaps Ratcliffe's mastiffs who had grown attached to the youth and vice versa.

Instead, Smith found his friend lying on his cot in a fevered and weakened state with Dr. Wilkinson in attendance.

"It looks like a calenture." The doctor applied another cold cloth to the patient's forehead. "I fear he will not be able to govern much, not for several days at least."

"He has been vomiting? He is incoherent?" inquired Smith.

"Aye, but he is of a strong constitution; I believe he will rally."

"But not for several days," Smith said thoughtfully. "That would leave the Company in Ratcliffe's hands when I am gone. Something must be done."

"But what? You are leaving any moment. Do not fear. Ratcliffe will not have much to say or a chance to say it and if he does, I shall intervene. Master Percy, Master Hunt and I will see to it that Master Scrivener here is given all the power and respect due an Acting President. You may rely on us, Captain. Ratcliffe has few friends at the moment."

"So I see. Prayer is the only aid I may provide, then. I shall return by September 10th, you have my word."

"You are taking Mosco with you?"

"Aye. He is as good an interpreter as anyone could want. I know enough Powhatan to be understood and to understand, but he knows the variations and subtleties. He is a true blessing."

"Good luck, then, and God speed, Captain. I hope you find the passage to the South Sea."

"What's wrong with these men, Bagnall?" Smith pointed to the eight men stretched out on the deck in semi-consciousness.

"They are not seasoned, yet, Captain. They have been puking all night and now are as weak as kittens." Bagnall shrugged his thin shoulders.

Yesterday, sailing northward past the Potomac and the point where their dwindling food supplies on the previous voyage had signaled a return to Jamestown, Smith had spied a split in the Bay where four large rivers converged. The first two rivers had led nowhere and now the barge was on the open Bay and dawn was coming over the eastern shore, all glowing pink and promising another hot day.

"All newcomers, eh? They will heal soon enough." Smith scanned the waters of the Bay.

"Aye. That, or they'll die."

"You are an optimistic sort, Bagnall."

"Just thinking of last summer, that's all." Bagnall didn't mention the fire and the thirty men who died from exposure in January and February. That was different.

"Captain! Naturals coming!"

From the eastern side of the Bay, eight canoes, each carrying five Naturals, bore down on the barge. Smith moved quickly.

"Fetch the tarp, Bagnall, and cover the sick! Make haste! Profit, you and Powell and Pising gather their hats and muskets. Bring them here." Smith darted to starboard and jabbed a finger along the railing.

"Now, all of you, lodge a musket brace in the deck here and here. Good. Put a hat on each. Now you stand here, Profit; you here Powell; you here Pising; and you here Bagnall." Smith placed each man between the braces and gave each one two muskets. "There. Do not fire until I tell you to do so."

Sailing into the path of the canoes, Smith stood in command at the front of the barge, musket and sword in hand.

The sight of such a large boat in full sail with the sun glinting off the muskets gave the canoeists pause, and, before the barge could gain much distance, they swiftly turned around and paddled for shore.

Smith laughed and sailed forward, instructing his musketeers to maneuver the barge toward the same shore.

"*Wingapo!*" he cried, trying the Powhatan greeting. The Naturals stared from the shore.

Smith gestured and smiled and indicated he was coming onto shore. He had Mosco tell them to leave their bows and arrows on shore. Two of them did this, but their comrades remained armed.

Powell threw out the plank and Smith bounded down, arms open and smiling as if he were about to meet King James.

"A present for you!" Smith said and placed a tiny bell in each outstretched palm.

They tested the bells as Smith mimed the action required to produce the bright, clear tinkling. The guests were pleased enough to raise their gifts for the others to see and soon the entire complement of Naturals was gathered around Smith and acting as if he were an old friend.

Between Mosco's labored interpretations and the Natural's hand motions, Smith divined that these were Massawomekes—with no connection to Powhatan at all—who were returning from a raid on their enemy, the Tockwoughs, on the eastern shore.

Smith could see the bearskins and meat, venison, fish, bows and arrows, clubs and shields in their canoes. A handful of bells later, Smith had possession of all and, bidding a delighted farewell to his new friends, decided to anchor there for the night.

When no Massawomekes appeared the next morning for further trade, the barge continued on its way to the third river for discovery.

"Four of the sick are ready to stand again, Captain," said Bagnall at breakfast.

"Good! There is hope yet for the other four!"

Upon entering the river, a repeat performance of yesterday's encounter with barterers seemed imminent.

"*Wingapo*!" saluted Smith, hoping again that the language would be recognizable to this new band. Smith and Mosco came on shore, backed once again by muskets and swords on display.

Mosco carried on a conversation that ended with the Naturals turning in awe to Smith and bowing.

"What the hell did you tell them?" demanded Smith, bowing back.

"I told them you had won the Massawomeke supplies in battle. They are Tockwough. They are most impressed." Mosco grinned.

"You are the devil! 'Tis a good thing you are on my side and can be trusted. Thus far." Smith grinned back.

Smith then had Mosco ask the question most pressing.

"It seems, Captain, that the four rivers at the head of the Bay all lead north to Can-a-da or to the east and the ocean," related Mosco. "We shall find no passage to the South Sea from here."

Smith, disappointed, asked no more questions but allowed the Tockwoughs to take them to their village for a feast which was, as all Natural feasts seemed to be, long and satisfying and full of dancing and merriment. On their way back to the barge, Smith withdrew several small brass Anglican crosses and handed them over to Powell and Profit, telling them to be back by dark.

Powell pounded in the last nail on the last cross as Profit finished carving their names and the date on a prominent pine. "That should tell the damned French and Spanish who owns what here! And they can tell the damned Pope!"

Meeting the others at the waiting barge, Powell and Profit found the other voyagers ready for a good night's sleep and a fresh start in the morning. All the sick had recovered, much to Bagnall's amazement.

A quick voyage up the two rivers that turned east, and then it would be time to turn back toward Jamestown. Smith consoled himself with the fact that this voyage had at least borne out that the Chesapeake was not the place to look for the passage. Knowing where not to look could be just as important as knowing where to look, he thought. There is but one more river to navigate—the Rappahannock—and that shall be the end of our discovery of the Chesapeake Bay. I at least shall have a worthy map to send back to England.

Sailing down the Chesapeake toward Stingray Isle, the crew enjoyed the breezes, the sun, the saltwater air and the sense of freedom that comes with being allied with a man who knows how to handle natives.

As they passed the place where the stingray had incapacitated the Captain, Smith moved the dressing aside on his wrist and noted that the scar was less purple and angry than even the day before. It hardly hurt at all anymore.

Thirty miles up the Rappahannock they came upon a group of Naturals mending their weirs.

"I know these men! They are my friends!" cried Mosco, asking permission to stop. "Do not worry, Captain. They are Moraughtacund, part of Powhatan's kingdom."

Mosco chattered easily with his old acquaintances as Smith and the crew stretched their legs on land and left notes in tree holes. These notes, like the crosses up river, were intended for any English – or Spanish—who might come by later. King James I claimed all of Virginia, even if no one knew precisely how big Virginia was.

Smith was the first to return to Mosco and his old friends.

"We shall continue, then, to the other side of the river and visit the Rappahannocks," Smith announced when all had gathered by the shore.

"Oh, no, sir! We cannot!" exclaimed Mosco.

"And why not?"

"The Rappahannocks are enemies to the Moraughtacund. They have recently stolen three of Rappahannock's women. No friend of the Moraughtacund is a friend to the Rappahannock!"

Smith said nothing at first. Mosco wants to keep the trade for his friends, that is all, thought Smith. "No, we shall go, armed and ready for resistance as always. Mosco, you may stay here if you fear them."

Mosco's face flamed at the idea he might be a coward and immediately he answered, "I gladly go where the Captain goes. But before we leave, we must make one change to the barge, if the Captain agrees."

Across the river, a few miles further up stream, Mosco identified at least fifteen Rappahannocks standing on shore near four canoes fully loaded with baskets of food and skins, ready to trade. They were expecting Smith to stop and trade.

Waving Smith's barge to a landing, the Rappahannocks laughed and urged the English to come closer.

Smith stayed his distance and shouted for the Rappahannocks to send a hostage in exchange for one from the barge.

"A sign of love and good intentions," he said himself for he did not need Mosco to translate so elemental a phrase for him.

Eventually a canoe floated up to the barge carrying five unarmed Rappahannocks with one more to exchange. Smith selected Anas Todkill out of the volunteers to go. Todkill had come to Virginia as John Martin's servant but when the Councilor had returned to England, Todkill had petitioned to stay. He was articulate and intelligent, the right choice for such a mission.

"Should you see signs of an ambush," whispered Smith to Todkill as he made ready to leave, "make your way back here as fast as your feet will carry you and give us warning."

"Aye, sir, that I shall," answered Todkill. "Nothing would bring me more happiness than to be whole at the end of this day."

With that, the English had one hostage and the Rappahannocks the other. While the leader was engaged in discourse with Smith over the barge's location, Todkill wandered slowly toward the woods and had made it a hundred yards when he spotted fifty armed Rappahannocks hiding behind trees. Trying not to alarm his hosts, he nonchalantly walked back to shore.

"Perhaps I had best return to the barge, Mister Rappahannock, since they will not come closer. Our agreement seems to be over."

The leader turned in disgust and barked an order for two of his fellows to carry Todkill away.

Todkill drew a deep breath as the braves grabbed his arms and yelled, "Ambush! Ambush!" Someone clamped a hand over his mouth.

On the barge, as the English raised the cry of alarm, their own hostage dove into the river and swam for shore.

Powell drew his pistol and fired.

The swimmer slowed down; before the smoke from the shot had cleared, blood spread over the river's surface, and the hostage ceased to swim and floated face down in the brackish water.

Every man on the barge fired musket and pistol onto the shore, and every Natural on shore shot off arrows as fast as his hands could fly. Todkill, fearful of being struck by either a musket ball or arrow—or both—dropped to the ground and lay as still as he could, feigning death. From this vantage point he could hear but not see the battle, so clamped his eyes shut and prayed.

Minutes felt like years. Eventually silence surrounded him. His heart pounded. Determined to remain as he was until someone, English or Natural, came to retrieve him, Todkill prayed some more.

Heavy footsteps cut through the spiritual moment and cautiously Todkill turned his head in their direction. He heard English voices calling out to each other as they searched the bodies on the shore for his own.

"Over here! I'm here!" Todkill shouted as he tried to raise himself to a sitting position, an easy task made difficult by the body draped over his legs. In the turmoil of the battle, he had not even noticed it.

Pushing the limp, bloody native away, Todkill staggered to his feet and shouted again, this time winning a response from his comrades.

"Are you hurt?" asked Powell, the first to reach him.

"No, I do not think so."

"But you are covered in blood! Are you sure none of it is your own?"

Together they patted down Todkill's shaking torso and legs until they were satisfied he had not suffered any lasting damage.

"What about ourselves? Have we lost any man?" inquired Todkill as they made their way back to the barge, stepping over and around slain Rappahannocks and bloodstained ground as much as possible.

"Not a one, by God, not a one. That French-Injun is a God damn genius. Putting up the Massawomeke's shields as a forecastle was our salvation. We fired from behind the screens while the arrows bounced off. Hundreds of arrows and not one injured Englishman! The King should make him a knight, even if he is a Frenchman."

The King not being present, Smith gave Mosco the four canoes floating nearby and as many arrows as he could gather from the battlefield for suggesting they rig the shields—small sticks tied together with hemp string and woven tightly with silk grass—on the barge.

"Lighter, more effective against arrows—what more could a man ask?" declared Smith to Todkill who was admiring the shields.

"You'll hear no noise from me, Captain. We have been here more than a year and no Spanish has yet come round the bend, but we see savages every day." He looked closely at the woven apparatus. "They do not look very English, a course."

"I don't care what looks English, Todkill. I only care about what works."

Whooping and hollering in triumph, Mosco helped himself to as many arrows as he could carry at once and dumped them into one of his canoes. His joy was a delight to see and Smith gladly thanked him again for his assistance.

"Now, let us fasten these remarkable shields about the gunwale. We know they repel arrows well enough and that will both give us protection from flying arrows and hide us from view so the Naturals will not know how many we are," Smith said with satisfaction. "Mosco, if you have your fill of arrows, we must be off."

Twenty-five miles more upstream they sailed. When the river narrowed, the shoreline became rugged on the left, small white cliffs the home to three small native towns; the right shore remained a marshy, low plain dotted with bushes and brush.

All was quiet here. No sign of trouble in any form. The weather was clear and hot, the water bubbled and churned but was not a hardship, the wind blew steadily from the southeast, and life itself seemed serene.

Mosco was standing by the shield-encrusted gunwale when he heard a whizzing sound. Seconds later he watched several dozen arrows hit the side of the barge or fall short into the river.

"Rappahannocks!" he cried, throwing himself prostrate on the deck.

All on board were instantly armed and started firing blindly onto the shore, for no Naturals could be seen.

Smith squinted and looked hard at the shore. At the first volley of shot, the bushes stood up and ran. Forty-some Rappahannocks, kicking off branches, jumped up when the guns fired and then crawled away into the marsh reeds.

"'Fear not, till Birnam Wood do come to Dunsinane,'" quoted Smith.

"What are you talking about?" asked Todkill.

"I saw a play in London before we left in the year six. About the Scottish King Macbeth. He was told not to fear until a forest in one part of Scotland came to his home."

"But how can a forest move?"

"That is the riddle. Macbeth thought it could not be done, and so he feared no one. Until the enemy army disguised itself with branches and when it moved, it looked as if the whole Birnam Wood was on the march. Just like now."

Todkill shrugged and let out a faint "oh."

Smith smiled to himself and ordered the guns to cease. Unlike Dunsinane, his barge and men had been saved; Massawomeke shields were worth more than a passage to the South Sea at that moment.

The next day, having reached the place in the river where the barge could travel no further, Smith landed and, leaving a sentinel on board, marched his crew on shore to examine the soil, look for spring water and herbs, and mark the territory.

In the midst of carving names and fixing brass crosses to trees, an alarm went up.

The men dropped everything to arm and used the safety of the trees to both hide behind and shoot from. Smith had taught them well.

The Naturals, of unknown tribe, skipped from tree to tree to shoot their arrows and dodge the musket balls.

Mosco, seeing his quiver now empty, ran to the canoes that were tethered to the barge and, refilling his quiver, began delivering arrows with such speed, fierce yelling and movement from tree to tree that the attackers believed him to be ten attackers, not one.

The attackers disappeared as quickly as they had arrived, with Mosco following them as far as he could see them running. Having lost them, Mosco returned to the English.

A groan of agony stopped them as they gathered their belongings to return to the barge.

The groan increased to a cry and Smith followed the sound to the side of an injured Natural. Mosco arrived two steps behind.

"Let me beat out his brains!" cried Mosco, enraged, grabbing the club he kept tied to his breechcloth.

"No!" commanded Smith pushing him aside.

"But he is our enemy!"

"Battle deaths are their own transgressions; killing when the battle is over is outright murder. Mosco, you acted bravely and valiantly just now, and I thank you for your loyalty, but do not touch this savage or you will forfeit your own life."

Mosco's eyes lost some of their hate, and he lowered the club in obedience to the English captain. Todkill helped the wounded youth to the barge for his knee had been laid open by musket fire, though it did not appear that the ball had lodged anywhere on his person.

On the barge, Bagnall staunched the bleeding and wrapped the knee in linen strips. Mosco, having contented himself with collecting more arrows, returned to find the captive eating berries and willing to chat.

Mosco agreed with equanimity to interpret once again.

"My name is Amoroleck and I am from the Hasinninga people," the wounded boy began mildly, happily selecting berries from his palm, "of the Manahoac realm. Four of our werowances—Stegar, Tanxsnitania,

Shackacoma and my werowance Hasinninga—have come to hunt at the village we call Mahaskahod."

"Why did you attack us when we come peacefully and seeking your respect?" asked Smith.

"We have heard you are a people come from under the world to take our world from us."

"And how many worlds do you know?"

The injured native paused and looked directly at Smith when he answered, "Just what the sky covers. Manahoac, Powhatan, Monacan, and Massawomeke who live higher up in the mountains."

"And what is beyond the mountains?" asked Smith with great interest.

"The sun, of course. There is nothing else to know because the woods have not been burnt yet and so we cannot travel there."

When pressed about the various tribes he had mentioned, the prisoner acknowledged that the Monacans were friends and neighbors and did dwell as they among the hilly countries by small rivers, living on roots and fruits, but chiefly by hunting. The Massawomekes lived by a great water and had many boats and so many men that they made war with all the world.

"Where are the kings you said have come hunting?"

"Some have gone hunting, some came fishing here which is how we saw you. Tonight they all will meet together at Mahaskahod. You come, too, and meet my king," said the youth smoothly. "You should stay tonight. You will be welcomed as friends for having been good to me. I am brother to Hasinninga."

Mosco translated this last speech and then spoke to Smith in English.

"I do not trust him or his people. We should go."

"We shall go when it is dark. In daylight, those high cliffs we will pass are an uncommon advantage to those who would shoot us from above. We shall travel at night to prevent this advantage. Let us make ready to leave and defend. If these kings come in peace, we will be ready for that as well."

Night fell and the barge pushed off downstream. Within minutes, arrows fell about the boat, making little zipping splashes.

"Mosco! Amoroleck! Tell them we want peace and a parley," commanded Smith.

But the great din made by the attack was so distracting that none heard what Mosco and Amoroleck tried to tell them. After that, only the sound of musket fire came from the barge.

Twelve miles this scenario played out until, when dawn broke, Smith and his men found themselves in the middle of a small bay, out of danger.

"Throw out the anchor and let us have our breakfast, men. No one deserves a better!" declared Smith, rubbing his hands together in anticipation.

Refreshed and out of arrow range, Smith ordered each man to untie a shield for himself and to draw swords. Placing them thus armed along the side of the barge facing the shore that supported the Manahoacs, Smith directed the prisoner Amoroleck to stand in the midst of them, and, through Mosco, instructed him as to the discourse he would now have with his fellow Naturals.

"Listen to me, brothers!" said the Natural as loudly as he could so his voice would carry across the water. "I was wounded yesterday and would be dead today if not for the kindness of these men. There is a Potomac here who loves the English as he loves his life and would have slain me had they not prevented him. If you my brothers will be friends with the English, I will have my freedom and you will not be hurt. The English have been very kind to me. I ask you to be kind as well."

A few minutes' consultation on shore produced the desired effect. Every attacker, save two, hung his bow and quiver upon some tree branch. The two remaining braves each tied a bow or quiver onto the top of his head and started swimming out to the barge.

The dripping natives solemnly handed Smith their weapons and waited for instructions.

"Go back, friends, and tell the other three werowances to do the same. When done, King James of England, the king of our world, will be your friend. We are his people, and we shall be your friends. I will wait here. When I see your four kings on the shore, I will come to them and deliver Amoroleck."

By noon, all four kings stood on the marshy shore, all weapons on the ground. After trading bells and beads and Amoroleck for tobacco bags and pipes and bows and arrows, Smith steered the vessel downstream, saying, "To the Rappahannocks! We have unfinished business."

Chapter Twelve

End of a Voyage

Back down the Tappahannock River the little barge sailed, crowded with men, supplies, bows and arrows, skins, and furs won through friendship and trade.

At the Rappahannock village, the once-belligerent natives now welcomed Smith and his men with awe when they saw the Manahoac weapons in Smith's possession.

"They think you won them in battle, Captain. They cannot believe the Manahoacs, enemy to every tribe on the river, would ever trade with you. You had to take the weapons by force," said Mosco.

Smith grinned. Better and better. "Let them think that, if they like. I see no reason to tell them any different."

"The Rappahannocks wish to be friends with the Captain." Mosco clearly distrusted them, but he said nothing more.

"Friends we shall be, of a fashion." Smith, his face hard as quarry rock, turned to address the Rappahannock braves who had met them as the river's edge. "You have twice assaulted us when we only wished you well and did nothing to give you reason to attack. We will now have to burn your houses, destroy your corn, and forever hold Rappahannocks as enemies unless you can give satisfaction."

"What do you want us to do?" asked one of the braves.

"First, bring me your werowance's bow and arrows. Second, do not come into my presence armed; it gives me great offence. Third, you shall be friends with the Moraughtacunds who are my friends. In pledge of this friendship, you are to give them your king's son. When all this is done, all Englishmen shall be your friends."

As Mosco translated, the faces of the Rappahannocks showed no reaction.

But, they could not very well challenge a man who could defeat the Manahoacs so easily; and so it all passed as Smith had demanded, except one thing.

"I have only one son, Smit," said the werowance. "I cannot live without him. I will give you the three women Moraughtacund stole from me instead."

Not that I need three women, Smith thought. But maybe I can use them to bring the two enemies together. He accepted the offer.

Four canoes of Rappahannocks, including the werowance, followed the barge back up river to Moraughtacund. Mosco freely handed out bows and arrows from his abundant collection to the joy of his Moraughtacund friends.

Moraughtacund brought forth the stolen women. The oldest was slightly younger than Smith, with gentle and unafraid brown eyes. The second, shorter and rounder than the first, was probably five years younger and showed no emotion at all. The last was youngest and prettiest, a lass not out of her teens. They all wore the ubiquitous leather apron and tattoos on their arms and legs.

Smith called for Moraughtacund, Rappahannock, and Mosco to step forward as well.

To each of the women, he placed a great strand of beads around her neck.

"Rappahannock, take her whom you love the best," directed Smith.

Rappahannock, surprised, did not hesitate to choose the older woman with the soft eyes.

"Moraughtacund, choose now whom you love best."

Moraughtacund reached for the hand of the rounded young woman.

"And Mosco, you take this sweet young creature for yourself." Smith was happy to have settled the matter to the satisfaction of the men, if not necessarily the Rappahannock women.

Six hundred Rappahannocks and Moraughtacunds shared the feasting the next day and, with much singing and dancing, they bound themselves in friendship to each other and to the English.

Smith said good-bye to the werowances first and then looked for Mosco who had decided to stay with his friends and new wife.

Todkill, seeing tears glistening in the eyes of his usually stoic Captain as he climbed on board, inquired if all was well.

"Indeed," answered Smith, blowing his nose. "Mosco just told me that he has changed his name to Uttasantasough."

Smith ordered salvos be shot over the river to honor their new friends and stood facing the shore for as long as Mosco—now Uttasantasough—could be seen.

Todkill discreetly turned his face so that Smith could not see his own eyes filling. No finer tribute could be paid to the Captain.

Uttasantasough was the Powhatan word for *Englishman.*

"By my calculation, Todkill," Smith said later on, "it is too soon to return to Jamestown. I want to return in time for the elections, yes, but not before that. Let us turn toward the Nansemonds and Chesapeakes. Is it not just that we should be as well known to our close neighbors as we are now to the distant ones?"

No wind stirred, so the crew rowed pleasantly into Gosnold's Bay and anchored for the night.

Yawing and pitching of the barge jarred every man to full consciousness as the sudden wind threw passenger against passenger and tossed anything that was not tied down into the churning water. Never had such a squall started so suddenly and never were men so aware of the need to bail.

Giant streaks of lightning broke the blackness and Smith bellowed orders for half the crew to bail, the other half to row for their lives to Point Comfort. The shore was visible only by the great bursts of light, and Smith knew enough to be grateful despite the terrifying roar of thunder that accompanied them. Surely they would have crashed upon the shore and perished if not for the lightning. At Point Comfort, the mouth of the King's River, they came ashore and waited out the storm.

They refreshed themselves in the calm light of day, assessed what had been lost (nothing of consequence) and what had not (lives and food supplies). A few miles up, the barge detoured first onto the Elizabeth River and then south onto the Nansemond River and into the country inhabited by Nansemonds.

At the mouth of this small river, the adventurers spied seven Naturals mending their fishing weirs; upon seeing the barge of English floating their way, these fishermen fled.

Todkill jumped off the barge onto the shore and made a conspicuous noise in leaving bells near the weirs. The barge pushed off and it wasn't long before the Naturals returned to their weirs and, seeing the bells, began dancing and singing and motioning for the English to come back.

One fisherman invited the white men to come to his house, and he climbed aboard the barge to show them the way. His friends trotted along the shore, waving and smiling.

Seven or eight miles up, they all could see on the western shore large cornfields and a little island with an abundance of corn. Here was his home, said the traveler, and wouldn't Smith and his friends come in to meet his family?

"But where are the people of the village?" asked Smith, wondering why everything was deserted save this man's house.

"They have gone hunting," assured the host.

Smith passed out bells and beads and other gewgaws that contented the wife and child.

The host's friends begged Smith and his crew to come visit their houses, which were but a little higher upriver. Smith agreed but only after he noticed that his host had disappeared.

"Tis strange, Todkill," said Smith as they walked back to the barge. "I don't like it. It is not natural for the women and children and old people to be gone hunting."

The remaining friends paddled a canoe beside the barge until the river, already small, became even more narrow and confining.

"Come aboard with us!" called Todkill. Under his breath he added, "You lying bastards."

"We need our bows and arrows first. Then we shall all go with you."

They came back to the shore, armed, and refused to board the barge or the canoe but persisted in urging the English forward. Smith's suspicions sharpened. "Keep your matches lit and weapons ready, lads."

Seven canoes appeared behind the barge, each full of Nansemonds bearing bows nocked and ready for shooting.

From both sides of the narrow river, hundreds of arrows pelted the barge's shields. Two or three hundred Naturals shot and reloaded and shot again and again while the English fired from behind the Massawomeke shields and rowed toward the King's River with all their power.

Musket shots hit the canoes with such ferocity and abundance that the occupants leaped into the water and swam for shore, allowing the barge to sail by without hindrance. Twenty shots later, the canoeists had all landed on shore and were shooting from behind trees to make their archery count.

As the river grew wider, the arrows fell considerably short of the barge. Smith laughed.

"Grab the canoes!" he shouted. This his crew did with snorts of satisfaction as they headed for the little island they had first visited.

Once anchored, half the men remained on the barge with muskets ready while the other half gathered on shore with axes and hatchets.

"Smash them," ordered Smith in an unnaturally loud voice. "Smash them to bits so small no one will ever know they were dugout canoes."

Todkill and his men hacked away at the dugout canoes, sturdy and time-consuming to make. The Nansemonds could not easily replace these craft.

With the destruction in progress Smith pulled Todkill aside. "Light five torches and make them substantial enough to be seen from the other side of the river. I want them to think we are ready to burn their corn."

"But so much corn would feed the company for a month!" protested Todkill.

"I said I want them to *think* we are going to burn it. It is far more prudent to take it with us. If they think we are willing to incinerate it, they will not see how much need we have and that puts us in a powerful position. Go to it, men; chop and keep those firebrands ready. Let us see how long it takes to gain their notice."

Before one canoe was halfway reduced to kindling, twenty braves paddled furiously across the river in the only canoe they had left with signs of peace, laying their bows and arrows on the ground in front of Smith.

"Peace we can accept, if you will bring me your werowance's bows and arrows along with a chain of pearl. Also, we will come again and you will give us four hundred baskets of corn or we will break all of your canoes and burn your houses as well as the corn. You do these things and we shall let you have your boats and homes and a portion of your corn. Do you agree?"

One brave stepped forward to answer, "This we shall do, but we need another canoe."

Smith paused, then nodded. Todkill untied one of the dugouts and pushed it into the current saying, "There you are. Swim after it if you would have it."

"We shall continue destroying these other canoes until you have fulfilled the bargain you struck," Smith said, jerking his head at the axe men who restarted their efforts.

"No! No! Please, English, do no more!" cried the leader. Turning to his people he instructed every one of them to run, fill baskets and run back to save the canoes.

Smith said to his men, "Slowly, slowly! Look busy, make noise, but do little damage. How heartless do you think I am? I do not wish to destroy them; I only want the Naturals to think I am capable of destroying them."

Todkill and his men grinned and then put a great deal of energy into not reducing the canoes to tinder.

Within a half hour, the barge was laden with as many baskets of corn as it could hold.

"That should hold us for a while," said Smith, exhilarated by the control and power he felt when dealing with the Naturals.

Thus fortified with corn and spent from the exploration of the Chesapeake Bay and Natural meetings both friendly and fierce, Smith and his entourage sailed up the King's River, around Hog Island, and into sight of Jamestown.

Smith, seeing the fort, now dreaded the coming year and resigned himself to the notion that his time and energies would have to be devoted to governing the Company as best he could.

He had never expected nor wanted to be elected President. Duty called and he would do his duty even if he weren't sure just how that would be accomplished with a sickly company, a barely existent Council, and no idea of when the next Supply would show up.

It was September 7th when Smith's barge returned to Jamestown, three days before Council elections.

"By God, it is good to see you well and in command," declared Smith to Scrivener who had come down to the shore to greet the crew. Scrivener, whom Smith had last been seen in a sweaty delirium, bounded with the health and vigor that a youth of his age should have.

"I am well, 'tis true, praise be to God. And you are all well? You have all with you who departed with you?"

"Aye, and I have much to tell you and Ratcliffe, for the Council will be happy to hear all I have discovered."

Smith directed the crew and some others to unload the barge while he walked back to the fort with Scrivener. "You look well indeed, Matthew!"

"Thank you. I am much recovered, but I have unhappy news. Ratcliffe is in the brig for mutiny."

Smith stopped abruptly. "Good God."

"I was still recovering from my illness, two weeks after you had departed, but was feeling well enough to eat with the Company. I came in to find Ratcliffe sitting at the President's seat and learned that he had apparently been doing so all during my convalescence. No one had said a word to me about it. When I asked him to move, he flatly refused. With the Company watching, it was more than just inconvenient."

"I can well believe it. He was trying to steal your authority without actually challenging you openly. What happened then?"

"He sat with a smirk looking at me standing there looking at him. The company stopped everything to watch us. I summoned the guard and he snapped his fingers. Ten of our company came to stand behind him.

"We stared at each other, not a word passing betwixt us or anyone else, until five of the guards appeared muskets in hand. They stood behind me, Master Percy, then Master Hunt, and then Wilkinson joined me. I ordered Ratcliffe's arrest for mutiny, but let the other ten go. Ratcliffe had to be removed bodily for he would not go otherwise. His language and struggles against the guards who carried him out were pitiable, but I am happy to report that he has stayed in the brig from that moment till this, though it hasn't been a quiet incarceration."

"I thought he was too eager to have me gone. But you fulfilled your duties with courage and dispatch, and I wager Ratcliffe did not expect you to do so."

"I hate to think what would have happened had not the other gentlemen been there to support me." Scrivener shuddered.

"A man can only lead if someone is willing to follow. Well done! And now we are ready for legal elections and we shall see what becomes of us all as I shall be President and you shall be Council. We can hope that the next Supply brings news of more Councilors being named. If I had the power, I would add Percy, Hunt and Russell immediately. Two men are not a Council so much as a friendship or partnership—or a tyranny, in some cases. I am ready to lead," Smith said with a sigh. "Let us see who follows."

Chapter Thirteen

A New Regime

Smith, accepting the patent letters in a formal ceremony on September 10th, 1608, immediately issued orders that set the company to work repairing the church, re-roofing the original storehouse and building another. Smith, with Scrivener's assistance, reorganized the sentinels and watch squadrons, creating a regular cycle of shifts that did not unduly tire anyone, thus eliminating sleeping on watch which had become habit as much as anything else under Ratcliffe's tenure.

Moreover, to the delight of Smith's disciplined military mind, the entire complement of Company men, gentlemen and laborers, sailors and captains, now drilled and trained each Saturday in both weapon use and native-style warfare.

Percy, though not officially on the Council, found himself a Lieutenant by Smith's command, and Smith hastened to send him with a barge to the Nansemonds to trade for corn. With unrestrained eagerness, Percy made ready, set sail and returned within two weeks not only with a barge laden with the golden kernels but also in the company of Admiral Newport and seventy new colonists in the *Mary and Margaret*.

Amid the disembarking and mingling of colonists, there suddenly fell a hush. Standing at the top of the ship's rail, about to set a dainty foot on the gangplank, was a woman.

Every man on the island swiveled his head in her direction and dropped his jaw, like marionettes controlled by one master puppeteer. And she, well aware of the scene before her, smiled stiffly and gripped her husband's arm. Her steely gray eyes were riveted to the nape of her husband's neck as the two of them descended in tandem onto Virginia soil.

Modestly dressed in good cloth that had neither holes nor worn spots, they appeared to be in their late twenties and as they moved down the gangplank a collective gasp rose from the watchers. The woman's head snapped up. She knew they were not gasping at her.

At the top of the rail, a few feet behind the couple, a young girl was tiptoeing at the rail, her copper curls bouncing out of her cap. And though she could not have been more than thirteen, her figure was womanly and full.

The married woman snapped at the girl. "Anne! Anne! Come down, I say. And take care not to fall. All I need is for my maid to fall into the river on our first day in the New World." She shooed away the colonists who had hitherto been struck motionless and now stood in her way. "Out of my way, you curs! Have you never seen a woman before? What would your mothers say?"

Anne, casting her eyes on the ground to avoid meeting the untoward stares coming her way, did as bid. As she reached the main gate of the fort, her mistress and master plowing ahead without her, a voice boomed in her ear causing her to jump.

"Let me help you with that, little bird." Read smiled gently to counter the unintended volume of his greeting and removed the bags from her hands. Anne smiled back shyly and nodded her thanks.

"We'd best hurry. My lady does not like me to be late for anything."

"I could guess that one."

Anne strained her neck to see over the crowd. "Where did they go, do you suppose?"

"It's not a big place, as you can see. I'm sure we can find them. All newcomers meet in the church for a prayer and welcome speech from the President. Off you go, that a-way. I'll see to your bags. They'll be right with me by the forge. Not to worry, little bird." As he watched her disappear into the church, he began to whistle.

Included among the new arrivals were a young nobleman, Francis West, and two new Councilors, Masters Waldo and Winne. West, his forest green doublet and breeches made of silk trimmed in gold, was not to be a Councilor but apparently would be part of all issues the Council considered. From the disinterested look on his face, Francis West did not seem to mind this arrangement, though it was difficult to say whether his attitude truly reflected his feelings or was a studied approach to life as a nobleman.

Waldo, a jolly looking man of middling height with thinning pale hair cropped in such a way that when he removed his sugarloaf hat he had the appearance of a gosling newly hatched, observed that the buildings with their thatched roofs and mud and stud construction were more rustic and less comfortable than he'd heard. But, he supposed, all reports from foreign places were exaggerated. Catching Winne's wandering eye, Waldo held it in a brief moment of mutual understanding. No one had fully believed the stories circulating about Virginia, but this was worse than expected.

Winne was reserved and hardened. Not in a bitter way, but with the rough, calloused demeanor of a career soldier who has seen more of battles than of home. He was about Waldo's stature but without the twenty pounds or so on Waldo that gave him a softer look. Winne was all sinew with long arms and legs out of proportion to his torso. Both men were waiting to hear from the President what they needed to do.

Newport had brought with him a private commission, unbeknownst to anyone until this moment, and was informing the Council of its contents. Ratcliffe, at Newport's insistence and Smith's acquiescence, was reinstalled as a Council member and now sat in relative obedience at the end of the long table, his chin imbedded in his starched ruff.

Newport finished his remarks. "I am not to leave here, gentlemen, until I have accomplished at least one of three tasks. I must either find gold—real gold, genuine gold this time, although a marketable substitute would be accepted; something worth two thousand pounds at least. If not gold, then a definitive, verifiable route to the South Sea. If neither gold nor passage, then one survivor from Raleigh's lost colony in Roanoke would give us our due.

"In addition, the King's Council is greatly interested in gaining control over the despot Powhatan who rules so much of the land here. He is to be crowned and deemed subject to King James in a coronation ceremony, and given gifts sent by His Majesty King James. We are to befriend him, make him one of our own, rather than antagonize him or his people. War is to be avoided at all costs. This is the basis of our *Instructions*." Here Newport looked at Smith directly. "It is the King's Council's command."

No one, either new or old, said anything in opposition to this. Smith agreed with it in spirit; it was in the implementation of the idea that they differed, but he had been told in a letter brought by Newport and handed to him on arrival that he, Smith, was to obey Newport's every order while he was present.

"So the first mission is to visit Powhatan and crown him under His Majesty's command. When that is done, we shall travel up the King's River and see if any passage to the South Sea lies beyond the Falls as we were told last year. Since Captain Smith tells us that the Chesapeake Bay does not bear out any passage, we must turn our attention northwest. Finally, we need to establish a new operation; I have brought with me several Polish and Dutch tradesmen with talent and skill. The area being so rich in pitch and tar, the

King's Council has ordered us to try our hand at glassmaking. If gold does not present itself, then we must make profit where we can."

The rest of the meeting was taken up with Smith's formal presentation of the map he had made from his voyages and then the informal telling of stories about Virginia, London, sea travels, families, and home. Late into the night they disbanded, heads spinning with new information and old wine.

"You did not tell Newport that Powhatan will not welcome this coronation, Captain," remarked Scrivener as they walked back to their lodgings. "He is sure to find out very soon."

"Aye, but you heard all that has gone into this plan – the crown, the red cloak, the silver, the clothes, *the bed*!" He chuckled at the thought of Powhatan in an English four-poster bed and horsehair mattress. "Telling Newport not to follow through would have been tantamount to calling the King a fool. You and I know Powhatan will not be tricked into thinking he is a subject to anyone. Best to let Newport find this out on his own. He would never believe me anyway, and then I should be labeled more of a troublemaker than I am thought already. Let us watch for ways to be useful, but other than that, be silent."

Pulling on Scrivener's arm, Smith halted. "Of all the cargo Newport brought with him, there are no medicines, no munitions, no food intended for the Colony. Just more colonists! How will we care for, feed and defend so many with so little?"

With seventy newcomers the Colony now numbered two hundred. Newport insisted he would be taking 120 with him on both his journey to crown Powhatan and his discovery of the Falls.

"But, sir!" cried Smith when he heard. "How can pitch and tar, wainscoting, clapboard, glass and soap ash be made if there are none here to do the work?"

"You will have the remaining eighty men, Captain. That should be sufficient to begin."

"We will need more food, sir. You can see we do not have enough even now."

"I will take the pinnace with me and procure twenty tons of corn from Powhatan and then twenty more tons when I explore the Falls. You may, of course, have a proportion of the ship's store, if you like," Newport answered evenly.

"But surely you do not require so many men in attendance with you. Pray, take only twenty and leave the rest here to work."

"Captain, you only wish to hinder my journeys so you may take up the matter yourself."

Smith started to protest again.

"Furthermore, I shall have 120 because your cruelty to the Naturals has made it necessary for my own protection. They are desperate because you have made them so. I cannot imagine how you could be so blatantly barbarous in your treatment of them when the *Instructions* are quite clear on how they are to be welcomed into our society."

Here Smith thought to check himself. Argument was futile; Newport was not inclined to change to his opinion regardless of anything he could say.

"I am more than willing to assist you as you deem necessary, Admiral, for your authority here is unquestioned. The coronation journey will take a great deal of time, and the unsurpassed largess of the gifts will require you to sail to Powhatan's village. That would be a one hundred mile voyage compared to the twelve-mile walk needed to reach Werowocomoco by land. Allow me to entreat Powhatan to come here instead."

Newport, ready for resistance, was visibly soothed at this turn of the conversation. "I think that an excellent idea. Excellent. He, as subject to His Majesty, should come to me, the King's representative. Aye, go tomorrow then, and report back as soon as you are able."

With Captain Waldo, Sam Collier and two soldiers to carry a canoe, Smith set off over the marshes and woods for Werowocomoco. At the Pamunkey shore, they all climbed into the dugout and paddled to the other side and Powhatan's village.

As they approached, Pocahontas ran out to greet them.

"My father has gone hunting and is thirty miles from here. I will send a messenger to him and you shall stay here. You are most welcome."

Pocahontas led them to her mother who, seeing the necessity for entertainment, quickly issued whispered orders. Pocahontas's mother then led the four men and Sam to a cleared plain, just outside the village. Mats lay around an open fire in a fair field, and Powhatan's villagers collected themselves by the fire. Encouraged to sit, the visitors obliged their hostess and waited.

Fully a half an hour went by. Waldo and the soldiers, not knowing what might transpire, raised eyebrows and mouthed questions, but Smith merely laid a forefinger to his lips and shook his head.

Twigs snapped in the nearby woods and such a shrieking and hideous wailing came next that Smith and Waldo scrambled to their feet, each grabbing both their pistols and an old man as shields. Sam stood behind one of the soldiers, each having drawn his sword.

Pocahontas, seeing their alarm, ran up to Smith and, laying a gentle hand on his arm, begged him to be at ease. "No harm is coming, I promise."

Smith relaxed his grip on the old man who shuffled away as soon as he was free. The villagers surrounded him, old men and women, children of every age. Hardly the setting for a massacre, he realized, and urged his companions to sit down again.

The horrendous wave of noise coming from the woods took human form. Out of the woods ran thirty young, naked women. Each was painted in a different manner, some white, some red, some black, some parti-colored, but all had horns tied to their heads. The leader, athletic and lean, not only wore the horns, but also an otter's skin about her middle and another hung from her left arm. A quiver of arrows bounced on her back as she ran with more arrows and a bow in her right hand. The rest of the painted women all carried a weapon—a sword, club or pot stick.

Smith did not react, but Waldo, Sam and the soldiers had never witnessed anything quite like it. Waldo's mouth dropped open, Sam's eyes were fixed on the bobbing bosoms before him, and the soldiers' breath grew heavy and quick.

Continuing the shouts and cries, the women rushed among the trees, casting themselves into a ring about the fire. Singing and dancing, they fell on the ground and wriggled in mock passion, then rose to dance and sing again, only to fall down and repeat the spectacle.

At the frenetic end, four or five women clasped a man by the hands and arms and lead him to a house. Sam, who was not yet a man in their eyes, was left with the villagers.

Smith found himself being pressed and crowded by five women all pleading, "Love you not me?" Two were at his back, one at his calf and one at each ear whispering enticements that could be understood by any man from any part of the world.

Smith extricated himself as politely as he could and quickly found Sam still sitting by the fire.

"Don't you like women?" asked Sam, poking a stick at the coals.

"Why, yes I do," laughed Smith, "but, frankly, one at a time, and I like it to be my idea. Besides, our bodies are God's temple, meant for marriage and procreation. I cannot in conscience partake here and still be worthy in England. Good Christians know this and follow, Sam, even when God seems most distant and sin hovers at your knees; remember it always."

"Why have you never married, then, Captain?"

"Truth to tell, I never met a woman I wanted to marry. Oh, I have been tempted to bed a few. There was that Turkish lass…" Sam threw up his hand in mock horror and begged Smith not to tell that story again. "But marry? No, marriage is a huge responsibility; you have to provide goods, a home, clothes and food. I left home at sixteen, you know, with nothing but what I wore. I have nothing to offer a lady. And besides, I have been taken prisoner by pirates, made a slave to a Turk, befriended by a Hungarian prince and now I am in the New World with the South Sea Passage just waiting for my name to be attached to it! No woman has ever made me so dizzy for love that I have forgotten all that or God's Commandments."

"What about the commandment against killing?" asked Sam. "Begging your pardon, Captain, but you've killed right many men."

"The commandment is 'Thou shalt not murder,' and so far I have not murdered anyone. Self-defense and justice served are not murder, lad. Otherwise good men would be fodder for criminals and tyrants. No, I have not murdered anyone, not here, not in Turkey, not in England, not anywhere. My conscience is clear, and I work to keep it that way. 'Tis not always the easy way, but it is God's way, and if I plan to stand before Him someday and for all eternity, I prefer to be worthy. This life will seem but an instant."

The rest of the English, rumpled and flushed, did not reappear for two hours.

Baskets of fruit, platters of fish and venison, beans, peas and every good thing to be had was laid before the English who ate and drank till they could abide the sight of food no more. The maidens who had been so attentive in the previous hours continued their singing and dancing throughout the meal.

"Is this how you were treated last winter, Captain? Such delight! Such lovely company! You must not have wanted to leave!" declared Waldo, his cheeks rosy, his eyes drooping.

Smith smiled. "Although I have seen this type of exercise in general, Captain, I was never offered so much at once. My time with Powhatan was mostly as a prisoner. We are none of us prisoners today. Unless it be of love."

The next morning, a horn sounded, and Powhatan arrived with his entourage carrying dozens of freshly killed deer.

In his longhouse, Powhatan received the visitors with great dignity but no warmth.

Smith spoke first. "My father Newport has returned from England and has brought you many gifts from our King. I am here to invite you to Jamestown to receive these gifts and to have counsel with my father. We will help you take revenge on the Monacans as we promised. We also wish to see the land over the mountains, so we may find the great water of the South Sea."

Powhatan answered, "Your king has sent me presents, but I am also a king and this is my land. Eight days I will stay here to receive them. Your father is to come to me, not I to him. I will not bite at such bait. As for the Monacans, I can revenge my own injuries. As for any salt water beyond the mountains, any of my people who told you it is so were lying. I know of no such water. I will show you." With that, Powhatan drew upon the ground with a stick the layout of the land beyond the mountains, so far as he knew it. No salt water was connected to any river in his realm or beyond for several days journeying.

Smith and his party returned to Jamestown with the not-surprising news that Powhatan would not come hither and that the South Sea was not to be found.

Irritated, Newport commandeered three barges, plunked the royal gifts upon one, and growled for seventy men to follow Smith overland while he sailed down the King's River and up the Pamunkey with another fifty musketeers.

"Have you ever seen a coronation, Captain Smith?" inquired Winne, his long legs stretched on the bank, as they sat by the Pamunkey waiting for sight of the barges.

"I have not. Have you?"

"No. I do not believe any of us here at Jamestown have been so honored. I can only wonder what this coronation will be like, then."

"As we have nothing to compare it to, it will be a wonder for us all. I should think that because the language barrier it will be a…short ceremony."

"Will Powhatan understand? You have mastered most of their language. You can make him understand."

"He will understand enough to be angry, even without my help. If Newport manages to place a crown on the man's head, I will be nothing if not amazed." Smith snorted. "I wish I could have persuaded Newport to come with fewer men. He is anxious to follow the *Instructions* that say we are not to offend. I would be more than offended if I saw hundred and twenty armed Englishmen arrive in *my* village."

The barges arrived and, having landed safely on the far side of the Pamunkey, the entire cortege labored to Werowocomoco.

The basin and ewer, each of finely crafted silver, made a small but noticeable impression on Powhatan. At the enormous black walnut bed with its four posters and heavy velvet curtains, dark and blue as the night, now assembled and on display, he nodded in amused regal acceptance.

As Hunt read aloud the proclamation, Newport produced a long, heavy, scarlet cloak. As he approached Powhatan, the great werowance stepped back and refused to let Newport nearer.

Pocahontas stepped forward and whispered in her father's ear. The wizened features relaxed into understanding. He accepted the cloak and the words that went with it, even though he did not fully comprehend them all.

When Newport pulled a copper crown from an elegant rosewood casket, Powhatan held out both hands to accept the gift.

"Oh, no. Powhatan must allow me to place the crown on his head!" exclaimed Newport, withdrawing the crown from Powhatan's reach. "And you must kneel. That much is a requirement."

Smith tried to explain in words, Winne pantomimed kneeling, and Newport ordered the man to his knees.

Powhatan refused to move.

Using quick hands and soothing voices, Winne, Waldo and Scrivener managed to press the old man's shoulders forward for two seconds together; Newport snatched the moment to place the copper crown securely upon the werowance's head which jerked up in abject fear when the fifty musketeers, who had been positioned beforehand, fired their volley into the woods at that precise moment.

The great leader remembered himself and bore forth to thank Newport for his kindness before plucking off the crown and cloak and tossing them to a servant who quickly carried the English trappings away. The English began to load the barges with corn that was half gift, half purchase.

Before the barges sailed, Powhatan reciprocated the gifts.

Newport, holding the worn moccasins by the heels, noted the thin soles and missing beads. The feathered mantle, too big by half to be wearable and one of dozens Powhatan owned, was also showed signs of great wear, but Newport's face shone in admiration of the werowance's generosity.

Ah, thought Smith. Powhatan is no subject to His Majesty any more than I am to King Philip of Spain. All the copper crowns and wooden beds in

Europe will not make him so. He knows it. I know it. Alas, Newport does not. It was time to return.

Werowocomoco hummed with preparations. Every house was cleaned and repaired; every child coached on proper behavior; the fields were weeded and straightened; every fathomable detail attended to. Powhatan had called a council of all the tribes in his federation. The Nansemonds, the Pasbeheghs, the Pamunkeys—all leaders had come to hear what Powhatan had to say.

Outside his majestic longhouse, Powhatan sat upon his many mats, surrounded by hundreds of his wives and children and every werowance in his realm.

His voice, strong and confident, thundered through the village. "I have been wrong. When Smith and his father Newport came here, I adopted Smith as my son, thinking we could bring these white men into our world and they would be as family. There were only a few of them and many died that first season. We could not let the rest live in such wretched conditions. They were alone and needed our help.

"But Smith was not truthful when he said his father Newport was coming to take him back. More English have come, few have gone back. They tried to make me subject to their king and I would not let them.

"We tried killing them and stealing from them but more English still come. Our arrows cannot match their guns and cannons. They have one weakness and we shall take advantage of it. They will not live long without our corn. No more shall we trade for food with Smith or his kind. No one in our kingdom will give one kernel of corn nor one crumb of bread, not in trade, not in friendship. If we cannot win a war of weapons, we shall win a war of survival." Here he paused. "Smith is their leader; Smith is the one whose death would devastate the English. Here is my plan."

Determined to disregard the details drawn so beautifully by Powhatan, Newport, along with the Council, Lieutenant Percy, Captains Winne and Waldo, and Master Francis West, lead 120 men to sail up the James River to the Falls he had last seen in May 1607.

Smith, he deemed, would stay behind and, with the remaining colonists, lade the ship with cedar clapboard. Feeling the slight of being left behind and realizing that the Admiral was an ally no longer, Smith found consolation in Powhatan's assertion that no South Sea Passage existed here or in Monacan country. Going on this discovery would prove a waste of time, and Smith had little temper for that.

Left with the four score colonists, Smith began the clapboard endeavor with a passion. Sam was among those still at the fort.

"I am not one to say 'I told you so,' Sam," remarked Smith as they worked on a large cedar tree. "Yet, I shall be tempted to say it when the Admiral comes back empty-handed." Another chop and the tree fell.

Not many days later the pinnace and barges returned, without gold or passage. Colonists tumbled off the vessels, complaining loudly about the work, the futile voyage, and the lack of food they had endured. Storming past Smith who was hauling cedar to the *Mary and Margaret*, Newport pulled off his glove with his teeth and demanded wine of his manservant before he was halfway to the gangplank of his ship.

After supper had been served and bellies were full once again, Smith announced that the able-bodied were now to begin the glassworks, as well as the massing of pitch, tar, and the making of soap-ashes. A tired groan rumbled through the dining hall, but Smith was not to be distracted.

"And thirty of you, the names of which I post here, will come with me downriver to learn how to cut down trees, how to make clapboard, and how to lie in the woods without endangering yourselves or others. 'Tis time you learnt a valuable skill. Scrivener, I leave the rest to your charge, along with Waldo and Winne. Make the best of your time and you will not disappoint."

Thirty gentlemen, all raw and untested, watched Smith take down a fair-sized cedar while issuing instructions on the hand position, angle, and balance that would result in efficient labor. After a few tentative chops, all imitated Smith to perfection. A roar of appreciation followed the thunder of a fallen tree and Smith, happy that the men took pleasure in the work, joined them in their efforts.

"Jesus Christ! God damn it to hell!" began punctuating every third blow as rough axe handles chafed and blistered soft hands.

Smith halted the work and called the men to his side.

"Blasphemy will not be tolerated here or anywhere I have charge. Sam, you are to count each man's oaths from now on. At the end of the day, for every oath a man swears, a can of cold water shall be poured down his sleeve. Now, go to."

Within a week, not one oath sullied the brisk November air and Smith noted a convivial spirit and general enthusiasm for honest labor well done taking root in the men who toiled beside him. And he was equally enthusiastic, for he asked them to do nothing that he did not do himself.

Returning to Jamestown a week after that, Smith found that under Scrivener, Waldo and Winne the various industrial trials had made gains enough to put samples of pitch, tar, frankincense, and even glassware onto the *Mary and Margaret* which would soon depart for England. Adding the clapboard just made by Smith and his gentlemen-laborers, there was profit enough in fact and implied to satisfy the King's Council, at least for now.

And yet when Smith ducked his head into the Company storehouse he was dismayed to see not one basket of corn had been added in his absence. No fresh meat was evident, nor any other signs of victuals. They had been busy indeed, but too busy to notice that they would not be eating next week.

"How could you not take note?" demanded Smith of Scrivener, Winne, and Waldo. "What were you planning on feeding the Company on Sunday?"

"We thought...That is, we didn't think..." started Scrivener, uncomfortable at being chastised for something that was not his responsibility. "The Admiral has sent out barges for food; they have not come back in yet."

"Where is the Admiral?" asked Smith in exasperation.

"He and Ratcliffe are on the ship. They never come into the fort unless there is a specific reason, not even to dine with us," said Winne.

"Very well, then. Let them stay there. As for me, I am taking two barges and eighteen men to the Chickahominies. They will give us corn or be sorry for not complying. Scrivener, you are to come along, too."

The Chickahominies met Smith's barge at the shore with bows, arrows, and scornful looks.

"But I have not come for corn," Smith said. "I have come for revenge against my imprisonment and the murders of my brothers last year. Your people captured me and handed me over to Powhatan after you killed my men." Calling his soldiers to arm, they charged the Chickahominies.

A hundred yards later, the English were alone.

An hour later, ten unarmed Chickahominies came from the woods toting baskets of corn, fish, and fowl.

"One hundred bushels of corn by tomorrow morning or we will burn your village and take the revenge I came for!" cried Smith.

At dawn the next day, the Chickahominies delivered the required bushels along with complaints of poverty. Smith would not listen. Scrivener watched it all, noting the Naturals' belligerent meeting and how Smith handled them all. True, thought Scrivener, he did not injure anyone nor burn any village; he only promised to. But Scrivener did not like what he had seen. Smith was hard, unyielding, uncompromising. And threatening to burn a village is about as bad as actually doing it.

Directing the Chickahominies to load the barges, Smith instructed the soldiers to pay for the corn with beads and bells. These the Chickahominies accepted with little joy.

One brave heaved a large bag of beads into the river and yelled from the shore as the barges sailed off. "We cannot eat bells and beads!"

"Stay where you are, Captain," said Ratcliffe with an arch of his left brow, his receding chin unusually forward.

Smith, guiding the men as they unloaded the corn, stood on the riverbank.

"I had not planned on going anywhere. And what service can I do for you, sir?" asked Smith pleasantly.

Newport stepped next to the Captain and waved his hand toward the *Mary and Margaret*. "We cannot allow you to enter the fort, Captain. You are under arrest for leaving the fort without my knowledge or consent. This is mutiny and you shall be accountable."

The men unloading the barges stopped and looked at each other. Without a word, they dropped the baskets and unsheathed pistols, knives and swords. Before the Admiral had finished this speech, they were armed and ready by Smith's side, a dozen hungry men who were not going to be deprived of victuals, now or ever.

"Admiral, sir, are you sure you did not give consent?" asked Todkill, pushing forward, testing the sharpness of his blade with his thumb. "I remember well hearing the Captain tell you where he was going and why. You were glad to see him go and you wished him well on his journey."

Newport, surrounded by two-dozen gleaming weapons in the hands of touchy men, faltered. "I seem to recall some reference...aye, I do." He glanced over to Ratcliffe who was similarly taken aback. "Ratcliffe, I recall that conversation now. Of course. Best we leave these men to their work. That will be all, Captain." And he retreated to his ship in consternation and defeat.

"We know who feeds us and who don't, Captain," declared Todkill, laying aside his sword. "You are our President, proper and just, and he shall be gone soon."

"Indeed he shall, but it will not be soon enough," said Smith, scowling at the backsides of Newport and Ratcliffe. "His sailors have eaten much and produced little during their stay. Would that they had departed two weeks after they arrived for it would have kept food in our mouths a little longer."

Food was not the only concern Smith had about the Admiral's stay at Jamestown. Before the *Mary and Margaret* had arrived fourteen weeks ago, the Company owned three hundred axes, hatchets, chisels, mattocks, hoes and pickaxes. Now there were but twenty. Soldiers bartered away knives, shot, powder, pike heads – some not even their own—to any Natural who gave furs, baskets, squirrel pelts, and even small animals for pets in return. The soldiers then traded these commodities to the sailors for butter, cheese, beef, pork, aqua vitae, beer, biscuits, oatmeal and oil.

Smith, searching for the truth of the matter, asked Read one day where he had obtained the handful of biscuits and gobs of cheese he was eating.

"Why, 'tis just a present me mother sent to me," Read said with a laugh, picking up a crumb that had fallen on his doublet.

Smith growled at Newport at the last Council meeting before the *Mary and Margaret* sailed for England. "Your sailors have made this town a veritable black market of underhanded deals with the devil! Our soldiers followed in fashion and now, instead of saving our precious powder, knives, pikes and all for our defense, we have given the savages more than enough to use against us if they would. If you but whisper some excuse and beg acquiescence, I am ready to send the ship back without you and make you live in Jamestown for a year so that you might learn to speak of the experience with understanding!"

Newport was unusually quiet for a long time. Never had he seen Smith direct such outrage at him before; it gave him pause. "I confess I have been too lax in their management and, if I had to do it over again, would curb their trade," he finally said. It gave him no pleasure to admit that for all his haranguing about the *Instructions* and following the letter of the law he had looked the other way when his sailors bartered. "But we shall be gone soon. John Ratcliffe is coming with us. He has asked to return to England, and under the circumstances I thought it best to accommodate him."

"Go, then, in God's peace, and our friendship, Admiral, and when you come back let it be with supplies aplenty for the Company Store—and a few good carpenters."

Newport, who had once admired Smith, now felt kinship with Wingfield, Martin, and others who had been on the receiving end of Smith's righteous anger, and the feeling did not please him. Knowing a man is right does not make it any easier to take his criticisms. And why, damn it, did Smith always have to be right?

Newport said his good-byes and left the next morning with Ratcliffe at his side, Smith's maps and letters in his cabin, and a cargo of goods both whole and in sample that should please the King's Council, but instead of leaving provisions for the hungry Company to survive another winter, Newport, peevish after the previous evening's discussion, appropriated three hogsheads of victuals from the Store to feed himself and his sailors on the way home.

As the *Mary and Margaret* sailed down toward the Chesapeake, an idea came to Smith. They needed food, they must have food, and yet the *Instructions*—and therefore the Council, for Waldo, Winne and Scrivener were of one mind now and overruled anything Smith might propose that went in opposition to the eternal *Instructions*—would not allow any means but trade to gain victuals from the Naturals.

No persuasion could convince Smith that starvation was nobler than force. Powhatan had decreed that his people shun Smith and the English. If Powhatan won't trade, thought Smith, then we'll simply have to take what food we can from him. And the *Instructions* be hanged.

Before Smith could act on this decision, there came a rare and most pleasant diversion: a wedding.

As autumn had glided into early winter, James Read had courted Anne Burras, the copper-haired maid. In truth, Read had warned off, hot poker in hand, at least a dozen other suitors, and Anne felt her best interest lay in marrying soon and being done with the process of fending off men. Read was not so old as to be unattractive, and he was by far the strongest man in the fort with the exception of perhaps Captain Smith who always looked to Anne like he could throttle a small cow with one hand. And Read, whose temper had been wrested out of him on the gallows, was as kind and gentle as any man she had ever known. Anne obtained permission to continue as maid to Mistress Forest and be married as well.

Now the two plighted their troth in front of Master Hunt and the entire colony. As the pair declared their intentions and made their sacred vows of love, obedience, and devotion, Anne's round face was as expectant and open as Read's was tender and enthralled. They left the church, supped and danced with the colony before being escorted, accompanied by horn, drums, whistles and laughter, to the tiny house by the forge.

The festive nature of the day had not deterred Smith in his mission. Rather, the sorry wedding feast of corn mush and old bread had steeled his resolve to take what would not be bartered. He said as much to the Council as they prepared to retire.

"You simply cannot," Waldo replied. "It is expressly against the *Instructions*."

"It would lead to war!" exclaimed Scrivener.

"And yet if we do nothing, we shall starve." Smith was adamant. "We have only a few weeks of corn left and, since Newport sailed with most of the oil, beer, and oatmeal, we are even worse off than we were before he arrived. We must do something to have enough food to survive the winter. The Nansemonds promised to plant for us this spring, and we can dig and plant on our own, of course, but that is next autumn's crop and does us no good at present. Surely you see we must obtain food from the Naturals."

"Powhatan has told his people not to trade with us? That is a certainty?" asked Winne.

"As certain as King Phillip is a papist." Smith spat upon the ground, narrowly missing Winne's boots.

"The Council cannot permit you to force trade, Captain. You are outvoted on this matter."

"Then what is to be done?" asked Smith with patience.

They made no reply.

"When you are hungry enough, you will allow me to go."

A week later, Powhatan sent a messenger with a surprising offer: if Smith would come to Werowocomoco and build him a house, give him a grindstone, fifty swords, some pistols, a cock and a hen, copper and beads, why, then Powhatan would load Smith's ship with corn.

"'Tis a trick!" exclaimed Sam to his master. "Surely he will not load our ship with corn!"

"He might. He surely wants us dead. Starvation will take some time and if he can lure us onto his territory he may kill us swiftly and with little inconvenience to himself. If we come and build him a house first, all the better."

"Then we dare not go!"

"Oh, but we shall," declared Smith, "and we shall use the invitation to our advantage."

Forty-six volunteers, men who knew Smith would not return empty-handed as others had, lined up that frosty December morning eager to join Smith on his journey to Werowocomoco. Smith sent three Dutchmen—Franz, Adam and Jan—overland to begin construction on Powhatan's house as quickly as possible.

With Smith on a barge and Francis West, the bored nobleman, commanding the pinnace, they pushed off and sailed downriver to Kecoughtan, intending to buy enough provisions to last two weeks. A week of wind, rain, then frost and snow prevented the English from leaving which caused them to make merry over Christmas in the warm houses of their friends. Fish, oysters, fowl, venison, and bread kept them from being hungry at any time during their stay, and many of the volunteers thought how pleasant it could be to live among the Naturals if the Company should continue to prove a poor provider.

As the New Year drew near, the English inched their way up the half frozen Pamunkey River toward Werowocomoco where, God willing, Powhatan's house was framed at least and the shipload of corn lay ready to be taken.

Chapter Fourteen

Treachery

"Captain, we're stuck," said Todkill, leaning over the barge and pushing at the frozen mud with his oar.

The frigid January winds had transformed the dark waters of the Pamunkey into peninsulas of ice jutting a half-mile from shore, and the icy ooze had turned solid as the river ebbed and caught the barge and pinnace, forcing Smith's entourage to wait for the next tide.

At Werowocomoco, the Dutch comrades began work in earnest on a house for Powhatan, clearing and shaping trees into the framework of a European home, and enjoying the warm, smoky fires and ever-present meals cooked by expert feminine hands.

Powhatan visited the site daily to watch the construction. After two weeks of observations, Franz and Adam, usually silent in front of the great werowance, decided to try a conversation and found that hand signals and a few well-chosen English words could convey volumes of sentiment on both sides.

Within an hour they had pantomimed their way to an understanding: the English were desperate for food, and the Dutch wanted refuge with Powhatan's people who had more food and men than Jamestown on the best of days.

"You shall stay here," declared Powhatan. "Do not be in a rush to finish my house. When Smith comes, he will see that you need to stay longer. He will not know you want to stay and so not try to force you back."

Franz, taking heart at Powhatan's welcome, tested the extent to which Powhatan would go. "If Smith were dead, all would be right. Do you not think so?"

Powhatan eyes darkened in understanding. "Captain Smit dead, yes."

Franz recognized a victory and translated for Adam and Jan, who, breaking into grins of relief, promptly sat down for a smoke.

"We shall wait here. Tell Powhatan Smith has come as bid, to trade for corn." Smith made himself at home in the longhouse on the outskirts of Werowocomoco, along with eighteen armed soldiers. Percy, West and the remaining travelers had stayed on the pinnace, waiting for Smith's direction.

The next morning, after feasting on the customary gifts of bread and fresh meat sent by Powhatan, Smith, escorted by several braves, arrived at Powhatan's great house for an audience.

Waving his arm in a wide circle, Powhatan signaled for his servants to offer more food, then demanded, "Why have you come, Smit?"

Smith smiled patiently. "You sent for me. You said if we would build you a house and bring you these fine gifts of tools and beads and such you would fill my ship with corn. I have brought all you desired, and you can see from your doorway here where my men build you an English house. Have you so soon forgotten your own words? Why, here stand the very messengers who brought your words to me!" Smith gestured toward the braves standing beside the aging werowance.

Powhatan waved aside the beads and metal Smith had lain before him. "I will trade corn for more swords and guns, not bits of copper I can gain for myself."

"I have sacrificed my own people's provisions to give you what you asked for. Out of love for you, I sent three men to build you a house, neglecting our own needs. As for swords and guns, I told you long ago I have none to spare. I am gravely disappointed, Powhatan, but I would rather not use force to gain what you have honorably promised. I would rather not break our friendship. But if you continue to treat me so poorly you will force me to do what I would rather not do."

Powhatan's face clouded. "I do not believe you. You have come to invade and possess my village, not to trade! Your guns and swords proclaim your true intent, Smit. My people fear to bring you corn, seeing you armed. Leave your weapons on the ship, Smit, and we can be friends and forever Powhatans."

"No."

"It is better to live peaceably together than fight," continued Powhatan. "I have lived through three great wars. I know the difference between war and peace better than anyone in my country. I am old and will die before long; I only wish peace for my heirs, my brothers and sisters. But messengers from Nansemond tell me you are come to destroy my country; my people believe this and dare not visit you. What good will it do to take by force that which you may quietly have by love? Why destroy them that provide you food? What can you gain by war when we can hide our provisions and fly to the woods leaving you to famish?

"Do you think I am so simple not to know it is better to eat good meat, lie well, and sleep quietly with my women and children, laugh and be merry with you, have copper, hatchets, or what I want, being your friend than to be forced to fly from all? To lie cold in the woods, feed upon acorns, roots and such trash, and be so hunted by you that I can neither rest, eat, nor sleep, but my tired men must watch and if a twig but break, everyone cries *'There comes Captain Smit!'*

"Then must I fly to I know not where and thus, miserable with fear, end my life, leaving my pleasures to such youths as you. Let this then assure you of our love and every year friendly trade shall furnish you with corn, and now also, if you come in friendly manner to see us – not with your guns and swords to invade your enemies."

Smith saw the subtlety of the discourse and answered plainly.

"The vow of my love both myself and my men have kept. As for your promise, I find it every day violated by some of your subjects. Because of your love and kindness and because we are grateful, for your sake only we have curbed our thirsting desire for revenge. Otherwise your people would know the cruelty we use toward our enemies; instead you know our true love and courtesy as our friends.

"And I think you can perceive that by our actions and by our great advantage of arms, had we intended you any hurt, long before this we could have affected it upon you.

"Powhatan is right. It is better to live in peace and trust. But in my country we always carry weapons; it is our custom. Without exception we gladly entertain your people with their bows and arrows at Jamestown, as we esteem wearing our arms as our apparel. Our greatest pleasure comes in fighting our enemies. For your riches we have no use. You may well hide your provision or fly into the woods, but we shall not so unadvisedly starve as you conclude. We have ways beyond your knowledge to find you." Smith paused to pull out the compass from his doublet pocket.

A flicker of anger passed over Powhatan's stony eyes. "No werowance in my realm, Captain Smit, do I use so kindly as I do you, and yet from you I receive the least kindness of any. Captain Newport gave me swords, copper, clothes, a bed, tools, or what I desired, ever taking what I offered him and would send away his guns when I asked. No one declines to lie at my feet or refuse to do what I desire, but only you. You who give me nothing but what you regard not, and yet you will have whatever you demand of me. Captain Newport you call Father and so you call me, but I can see you do what you like, and we must both seek to content you. If you are as friendly as you say, send away your arms that I may believe you."

Smith, tired of hearing the same song beat to a different cadence, drew a breath and spoke in a low voice to a nearby soldier. "Bring our soldiers here. I think Powhatan is passing time until he finds a way to cut our throats. I will trifle the time as well until you return with our men."

Smith addressed Powhatan in a voice deep with emotion and severity. "Powhatan, you must know as I serve but one God and honor but one King. I live not here as your subject but as your friend to pleasure you with what I can. By the gifts you bestow on me you gain more than by trade. Yet would you visit me as I visit you, you would know it is not our custom to sell our courtesies. Bring all your country with you as your guard; I will not take offense or deem it anything but custom. To content you, I will leave my arms and trust to your promise. I call you father indeed, and as a father you shall see I will love you. But the small care you show for me caused my men to persuade me to look after myself."

A movement in the crowd stopped the dialogue as a young brave broke through to whisper in Powhatan's ear. The old man, assuring Smith that he would return shortly, departed with the youth, leaving Smith surrounded by talkative courtesans and a mountain of corn-stuffed baskets.

Within minutes Smith was distracted by the heavy noises outside the house. Smith cocked his pistol in his right hand, drew his sword in his left.

"Out of my way! Out!" he cried, pushing his way through the crowd. Two naked braves grabbed at his arm and leg. Smith aimed his pistol and fired. The injured brave fell to the ground, clutching his foot, and watched in transfixed horror as blood poured over his hands. The entire household trampled over each other to exit before Smith, whose other assailant had let go, could fire another shot.

Outside, a hoard of muscular braves surrounding the house stared blankly at eighteen soldiers who had come back with Pising, lined up with musket braces and poles. Smith took command. "Prepare to fire!"

A change of heart rippled through the Naturals left near the great house. One native came forward to claim it was all a misunderstanding. Behind him came another, an ancient orator, who offered a great bracelet and chain of pearl to Smith.

"Captain Smit," said he, "our werowance is fled, fearing your guns and knowing more men would come behind you. He has sent these braves but to guard his corn from stealing that might happen without your knowledge. Now though some may be hurt, yet Powhatan is your friend and will forever stay so. Now he would have you send away your corn to your ship and, if you would have his company, send away also your guns which so frighten his people that they dare not come to you as he promised they should. We have brought many baskets of corn for your men to carry. We would be pleased to stand watch over your guns as you carry your corn back to the ship."

"Fire!" commanded Smith, who had first told the musketeers to miss any live targets.

Well-proportioned braves dropped their bows and arrows and took up the baskets themselves, leaving Smith to guard their arms instead.

By the time night fell, the ship's hold was full of corn.

"Come! We must stay another night," said Smith to his eighteen musketeers, "so let us make merry as much as we are able. Laugh and be of good cheer for no better offensive could be launched upon our enemies than to let them think we are so comfortable as to make sport of our predicament."

"Did you not hear a sound at the door?" whispered Smith to Todkill several hours later. Half the men lay sleeping, the other half waiting for their turn on the mats.

"Aye, a soft noise."

Smith arose and waved his hand to signal his men to continue to talk as if nothing were amiss. Cocking his pistol, he crept to the doorway where a large deerskin draped over the opening,

"Do not shoot! Oh, please, do not shoot!" came the cry from outside the door.

The flap flew open and in tumbled a familiar naked child, tears streaming down her round cheeks.

Smith released his pistol and bent down to comfort Pocahontas who was wiping her tears away with dirty hands, leaving dark streaks where tears used to be.

"There, there, little one. Do not cry so. What has brought you here in the middle of the night?" Smith offered his handkerchief.

Pocahontas smiled and sniffled, then reached up to lay her hand upon the Englishman's thick arm. "Oh, you must fly! My father sends a party even now, a feast, but they who bring it are to kill you with your own weapons during supper. Or, if they do not, all the power my father can make will come after supper and kill you then. Oh, Captain, you must leave this very minute!"

A smile, tender and gentle, curved under Smith's bushy mustache and beard. He was grateful for her warning and offered her whatever she desired that he could give.

"I cannot," said she, more tears spilling from her velvety brown eyes. "If my father knows that I have any toys or trinkets from you, he will know I have seen you and then I should be put to death. I came to tell you and I have done so. I must go back before someone notices I have gone. Good-bye, Captain Smit. Good-bye!"

With that, she disappeared into the night. Within the hour, Smith and his men heard the bustling noises of the Powhatans coming with the feast.

Ten lusty fellows with great platters of venison and other tasty meats soon arrived, begging the English to douse the musket matches. "The smell turns our stomachs, Smit," explained the first to enter.

"Come in, my friends," enjoined Smith, smiling and ignoring the request. "Sit yourselves down with us and let us all eat from the provisions you have brought. No, no, you first. I insist. Each of you taste of the dish in front of you. There. That is good, is it not?" Smith watched carefully to see if any man hesitated or balked at eating, but none did. He surprised the braves by then dismissing them and sending them back to Powhatan with this message:

"I know you have come here to murder us at supper, but I will not allow it. Be gone, back to Powhatan and leave us be. Tell Powhatan I await his arrival, for I know well that he intends to come back."

Several messengers came and went in the next two hours, the last of whom told Smith that Powhatan desired his house to be finished and one Englishman to shoot fowl for him.

"Pising, you are as fair a shot as any; you stay. Tell Franz, Adam and Jan to finish the house and come back to Jamestown as quickly as may be. We shall sail up the Pamunkey, to Opechancanough's village, for more corn, then stop here on our return, if the weather does not refreeze the river, to retrieve you and to settle with Powhatan. He will come back to Werowocomoco, and when he does, I shall be not long behind."

Powhatan sat unmoved among his advisors in a makeshift home of mats, a small fire warming the cramped interior and filling it with gray plumes of smoke. He had not decided what to do about the arrogant and dangerous Captain Smith. Werowocomoco was his home, the home of his people, the largest village in his realm, one that had been here four hundred years; no one, not even the exasperating Smith could keep him from returning.

Yet the great Powhatan could not continue to play verbal games with a man so clearly set on winning every match. Smith refused to yield even the slightest weapon and only offered toys and trinkets in trade, things that contented the simple-minded.

"What must Newport think of his son! Surely even the white man does not allow his children to disrespect and disobey a father's wishes." This Powhatan murmured to the young wife sitting at his knee. Other wives, young and unwise in the ways of Englishmen would not have dared answer, but this one had seen enough of the Captain and his comrades to venture a comment.

"Newport perhaps does not know of Smit's disobedience. He sailed away on his big ship and has not come back. Smit does not answer to anyone." Her tone was disapproving.

"No, he does as he likes and never fears the answer." Powhatan paused. "We can make use of that, somehow," Powhatan yawned widely and loudly, then let his eye rest upon the pretty, upturned face. "I think I shall go to bed and let my dreams tell me what to do." Taking her smooth hand in his, he led her to the mat covered with soft skins.

Later, Powhatan dreamed of his youth, the days before the white man was known to him or his people. Life was less troubled, less unsure, more...containable. War was infrequent and happened between familiar tribes when it flared at all. Powhatan versus Monacan, Monacan versus Iroquois, Iroquois versus...whoever. Now the English rooted themselves in a wooden fort and demanded their needs be met before anyone else's. The English with their strange smells and weapons and no women. No women!

Powhatan and his bodyguards approached the half-built house the Dutch were constructing. He called out in a deep, sonorous voice to the workers.

"Franz! Adam! Come to my longhouse and we shall speak."

The two men tossed aside their axes and gladly left the chill damp of the morning to sit with Powhatan in warmth and comfort.

"Are you happy here, my friends?" Powhatan asked, knowing their answer.

"Aye, Powhatan, we are," said Franz, looking and nodding at Adam who aped the action and left his friend to do the talking. "We choose to stay with you, if it pleases you. The Powhatan are noble and superior to the English."

"Good. We will defeat Smit and the English. Will you help?"

Franz did not hesitate. "Of course. Our King is not their king. We have no special ties to them. What do you wish us to do?"

Powhatan's eyes narrowed as he looked the two men up and down. They seemed trustworthy. He would try his trick. If it worked, then he would have more English weapons and goods than Smith would ever give up, and he could then rely on these traitorous men perhaps to do more later. If the trick did not work, he would be rid of them, and no harm would be done. It was worth the risk.

"Go back to Jamestown," began Powhatan, silencing their protests with a wrinkled brown hand. "Tell them that all is well here. Then say that Smit took all your swords, guns and powder and you need more. Ask for more tools to work on my house and more clothes as yours are wearing thin. You take all you can without making them angry. You understand?"

Franz chuckled and nudged Adam who again nodded in response. Franz said, "Aye, that should work. Smith has gone up river. We shall be in Jamestown and back before he even thinks about returning."

"Take with you these six braves to help you carry the arms and all you do take from Jamestown. Jan will stay here and enforce your pledge to return."

Captain Winne listened to the Dutchmen's requests, which had the air of sincerity and truth.

"Aye, well. Captain Smith certainly takes what he wants when he wants it. I have no doubt he left you unarmed to build a house among the Naturals. Stay for supper and we shall equip you with swords and what clothing we can. You say you need guns as well? Those too we can provide. You cannot be left vulnerable among the savages." Winne spoke with indifference and dismissed the men to gather what they could.

During supper, those men who had remained at the fort quizzed the Dutchmen about their adventures and life with Powhatan. By the last cup of ale, all but six had wandered off to their evening rituals. These six sat with the Dutch in convivial companionship for another hour or more, fascinated by tales of comfort, food, security and women—women!—that the Powhatan life afforded.

"I tell you, anyone here will starve and rot before next summer is over," declared Franz with disgust. "If I were a gambling man, I would bet my father's last dinar that Powhatan wins this one. He has three times the men in his village alone. And he commands every native within five hundred miles. Better to live with savages than with fools."

"Can not we come with you?" asked one of the companions in a low voice.

"Come with us? What would the good Captain Winne say if we all just walked out of here tomorrow? He would have us in the brig before we heard the gate close. No, you cannot come with us. But you can leave on your own and meet us at Werowocomoco at your leisure." Franz looked thoughtfully at the young faces in front of him. "You could help this moment, if you have the mind to."

"I have the mind to, but I also have the watch in five minutes. I'll be on the bulwark for the next four hours. I can help after that, if you still need it."

"The watch, eh? Will you be alone?" asked Franz with interest.

"No, we never stand alone. Keffer here will be with me."

Franz, seeing an opportunity that was too good to pass by, laid out his plan to the agreement of all present. It would be a long night.

Opechancanough was ready for Smith.

Twenty-five miles over land was nothing compared to sailing up river and marching inland. Powhatan had sent runners to warn his brother of Smith's approach and desire for food. Now they waited, bows and arrows grasped in hundreds of tense, warrior hands.

Smith, Percy and West selected twenty musketeers, left the pinnace by the frigid shore, and marched toward Opechancanough's village.

The homes stood silent and empty. No delicious odor of baking bread or smoking fish hung in the air; no children played; no women chattered. The village, once bustling with life and laughter, was a mausoleum, deathly still and cold even for January.

The twenty musketeers scattered to inspect the houses and found nothing except a lame old man, shriveled and leathery, with a boy of about seven squatting beside him. The old man started chanting when the English appeared at his door and the boy stared, unmoving and unimpressed by the strangers in front of him.

Smith was about to enter when the beating of drums and a loud clamor from the woods stopped him.

Opechancanough, surrounded by fifty braves with bows and arrows at the ready, appeared at the edge of the village. The winter breath of each warrior misted and rose, the only sign of life as they waited in motionless belligerence.

Smith, surprised but not awestruck, signaled for his men to follow him.

The two groups faced each other, the one barely covered in skins, the other clad from top to bottom in armor, wool, and leather. The first held bows nocked with arrows; the second, swords and pikes, pistols and muskets. Smith and Opechancanough stood at the center, neither speaking nor moving for several minutes, each staring into the other's eyes and waiting for capitulation.

Finally, Opechancanough waved his hand and from the back of the crowd came a young boy with a small basket of dried apples. This he laid at Smith's feet and backed away as quickly as he had come forward.

"Opechancanough," Smith began, "the great love you profess with your tongue seems mere deceit by your actions. Last year, you kindly freighted our ship, but now you have invited me to starve with hunger. You know my want, and I your plenty, of which by some means I must have part. Remember it is fit for kings to keep their promise. Here are my commodities, take your choice."

The werowance took kindly to this offer and, after selecting a dozen shovels, a multitude of baskets with fish, bread and more dried fruits emerged from behind the screen of guards. Happy trades concluded the brief visit with promises by Opechancanough of more the next day at his home. The English returned to the pinnace and barge, content that by evening the next day the ship would be filled to bursting with corn and other edibles.

Smith and his fifteen soldiers were halfway to Opechancanough's longhouse the next morning when the sound of snapping branches caused them to stop in their tracks. Running toward them from the barge was John Russell, a soldier who had held onto his corpulent girth despite the hard times, now breathless and frantic.

"Betrayed! We have been betrayed!"

Smith and his guards drew their swords and pistols.

Russell, his breathing less labored now that he had stopped running, swallowed hard, then said, "There must be two hundred savages circling the fields and house, Captain. Three hundred! We are outnumbered and outflanked."

The guards hearing this stepped forward and assumed they would be shooting their way to safety behind the Captain. A hard look met their cries for action.

"We cannot! This is my torment. If I escape and slay any in our way, our malicious Council will label me a peace-breaker and in doing so break my neck. I wish they were here to see these saint-seeming savages." He spat upon the ground and watched the spittle bubble up and freeze. "If we should each kill a man and proceed to the house, all the rest will fly. Then we shall have corpses at our feet, but no victuals."

"There is truth in that," huffed Russell.

"Their fury is the least danger to us. If we but discharge our pistols into the air they will not stay to see more. If by chance they do stay to fight, we will fight like men and not die like sheep. I trust in God to deliver us in battle; as you know, He has done so for me many times before. But first, I will deal with them to agree to conditions. Can you can stomach this?"

They could and said so with resounding confidence in one accord.

"Why, then promise me to be valiant and patient—for the spoils shall be ours!"

A mighty "Huzzah!" rose in the cold January air as Smith led his men to Opechancanough's longhouse, fully aware of the congregating masses outside.

"I see, Opechancanough, your plot to murder me, but I fear it not."

The werowance's eyes narrowed at Smith's opening remark and then widened in surprise as he marked the Captain laying his pistols and swords on the matted floor.

"As yet, your men and mine have done no harm," Smith continued, "but only because of my direction. I propose a contest. Remove therefore your arms. You see mine. My body shall be as naked as yours. The isle in your river is a fit place, if you be contented, for our battle, and let the conqueror of us two be lord and master over all our men."

Opechancanough's mouth dropped open in mute astonishment.

"Or, if you prefer, draw your men into the field here. If you have not enough, take time to fetch more—whatever number you will—and have each man bring a basket of corn against which I will stake the value in copper. Our game shall be winner take all."

Opechancanough, unused to single combat, said nothing for several minutes, then ignored the challenge and ushered Smith to the door saying there was a present for him. "I am not unkind, Smit. Come and see."

Smith knew better. "Russell, come here. You go out and see what present the king makes."

Russell, white and trembling, shook his head in disobedience, refusing to go through the door to almost certainly be greeted with a shower of arrows meant for the Captain. He simply said, "I would rather not."

Smith drew breath through his teeth, clenched his fists and rolled back his head.

The other guards and gentlemen in the group, seeing Smith's rage building, tripped over themselves to beg the Captain for the chance to go in Russell's place.

"Let me!"

"I shall go!"

"No, no, I should go!"

Smith found his voice and in a baritone laced with disdain snarled, "Coward! What unnatural blood runs in you that you would refuse this simple task? You would rather not? *You would rather not?* White-livered, onion-eyed cur! Out of my way! Powell, Behethland, guard the door. West and Percy, you stay with the others and take the house."

With that, Smith pushed the sniveling Russell into a corner. Two long strides placed the Captain next to the werowance whose satisfaction at the altercation had led him to miss the cocking of Smith's pistol.

With one hand, Smith thrust his pistol against Opechancanough's breast. With the other hand he grabbed the long lock of hair flowing down the king's brown back. Smith wound the black tresses around his fist and yanked hard enough for Opechancanough's head to snap back and his once-smug eyes to go blank.

His men, supposedly guarding their king, stood in shock watching as Smith took unprecedented liberties with their revered leader. No one moved nor said a word as Smith nudged his captive toward the door and out into the village where the sight of their king so pitifully at Smith's mercy drove each man to drop his weapons and vambraces at the white Captain's feet.

Smith could feel Opechancanough's pounding heart and saw beads of sweat appear on his beardless lip despite the temperature. Still, the old man's face was unmoved. Holding fast to both hair and pistol, Smith addressed the crowd.

"I see you Pamunkeys, your great desire to kill me and my long-suffering of your injuries has emboldened you to this presumption. I have forborne your insolences because of the promise I made before the God I serve to be your friend till you give me just cause to be your enemy. If I keep this vow, my God will protect me; you cannot hurt me. If I break it, He will destroy me. If you shoot but one arrow to shed one drop of blood of any of my men, or steal the least of these beads or copper I here spurn with my foot, I will cause revenge, and once I begin, I will continue so long as I can find one of your nation that will not deny the name of Pamunk. I am not now half-drowned with mire where you made me prisoner. Here I stand. If I be the mark you aim at, shoot he that dares! You promised to fill my ship before I departed, and so you shall or I mean to load her with your dead carcasses." He stopped to let the idea settle in.

"Yet if as friends you come and trade, I once more promise not to trouble you, except you give me the first occasion. And your king shall be free and be my friend, for I will not come to hurt him or any of you."

Minutes passed as the surrounding warriors waited for their werowance to make a decision, pistol pressed against his flesh and his hair entangled in Smith's fist. Finally, Opechancanough nodded as best he could against the force of Smith's hand.

Bows and arrows fell to the ground, and the braves ran for the woods.

Smith uncocked his pistol and released the werowance's hair. "Bind his hands and feet, Todkill, and confine him to his house for the night. Let us see what happens."

Soon great baskets of foodstuffs lay at Smith's feet and the people pressed the Captain for his favor. Content that he had been taken at his word, Smith retired after three hours of receiving gifts.

"I am tired. Behethland and Powell, you take my place. See that the victuals are properly stored, and take some supper for yourselves." With that, the weary Captain lay down on a mat next to a warm fire in Opechancanough's longhouse and fell fast asleep.

"Captain." The whisperer changed his tone immediately to an audible cry. "Captain Smith! It is I, Richard Wyffin! Do not shoot!"

Smith, wide awake and standing with pistol cocked, relaxed.

"Wyffin. What are you doing here?"

"I have sad news and, of all at the fort, only I dared come to tell you."

"Better have it out, then," replied Smith, "here where none can hear it but me."

Wyffin's worried eyes verged on tears. "Master Scrivener, a man you held in high honor and who we all thought regarded you the same, disregarded your orders to stay at the Fort, and some certain days after you left decided to set off for the Isle of Hogs and took with him Captain Waldo."

"Waldo went with him?" asked Smith, incredulous. "Scrivener was to be my second in all things. How quickly man does turn from one allegiance to another!"

170

"Aye. But that is not the whole of it, sir. Master Scrivener took Captain Waldo, as I say, but he also had with him Master Anthony Gosnold and eight others. And here is the sad part, sir. They have all perished! The barge was so overloaded it would scarce have survived the severe tempest that grew and that is what happened, as far as we can tell. No persuasion could restrain him, sir, not even a hundred doubting voices as they set off. They all drowned. There happened by several Naturals who found their bodies which seemed to encourage them to war with us." Wyffin paused to wipe his nose.

"Go on. What then?"

"As I say, none but I would volunteer to journey to tell you of this great treachery. I found Powhatan and lodged there only one night—but it was enough to tell me mischief is in the making. Pocahontas hid me for a time and sent those that followed me in the contrary direction. She is a most tender and generous little girl!"

"That she is. Go on, man." Smith could not believe Scrivener would betray him so.

"By her means and extraordinary bribes I have arrived here in three days time, sir, to deliver such tidings as I wish never to have known." Wyffin sat down upon a mat and stared at the fire, spent from his travels and the telling of his tale.

"Keep this news from our comrades. I shall tell them in my own time, when we are safely on the barge and away from Opechancanough's treachery. Right now, I need to think."

Chapter Fifteen

A Singular Arrangement

The next morning, Opechancanough met Smith by the barge as the English made ready to leave.

His weathered face masking any emotion, the werowance offered Smith a giant necklace, ten strands, with pearls the size of musket balls. "Stay for one last meal, Smit. You have time before the next tide. We are friends again."

Perhaps, thought Smith, fingering the necklace around his neck. He smiled at Opechancanough who did not return the courtesy. And then, perhaps not.

A half hour into the feast Smith's stomach churned and gurgled. Making himself belch only drew bile into his mouth. His innards twitched and cramped. "I am an idiot!" cried Smith, scrambling toward the woods in convulsions, heaving the contents of his stomach onto the snow.

Back at the feast, he grabbed his portions, charged the woods again and heaved his meal into the brush.

"Whatever is the matter, Smith?" asked Percy. "I've never seen you throw away food. What a waste!"

"Mine was poisoned, you dolt."

"Poisoned?" asked Percy, dropping the turkey wing hovering near his mouth. "Are you sure? I do not feel sick."

"Beyond doubt. Perhaps it was only my meal that was tainted, but I would not eat that if I were you. I cannot believe I was so foolish when I know better." Everyone pushed aside the meal and rose, rubbing their stomachs, tasting their lips for toxins, and wondering if they too would be running to the woods soon. "Let us take our leave and be done with this place."

"Are you not going to seek retribution?" asked West, incredulous. "No gentlemen would let such an insult pass!"

"No gentleman would, I suppose. But I am no gentleman, as everyone knows. If we fight, we lose our freight. We must have what we came for and that is enough to satisfy. But," added Smith as he moved toward the barges, mentally berating himself for letting yesterday's victory color his judgment, "we shall dine more carefully in their presence from now on, if we dine at all."

Opechancanough, who had watched this exchange with interest, realized that he would have to freight the ship and barge in earnest now. By the turn of the tide, the English had all they could come by from the Pamunkeys.

Back in his hut, Opechancanough sank onto his mat in disgust and sent a bowl crashing against the fire pit at the other end of the room. His brother Powhatan would have to find a way to eliminate the arrogant white Captain. Trying to kill him outright with knives or arrows had not worked; he was always guarded and always armed. Poison could suffice, if administered in the proper dose, at the proper time, and by the proper hand—someone Smith trusted, someone who was not a Powhatan.

Smith, giving the order to return to Jamestown, wondered how the Spanish had been so lucky as to have met with Naturals in the Indies and South America who mined silver and gold and kept well-manured fields with plantings enough for everyone, native or not. Here in Virginia the Naturals did not have more than could be brought from hand to mouth and certainly nothing of value to trade in England. No wonder the Spanish had not stayed here! Smith sighed. Surely more lucrative offerings lay beyond the rivers. The South Sea Passage! Smith cheered at the thought of winter's end and doing more than scrounging for food.

But for Smith to go on discovery again the fort would have to be self-sustaining and under good leadership, something that had perished in the King's river while they were gone. He had little hope of exploring any more until the Council was more than himself and Winne, and that required a new supply and new *Instructions*. And when would that be? Spring? Summer?

Smith sighed again. It was time to tell the men what waited for them at Jamestown.

The arrival of a pinnace and a barge's worth of food did much to raise the spirits of all in the fort who had spent the winter eating rotting or soggy corn.

"We were nearly deprived of all food till your return, Smith. How good it was to see you land and in possession of so much corn!" Delight bubbled on Winne's thin lips. "This is our first good news since January when we lost Scrivener and the others."

"Are all other matters, then, as ordered?" inquired Smith, his eye surveying the fort's interior: torn tents, debris strewn about the walkways, roofs in need of repair, chickens running loose.

"Almost." Winne hesitated. "Not quite. I mean to say, we seem to have a leak."

"A leak?"

"Most of our tools and a good portion of our arms are disappearing."

"Disappearing?" repeated Smith, trying to comprehend. "Whatever do you mean? Are we without arms?"

"Not precisely. Oh, the cannon are still where you left them and every man has his own sword and pistol, but the nearly all the Company pikes, powder, shot, swords, and tools have disappeared. Every search of the Fort yields nothing. No one is hiding them around here."

"Weapons and powder do not simply disappear, Winne. Use your head, man. Someone is stealing them. Do the Pasbeheghs still come and trade inside the Fort?"

"Aye. But they leave as naked as when they arrive. It would be hard to hide English weapons on their person."

"If not the Pasbeheghs, then it must be someone in the Company. That is the only possible alternative." Smith's face was grim. "Have you any notion of who that may be? If we know who, we may be able to figure out how they are stealing and what they are doing with the spoils."

"I know not, for if I did I should have done something about it by now," was the icy reply.

Franz shifted his weight as he leaned against the wall of the guardhouse. Colonists who passed by gave him no notice, for to them he looked like any other Natural that had come to trade. His hair was shorn on the right side of his head and pulled back on the left. His skin was dyed the same oily brown and, unless a man peered closely, his dark blue eyes could easily be mistaken for brown. He soon squatted on his haunches and drew meaningless figures in the dirt with a forefinger. Waiting was never his strong point, but he forced himself to mimic the patient attitude of the Powhatans with whom he had lived these many months.

Eventually one of the colonists stopped in front of him and asked him a question. Franz mumbled an answer and the two of them walked out of the fort and toward the river's edge, ostensibly examining a fishing weir downriver.

"Where the devil have you been?" demanded Franz. "We expected you and the others two months ago!"

His companion looked miserable. "We were on our way, on foot, when Smith's men met us on their return. We could not very well tell them where we were going or we would have been shot that instant, so we made it appear we were hunting and would be just as glad to join them on their return to the Fort."

"Well, I suppose it was for the best," said Franz. "I think you may be of better assistance now. Powhatan has offered great riches to any man who kills Captain Smith. I have King Pasbehegh and fifteen of his men camped with me upriver. You find a means to bring Smith to the glasshouse this afternoon and an ambush will do the rest."

"Tomorrow morning might be better. He goes there every morning to inspect the progress and speak with the men. 'Twould be easy to catch him then." The companion's voice rose in anticipation.

"Hush! Tomorrow morning then it shall be." Franz jumped to his feet and grabbed a line from the weir. "Here. Take the fish back with you or someone might start wondering what you were doing here all this time. Tomorrow, then."

Franz hopped upon the riverbank and ran along the shore toward the Pasbehegh village.

A few yards away young Sam cautiously rolled over on his side and peered from behind the cedar tree that had been his napping post just a few minutes before. The Natural who had spoken with the Dutch accent was but a blur on the shoreline, and his companion had already made it to the front gate with his fish. Sam blinked several times, stretched his neck and rolled his shoulders to soothe the kink in his muscles as he went in search of Captain Smith.

The early spring mist lay heavily about the Island the next morning as Smith and twenty of his best shots headed for the glasshouse. Over the isthmus they trotted in rows of four, pistols and daggers ready, Smith leading the way with sunlight bouncing off the extraordinary falchion in his fist.

When they arrived, no one was to be seen except the five glassmakers who were rebuilding the fire.

Smith surveyed the area, then barked to his men, "Follow the shore and find the traitor Franz among the Pasbeheghs. Bring him back to Jamestown where he shall find justice."

Alone, Smith turned toward the isthmus and the fort that lay beyond.

Early morning was his favorite time of day and he savored the fresh, clean air mingling with the damp woodsy odor of the forest floor as he scuffled along. As he cleared the woods and headed for the isthmus, a wild scream flooded his brain.

Rough arms wrung his neck; a heavy torso crushed his back, and a swift kick buckled his knees as he fell with his attacker still clinging to him. Over and over they rolled, Smith trying to unleash his assailant and grab his falchion at the same time.

The odor of bear oil was overwhelming at this close range and the naked arms and legs unencumbered by clothing wrapped themselves around the Captain in a vise that cut off his breath.

Icy water hit both with a force that loosened their grips for an instant. The river was shallow near the isthmus and soon the combatants staggered to their feet and found themselves knee deep in frigid spring water, facing each other as cold wetness dripped from their chins, noses and fingertips. Smith growled at his opponent, whose dark eyes glowed with hate.

Lunging, the attacker tackled Smith's waist. Smith grabbed the lock of wet hair streaming down the native's back and wound it around his fist, as he had not so long ago with Opechancanough. A snap of his wrist pulled the native upright and within inches of Smith's angry countenance.

It was Wowinchopunk, King of the Pasbeheghs.

The two warriors stared at each other in hard, breathless animosity. Grunting, Smith dragged the soggy assailant out of the river and to the fort.

Shivering under his river-soaked woolen clothes, Smith pushed the Pasbehegh leader toward a guard.

"Clap him in irons! He tried to drown me and for that he is a prisoner," barked Smith. "Take him from my sight before I take him back to the river and drown him myself."

Before he could turn toward a warm fire and dry clothing, Smith saw the gate swing open at the sound of a drum. In stumbled the hapless Franz, urged on by the soldiers sent to capture him.

Seeing Smith, Franz ran over to him and pumped the Captain's arm in obsequious gratitude.

"Thank you, sir! Thank you! You have saved me from the vile savages!"

Smith appraised the Dutchman's appearance from top to bottom and raised a questioning eyebrow. "Odd words from a man dressed as one."

"Oh, but I had to take on their ways. They forced me to live as they do. We were all held against our very will. Poor Adam and Jan are still captive! How fortunate it is that your men found me gathering walnuts as I made my way back to you after I did escape! Had they caught me, sir, they surely would have killed me. Thank you! Thank you!" And with that the man fell to his knees and kissed Smith's hand several times.

Wowinchopunk, listening to this rush of English-Dutch words, understood what was being said and stepped forward with a derisive laugh.

"Do not believe him, Smit. He was with me as we waited to kill you. He and his friends are not trustworthy. They brought English weapons to Powhatan and begged us to help him kill you and the other English."

Smith, plucking his hand from the adoring Dutchman, knew that the King spoke the truth; the Dutchman had obviously succumbed to the lure of what he saw as security on the other side.

"Take him away, and put him in irons, too. As for the King, we shall use him in trade with Powhatan—his life for Adam and Jan still in Powhatan's hands."

Sputtering denials and begging for assistance, Franz tripped alongside the King on their way to prison.

Every day for the next seven, the King's wives, children and friends came to visit bringing gifts and food that the fettered Wowinchopunk distributed liberally to win the English's affections. The children, round and merry, turned cartwheels and giggled freely once they had lost their natural shyness of white strangers.

Every day, messengers ran from Jamestown to Powhatan, offering the life of the Pasbehegh king for that of Adam and Jan. Each runner returned with much the same answer.

"The Dutchmen will not return," declared the first runner.

"The Dutchmen are not held against their will," said the second.

"Powhatan cannot bring unwilling men fifty miles on the backs of his men," the third stated plainly.

Smith was astonished.

"I don't know why you should be so surprised," said Winne. "Franz is a traitor. Why not the others from his country as well? What else can you expect from the Dutch?"

"More than this, to be sure. Now what do we do?"

"Your ways are too heavy-handed, my friend. You must be more accommodating to the Naturals and to our Company."

"What?" cried Smith. "*More* accommodating? You must be mad! Powhatan has a death warrant out for me and all the English, corn is scarce for them, and two-thirds of our Company cannot be bothered to rise and feed themselves. If we were any more accommodating we'd be dead."

"Your rash ways have offended and antagonized our neighbors."

"My prudent ways have saved our lives and provided us with food for survival. The Naturals respect me, as they did not any other leader here. I thought you had observed as much, Captain Winne. The King of the Pasbeheghs is our prisoner, and I shall have revenge upon his village. If we do not act quickly, they will take it as a sign of weakness."

"Let me go, then. I will take care of this matter," he said, silently figuring that he could do less harm than Smith with the same results.

The next morning, in the darkest hours of the night, Winne sailed a barge toward Pasbehegh.

At dawn, when the Pasbehegh came to the river to bathe and offer tobacco to their gods, Winne ordered a volley of musket fire into the village. As a soldier swam into shore and gained two canoes as prizes, from the barge flaming arrows sailed over the riverbank and into the King's house which was engulfed in fire within minutes.

That's enough, thought Winne as the villagers tried to save the house. His chest was heavy and his breath labored. Too much work, he thought. I should rest more.

"Good God!" cried Smith at Winne's return. "That is all? Two canoes and a house for trying to murder me?" Pushing Winne out of his way, Smith commandeered the barge.

At the Pasbehegh village, where the ruins of the King's house still smoldered, Smith and his soldiers lined up with swords, pikes and pistols, their armor glinting in the sunlight. They marched as one through the main street, taking seven prisoners and leaving seven of the strongest braves dead.

Firebrands made ashes of the houses in minutes. Leaving the cornfields intact, Smith confiscated every canoe, weir and trap, leaving at last with prisoners in tow. As he left, Okaning, Wowinchopunk's second in command, approached Smith.

"I come for peace," he said. "You have won this victory and have our werowance in your fort. But we have the corn and if you wish to have part of it, now or later, we must have peace. If you do not agree to peace, we will leave this country for land far away, and you will have no corn at all."

"Now that I have my revenge, I will agree to peace for corn. You do not have to leave. I will release your King, and he may return to your village. But know that I will not ignore injuries to me or to any of my Company. Tell your people that peace comes at the price of restraint and mutual respect."

"As you say, Smit. It is done." Okaning departed as he came, in straight-backed dignity.

Winne would not be happy, but the message was clear: do not mistake Captain Smith for an easy mark. His pulse was returning to normal, but relief mixed with exhilaration at doing well what needed to be done.

Chickahominies, always bolder than the Powhatan confederates, soon filled the void of harassment left by the Pasbeheghs. Now, in the early April days of 1609, sentries prodded two Chickahominy youths toward justice.

Smith, meeting them in the Church, drew a deep breath. *More thieves*, he thought.

"Severe punishment," said Smith to Winne, who had pleaded for leniency, "is the way to peace with the Chickahominies. They will not stop their thievery until the consequence hurts. Slapping their hands and ignoring the problem only emboldens them to take more with greater frequency."

The two thieves before the Council were brothers. A third youth, a friend, had escaped with a pistol. Smith had the youths sit on the pews while he paced in front of them, hands on swords and pistol, his boots echoing on the brick-lined floor.

"You," he pointed to the taller one, "you are to go back, fetch the pistol and bring it here before the sun rises." The youth smirked. "Bring it back or your brother here will die." The youth stopped smirking. "Do you doubt that I will carry out this punishment?"

The youth shook his head as the guard released his bonds. Rubbing his chafed wrists, he sped off toward the gate as the sentry bellowed for the guards to open it.

"Here then," said Smith to the remaining brother. "You are to remain in the cellar just outside. Guard, give him victuals and charcoal for a fire and keep his hands and feet shackled. We shall see if his brother values life more than he covets a pistol."

At the break of dawn, the returning brother dutifully handed over the pistol and went to retrieve his brother. Cries of lamentation startled the guard outside.

179

"What the devil have you to cry about?" demanded the guard, coming into the cellar. "Captain Smith promised you could..." Here he stopped in amazement.

The prisoner brother was prostrate on the dirt floor, his body covered in soot, his chin and cheeks streaked with spittle. His brother crouched beside him, moaning and rocking on his haunches.

"He's dead! He's dead! You killed my brother before I even came back!" The lamentations echoed through the fort while the guard ran to summon Smith, the doctor, and anyone else who might help.

Smith burst into the cellar, pulled up the wailing youth and knelt down to press his ear to the prisoner's chest. The faintest of heartbeats reassured Smith, and he sat up, thinking.

As the brother's cries continued to pierce eardrums everywhere, Smith grabbed his shoulders and shook him, saying, "If you swear never to steal again, I will make him well."

The youth abruptly stopped his mourning and looked at Smith in wonder. He said nothing, but his silence was more welcome than any answer would have been. Stepping back, he waited to see what Smith would do. No one he had ever known had the great power to revive the dead. Surely not even the marvelous Captain Smith could do that!

Smith stood for a moment, wondering just what he *could* do. The heartbeat he had heard was barely audible, but there it was, so he knew revival hung loosely about the young man, who had obviously succumbed to the smoke of the charcoal fire and could be dead in a matter of minutes.

"Fetch me some aqua vitae and vinegar," said Smith the guard, snapping his fingers. "Quickly!"

As the brother squatted in the corner, he watched the great Captain uncork a small clear bottle. The sharp smell caused the youth to avert his nose involuntarily. Smith pried the prone brother's lips and poured the pungent contents into the cavern of his mouth. Vinegar spilled out of the slackened jaw with no effect taken.

Smith opened a dark bottle of aqua vitae. The odorless, colorless liquid filled the unconscious youth's throat. This time, he gagged and swallowed and gagged again. With his first deep breath his eyes flew open and the remaining mouthful of alcohol spewed forth in a mist that covered his legs and the ground beside him.

Smith plied more of the drink into his patient. A few minutes later the thief was on his feet and staggering around the cellar. He coaxed his wobbly legs to the corner where his brother had risen in amazement and joy.

The one brother, sober and sane, propped up his sibling whose eyes were red from smoke and glassy from liquor. The patient tried to speak but all was a blur of slurred syllables. His movements were loose and uncontrolled, and he did not respond to anything said by his brother or by the English in front of him.

He was drunk.

Helping his brother to the ground, the sober brother turned to Smith and, instead of thanking him, he set to wailing again, in more consternation and sorrow than before. He had never seen such behavior, except in the hut where Powhatan boys became men; if this kind of living replaced Death, he'd rather have lost his brother completely.

Smith guided the sobbing young man to another corner of the cellar and said, "Calm yourself!" Smith could endure anything except hysteria. "I can remedy this, too. If you will restore your sense, I will recover him for you, I promise. You sleep here; your brother will sleep there, and in the morning, all will be as it was before. Do you believe me?"

The brother nodded his belief in the Captain's powers and agreed to stay with his brother for the remainder of the night, with a guard awake and watchful of the fire.

After breakfast, Smith gave each hale youth a piece of copper. "And tell everyone you see, from all of Powhatan's kingdom, that stealing from the English is not worthwhile and that Captain Smith can bring the dead back to life."

With that, the two youths bowed in wide-eyed obedience and ran toward home, eager to tell all they had seen and known in the last two days. Smith laughed and thanked God that the boy had not died and that a little aqua vitae could do so much.

"Mark me," Smith said to Winne, "they will be sending me every thief they have for punishment. I do not think we will have any more problems like this."

Doubtful, Winne said nothing, not even when Smith's prediction came true.

Winne lay on his cot, his head propped by pillows, the perfumer's pots clouding the air within the tent.

In the month since the Pasbehegh boy's resurrection, the colony had enjoyed relative peace and progress. Food was plentiful, the hogs had reproduced to number sixty and the chickens, now properly housed and penned, stretched their confines with five hundred. A cabal of second-sons still refused to do more than was absolutely necessary, preferring to let the thirty lesser sort toil and sweat for their comfort and victuals, but the relative prosperity echoing through the island gave Smith hope and a sense of true accomplishment. Winne would not agree to the measures that would remedy the contrary natures of certain gentlemen, but Smith was reconciled to that.

Now Winne had been ill for several weeks, much as Gosnold had. The same pale, pasty countenance blended into the white lines of the pillow. The same loose intestines and poor appetite followed by a weakening voice led Smith to have Bagnall and Wilkinson stand watch with the Councilor and to do all they could to heal the broken man.

Even so, two days later, Winne was dead.

Deep into the night after the funeral, Smith knelt on the woolen cushions by the altar rail, his head buried in his palms, his heart praying for guidance. The lone candle cast shadows that were his only company –the spirits of Winne, Waldo, Halthrop, Gosnold, Scrivener and all his comrades who had perished here in Virginia. Grief, heavy as granite, weighed down his spirit. Remembering why he was here in Virginia, why they had all come, knowing the risks involved, remembering that God helps those who help themselves, eventually comfort, small and persistent, crept into his soul.

And yet he dreaded what lay before him. Never in his life had he feared so much, never in his life had he been given responsibility over the lives of so many who held no respect for him or his authority. He knew what was right; he knew what needed to be done. He had always known. But he had been thwarted at every turn by circumstance or colleague.

Now no one remained to tell him nay, to call him a troublemaker, to push him aside in greed or opposition. West and Percy were advisors and so far and not been passionately for or against him, perhaps because they held no power in the Company nor patents.

His mind churned with possibilities. Oh, what good could come of this! Smith's heart, aching at the losses, still soared at the thought of a Company that was efficient, even-handed, and effective, one that had no dissension to mar the works and confuse the colonists.

In truth, he would not have asked for it, but now that sole leadership was his and his by law, by God, he would do what needed to be done. A course of honest labor and just rewards was the balm to soothe the ills of the Company. Discipline would be as plentiful as river water.

The next evening, Smith called together the entire Company to announce new policies.

"Countrymen, we have reached a milestone. Do not think that neither my pains nor the adventurers' purses will maintain you in idleness and sloth any longer. I speak not to all of you, for many deserve both honor and reward better than is yet here to be had. Although you have been allowed to decline your duties up till now, you see that power rests wholly in me, and you must obey. He that will not work shall not eat, except if it is sickness that disables him. One hundred and fifty idle loiterers shall not consume the labors of thirty honest and industrious men."

Read and Sam grinned at each other. Captain Smith had wasted no time in coming to the point. He never did.

"And though you presume authority here is but a shadow, and that I dare not touch the lives of any but my own, you cannot deny what is right and true. The Letters Patent I shall read to you each week, whose contents tell you the contrary. Observe these orders, without contempt, for there are no more Councilors to protect you or to curb my endeavors. He that offends should expect his due punishment.

"I shall also post as a public memorial every man's desserts to encourage the good and to spur the shamed to amend their ways. Let us look to industry and discipline and we shall improve our lot a thousand fold.

"Each day shall be spent in this manner: six hours of honest labor, three meals spaced appropriately, Morning and Evening Prayer observed as always, Sunday a day of rest after Services, and the remainder time spent in sport or leisure. For our survival, we shall hunt and plant and harvest; rebuild the Church roof; dig a sweet water well inside the fort; make nets and weirs for fishing; and build another fort on the south side of the river here for the colonists to come and as a refuge from invaders. For the Company benefit, in anticipation of Admiral Newport's return, we shall cut clapboard, make pitch, tar, soap ashes and glass samples.

"Any man who takes umbrage at these policies had best complain to his pillow and no one else. Again, any man who will not work shall not eat. The sick shall be tended to, as is our Christian duty, but no one else shall escape punishment for not abiding by these rules."

Smith was fortunate, he knew, to have as supporters the guards, the laborers, the military contingent. They knew his willingness to do what was necessary not only to survive but to thrive; they had seen who kept them in food.

His opposition lay in gentlemen who so far had refused to help with the day-to-day duties of survival. They were arrogant, spoiled, and insistent upon their rights as gentlemen to have others do their labor for them. Smith had no time for such useless men. His obligation was to the Company as a whole, as a moneymaking enterprise, as a fledgling colony, and therefore, to the King. If it meant being unpopular among the second-son gentry, so be it. The colony *would* thrive—by God's grace and intervention – and with Captain John Smith to hold the men to a higher standard.

The isthmus blockhouse, now fully manned with a garrison to prevent unwanted visitors from setting foot on the island, also doubled as a storehouse for the corn Smith had bought from the Naturals. Piles of corn ears were crammed into the little rooms, stored against the coming winter. This year's crop, if drought did not destroy it, would be added in a few weeks when they were on the unripe side and would store best. How blessed they were to have food in storage, and pigs, hogs and chickens multiplying in droves! The coming winter would not be hard, God willing and Smith providing.

But the drought did take a toll and when the harvest was gathered in early July, disappointed colonists rolled the few full carts to the storehouse.

Todkill and the Company cook pushed aside the large wooden doors, doors that had not been opened since early spring when the last of Captain Smith's barges had delivered its load of golden kernels.

Gnawed and raw cobs rolled against Todkill's boots. Dismayed, he stared dumbly at the mountain of rotting ears. From a hole in the roof, rats and rain had reduced the precious stash into a pile of mushy mold and half-eaten cobs. Rats had skittered and slipped their way into the darker corners when they heard the doors creak open.

"Not fit for pigs," said Todkill in disgust. "Someone has to tell the Captain."

"I suppose you mean me!" wailed the cook. "I'm not going to tell 'im!"

"Go to. I'll tell him." Todkill kicked a cob with such ferocity the walls rattled and forced an avalanche of cobs into the main room. "What a piss-poor job that will be." He paused. "We will have to set fire to the storehouse and drive the rats into the river with firebrands. Drowning them is the only way

I know of to be rid of them." He shook his head in weariness. "And we was making such good progress, too. Christ. What will the Captain say now? And what will we eat this winter?"

Kemps and Tassore, two Kecoughtans who had lived in the fort for the past six months willingly learning the white man's ways and language, stood with a ten-foot limb between them. Fifty turkeys and squirrels dangled in death, ready to be dinner or supper or whatever the white men needed.

"God be praised for sending you to us!" exclaimed the cook directing his helpers to gather the carcasses and take them to the cookhouse. "See, Captain Smith? A fortnight ago we were in despair. Kemps and Tassore have brought us fresh meat every day, enough to keep all two hundred of us from starving." He felt the plumpness of the turkeys. "You are decent fellows. A credit to your mothers!" Cook grinned and followed the swaying carcasses.

Smith turned to the young men. "You are both generous to a fault. We cannot offer much in return except our deepest thanks and gratitude. Without your services, we would be limited to sturgeon, nuts, and fruit, which is truthfully enough to keep us from starving, surely, but you bring us the meat that fortifies our bodies and souls. We are in your debt."

Kemps half-smiled but did not reply. Tassore gave a little nod and the two of them left to double the offering as they finished their day's hunting.

"Debt? Bah!" grunted a voice in the shadow of long row house.

Smith turned and squinted to see who had spoken. He saw two brown-hosed legs cross the dark line between shade and sun, legs sprawled and relaxed with no intent of rising. Smith leaned into the shadow.

"Stand up, man. Stand and answer me."

The legs slowly drew into the body and managed to prop up the frame of their owner, a thin youth of eighteen with a sallow complexion and curly black hair. His lips he forced into a line that hid his teeth. A stiff "sir" slipped between the line as he leaned his back against the brick wall and cast his eyes upon the ground.

"You are Dyer," Smith said rather than asked, looking the man up and down. "I recognize you from the last Supply."

"Aye," he said, eyes now on the horizon.

"William Dyer, you have something to say. Better have it out."

"I have nothing to say," answered Dyer turning his attention to the wall and fingering the mortar.

"You do not like Kemps or Tassore."

Dyer met the Captain's hazel gaze briefly and then resumed his exploration of the wall. "The savages that live here? I think they reek of heathenism, and I wouldn't eat a morsel of anything they brought in."

"And where do you come from, Dyer, that you have license to choose who cooks your meals? Are you a relation of the King?"

"I come from London, and we never ate with the servants, I can tell you that. No, they ate our scraps, and that is as it should be here. I am no pauper, no middle-class merchant, and I prefer to eat what white hands have prepared."

"Do you hunt, then? Can you shoot a turkey, fell a deer? Can you catch a sturgeon?" Smith asked. "No? Can you plant a row of corn? Harvest nuts or berries?"

Dyer snorted. "Indeed not, sir; that is what servants are for. I am a gentleman, and gentlemen to do not labor to feed themselves and certainly do not labor to feed the savages or lesser sort of English. They are to serve us; that is the natural order of things."

"Natural order or no," snapped Smith, "I am grateful to Kemps and Tassore and so should you be. They have worked daily, twice as hard as any Englishman, and taught us to order and plant our fields. Here in Jamestown we must all work together or we shall all perish. I suggest you think upon that idea; a growling stomach is the natural order of things when a man does not feed it."

"The savages bring us food, and I have goods to trade. Labor is not necessary when buying food is that easy."

"But at what price? What is the true cost of such a dealing? You would have us give them items of infinite value here in the wilderness—hoes, tools, kettles, nay, swords, ordnance and even our houses!—for something that turns to shit in a day's time? You are too simple."

Dyer's mouth clapped shut and his lips retreated into their hard line.

Smith paused, giving the surly youth a hard stare. "That is all. You may go."

Dyer lingered a while longer, deliberately smoothing his doublet and adjusting his ruff before departing. Smith waited, not moving an inch, until Dyer's thin form had disappeared around the corner of the church.

Angry raised welts of raw skin mingled with blood and crossed Dyer's back. His outstretched arms were tied to the palisade wall; his face and naked torso pressed against the rough-hewn trees. At the first lashes, he had muffled his cries, but now at the end of the dozen ordered by President Smith his head swam, and he did not know if his voice worked or not. He could feel nothing but the stinging whip and then, mercifully, the bindings falling away and thick hands on either side carrying him away.

The company, gathered as they were to view the punishment, stood in silence as the prisoner was taken away, and waited for Smith to speak. No one expected Smith's words to be soft or easy. Mutiny was punishable by death and Dyer was lucky: he was only flogged and only had to endure twelve lashes. Smith was well within his rights as President and Council both to have imposed the capital law upon the man.

Smith's face was hard and the muscles along his cheeks and brow were visibly tense. He stood on the north bulwark so he could see and be seen clearly by everyone, his voice ringing out in the stillness.

"Fellow soldiers, I did not think any of you so false as to report, or many of you so simple as to be persuaded that I either intend to starve you or that Powhatan has corn for himself, much less for you, or that I would not have it if I knew where it were to be had.

"Neither did I think any so malicious as now I see a great many of you are. Yet it shall not deter me: I will do my best even for my worst detractor. But dream no longer of this vain hope from Powhatan. I will no longer forbear to force you from your idleness and punish you if you rail. If I find any more runners for Newfoundland with the pinnace, let him assuredly look to arrive at the gallows.

"You cannot deny but that by the hazard of my life many a time I have saved yours when, might your own wills have prevailed, you would have starved, and would still have it so. As yet I never had more from the store than the worst of you; and all my own extra provisions you have seen me divide amongst the sick. This savage trash you so scornfully repine at, being put in your mouths your stomachs can digest it. If you would have better you should have brought it."

Smith paused to let his next sentence have full impact.

"And he that gathers not every day as much as I do, the next day shall be set beyond the river and be banished from the fort as a drone till he amend his ways or starve."

Despite the few who murmured the order most cruel, the remaining two hundred soldiers and gentlemen at last pulled themselves into reasoned labor and for a time that hot, dry July all seemed right. The corn may have been lost to rats or withered in the dry heat, but there were berries, fruits, fish, fowl and venison enough to be gathered, netted or shot. Smith turned attention to drying what fish and meat they could to store for the winter and to cutting trees to lade the ships due to arrive, surely, some time soon. The new arrivals would not find a fort full of wasted and starving colonists, not if Smith could help it.

On July 9th, with the full heat of day thrust upon them before matins had begun, there came a rallying cry from the eastern bulwark. A ship had been seen by Hog Island sentries, a signal fire blazed now on the shore facing the fort.

"To arm! To arm! Beat to quarters!"

Soldiers readied the cannon on the demi-lunes and aimed downriver; musketeers forced powder down their weapons, laid them on the forked end of their supports, and kept their matches smoldering. Spanish, French or English, until 'twas known who sailed up the King's River, all colonists need be ready for the worst.

To their great relief the ship that crawled toward them was neither Spanish nor French but flew the ensign of St. George.

Smith, standing on the pier, grabbed the captain's arm and greeted him with such joy that Samuel Argall was taken aback.

Argall was roughly Smith's age, perhaps a few years older, with wavy reddish gold hair that was far too feminine for the square face and weathered skin. He seemed happy to meet Smith of whom he had heard such varying accounts.

"Well done, well done!" exclaimed Smith, his eyes two half-moons of glee. "But is yours the only ship?"

Argall, his gray eyes simultaneously taking in the fort, his surroundings and the burly man who clasped his hand, replied, "For now. But let us talk over a glass of wine and let my sailors stretch their legs on your hospitable grounds."

Argall had sailed alone but not without news, and he was as anxious to share it as Smith was to hear it.

A bottle of port later, shared equally by Argall, Smith, Percy and West, and the details of Argall's journey flowed easily enough. "My commission was to try a shorter route from England to Jamestown and load my ship with

Virginia sturgeon, not to bring supplies, Captain, I am sorry to say. But you and your company may buy whatever extra we have of wine, biscuits and other such good provision that you should like—leaving us sufficient to return to England, of course."

Sam was at Smith's elbow and at the word "biscuits" a gasp of delight escaped before he could stifle it. Smith smiled and winked at the young man who was grinning in spite of himself.

"When did you leave London, sir?" inquired Smith.

"On the fifth of May."

Smith's jaw nearly grazed the table. "Did you say the fifth of May? Good God, that is but nine weeks!"

"Nine, strictly speaking, but seven in actual number. We had two weeks of calm that kept us from going anywhere. We headed west after the Canaries, avoided the West Indies –and Spain!—and here we are. Shorter and without the annoyance of defending ourselves along the way." Argall looked pleased.

"You shall be knighted for this, mark me."

"One has hopes, of course," said Argall smoothly, then changed the subject. "I have a letter for you, Smith, which I insist you take only after I tell you this: that you are well regarded by the Company and that your efforts here are not unrecognized." He handed over a parchment folded in thirds and sealed with the seal of the King's Council.

Smith read the letter carefully and then folded it neatly before placing it inside his doublet. "They are not happy with my harsh ways with the savages and wish I had returned the ships laden with gold and not wood." Smith sighed. "Ah, well. They would more fully comprehend were they here and not limited to the tales told by men who left in disgrace or resignation. Gold we have none here in Virginia and wishing will not make it so; and the Naturals have come to respect and obey and we live peacefully, if cautiously. There. You have done your duty in delivering their missive and I am grateful."

"There is more. I have saved the best for last. The King has agreed to – though it was not signed before I left in May—a second Charter. There is to be a Royal Council in England, much as we have now, but the power will lie with Sir Thomas Smythe who will be Treasurer and will have as his representative in Virginia a Governor."

Smith's eyes opened in surprise. "No more President of the Council?"

"No more Council."

Smith stroked his beard as Argall continued.

"A Governor—Lord De La Warr—will be the head of the colony. I believe you, sir, are his brother?" This last was addressed to West who nodded without comment. Smith hid his surprise as Argall continued. "Once the Charter is signed and, of course, delivered. But the most important part is this, Smith. No more sending only a handful of men to plant here. They have raised 40,000 ducats in subscriptions, with 650 personally subscribing and fifty-six city companies joining in. And *six hundred* have volunteered to come live here and make their fortunes! Men, women and children!"

Smith whistled. "Six hundred? Are they all coming at once?"

"I do not know. I do know that Sir Thomas Gates, Sir George Somers and Captain Newport were arranging for nine ships with six hundred people to leave soon, if they have not left already. Oh, and there is another requirement for new colonists. Each must sign an Oath of Supremacy of the Church of England."

Smith understood immediately. "Ah, yes. Kendall. No Catholics allowed. 'Twas to be expected, I suppose. Although a spy would sign anything, I should think, being without conscience."

Argall couldn't resist adding one last bit of news. "The Company has started advertising for young maids with household skills to come here as well." He grinned.

"Brides!" Percy's eyes lit up as the word blew past his lips. "A married colonist is a happy colonist, is that it?"

"And one that makes many more little colonists, if you take my meaning," said Argall, laughing.

"And a new Charter. Well, well." Smith stopped fingering his beard. "My term as President expires in September. Lord De La Warr is surely as capable and worthy a leader as any other man. I can return to exploring. But six hundred new colonists! They best come ready to work and feed themselves." Smith looked around the table. "With or without Catholics, spies or brides."

Chapter Sixteen

Mischiefs into Miseries

For the rest of July and the first part of August, Smith and his Company of two hundred bartered, jawed, traded and gamed with Argall and his crew to the extent that Argall's supplies were depleted and needed to be restocked before he could return to England. Argall was happy enough, being paid as he was, to keep company with the colonists till the *Mary and John* was packed with sturgeon, and Gates' nine ships had arrived to share supplies.

What corn could be harvested was placed in the new storehouse by the isthmus, Smith having cleaned the area with rat poison last spring and being watchful of other rats nesting where their brethren had died. The drought, so long and so severe, hampered attempts to have grain for the coming winter, but dried fowl, fish and venison were in abundance and might make up the difference.

With order, food, and discipline firmly rooted at last, the surrounding Naturals living in respect of the English, and the death toll fallen to a remarkable low, Smith was satisfied that he had done his best and that the colony would thrive with an influx of six hundred newcomers led by a Governor such as Lord De La Warr would surely be. He did not mind relinquishing the Presidency for he had never sought it, never considered politics his goal. His term would be over in a few weeks anyway. He had been brought to that point by God, he did not doubt it, and now God was bringing De La Warr and a new Charter which would likely allow him to return to the exploration he loved so well. Passage to the South Sea had yet to be discovered. God was good and Smith was grateful.

So when, on August 11th, the signal was raised that ships were making their way up the King's River, Smith's heart lightened, and a grin stretched his wiry beard and moustache into unaccustomed angles. The colonists poured out of the fort to greet the newest Virginians.

As seven dark shapes crawled around Hog Island, the thrill of anticipation that had arrested the gathered crowd gave way to stunned silence.

The two largest ships were missing both main masts and the sails were tattered and ripped to the point of uselessness. The smaller ships leaned unnaturally, some to port, some starboard. This was hardly a flotilla of fresh recruits; they were more remnant than whole cloth.

The pitiful ships edged their way up the natural channel and collected themselves around the end of the island where the *Mary and John* and *Discovery* were tied to the trees. As they maneuvered, Smith looked closely at the men who stood on the decks. There weren't many, to be sure. He blinked several times to clear away the cobwebs of old memories. He blinked again, and then he knew he was not wrong.

On the largest ship, the *Diamond*, stood John Ratcliffe. On the second largest, the *Falcon*, John Martin coughed into a handkerchief. And, on a smaller ship, Gabriel Archer stiffened his spine when he spied Smith. The name of the ship on which Archer stood hit Smith like a flagon of cold water on Christmas morning. It was the *Blessing*.

It couldn't be. Argall had said Gates, Somers, and De La Warr were coming! Not a whisper about Martin, Ratcliffe or Archer! Smith felt a lump in his stomach and uneasiness clouded his mind such that he did not remember their greeting or the next half hour as the three least welcome of colonists disembarked and introduced the ships' captains who had steered the little parade of sorry ships to Jamestown.

Four hundred men, women and children gingerly stepped upon solid ground for the first time in weeks, and in the confusion of passengers, supplies, whistles, shouts and staking a place to pitch a family tent Smith forgot about his worries. Many were sick and he was sure he heard someone say the plague was on board the *Diamond*, though he only heard it once in passing. There were no physicians or barber surgeons this time. He was watching the sick be carried off the ships on stretchers when a voice at his back caused him to turn. It was Sam.

"You're needed, Captain, in the church. I was told to fetch you."

Smith nodded absently and followed the young man, now grown tall and gangly as any sixteen-year-old might be.

Ratcliffe, Martin and Archer stood at the head of the church, not quite at the altar, but nearly so. The ships' captains, including Argall, were seated in the front row, as well as Percy, West and a few other gentlemen of means.

"What happened to your ships? Where is Lord De La Warr? Sir Thomas Gates? How many sick do you have?" Smith peppered the men with questions before he reached the end of the aisle.

"Smith, our story is long but you should find it interesting. Please, sit down. We will tell you all as it transpired, and you shall see the necessity of our situation." Archer sounded almost friendly.

"The King has decided that, to thwart Spain's growing presence in the New World, our colony needs to expand in greater numbers and in a shorter time than the Virginia Company could manage. To that end, he has sent nine ships—seven of which you see here—and six hundred colonists to inhabit Virginia, with more to come in the Spring."

"What happened to the other two ships?" asked Smith.

"I am coming to that," snapped Archer, dropping his friendly demeanor. "More to come in the Spring. As you see, we are seven when we should be nine. Somewhere south of the Bermudas a terrible hurricane swept us all off course, and it was only several days later and just a few days ago that we seven connected again. It would appear the flagship, the *Sea Venture*, was lost and all souls perished."

"Is it possible some survived?"

"Possible but hard to say if probable. No one saw it go down completely but we did see it heading for the reefs in a rolling sea. We did not see any survivors in the water, if that is what you mean."

Smith nodded.

Archer continued. "We seven, then, are here safely, if a little worn and in need of comfort and repair. The *Swallow* lost thirty-two to calenture in the heat of the tropics before the storm, and the *Sea Venture* carried one hundred and fifty or so. We have then a little less than four hundred colonists here, and though they be in a sorry state, they are ready to thrive." One of the captains grunted in dispute.

"The thrust of this story, Smith, is that a new Charter has been drawn up, and we are here to start afresh with a new government. Your services are no longer required. We thank you for your excellent work so far and wish you well."

Smith stood up and drew near to Archer and his comrades. He paced a few times in front of the altar, stroked the underside of his whiskers with the back of his fingers, and came to a halt in between the new captains and the trio who had caused so much grief in the past.

"I will gladly cede my position."

The trio smiled at each other.

"I will gladly cede the Presidency to the person who hands me the Charter and other documents testifying to the truth of this claim." Smith extended his hand and waited.

"We, er, do not have the papers *here*," replied Ratcliffe. "That is," he stammered, "they are not in our possession at the moment."

"Not here? Where then?" Smith was calm.

Archer found his tongue. "The Charter is with Sir Thomas."

"Since only the *Sea Venture* is lost—that and a little ketch tied to it—only one copy was lost. Bring me one of the other two copies. It is Company policy." Smith was calm, but resolute.

Archer, Martin, Ratcliffe and every captain seated there—except Argall who knew none of the particulars—remained unhappily silent. In a tight voice Archer finally said, "All three copies went down with the *Venture*."

Smith was incredulous. "No. No. No. That cannot be. No one would put all three on one ship! That is madness!"

Here the captain who grunted spoke up. "None of them—Gates, Somers, and Newport—the three highest officials we had—none of them wanted to sail on anything less than the flagship. Too much of a humiliation."

Smith was dumbfounded. "So you are telling me they all sailed on the one ship, knowing that all copies of the Charter were aboard? And that is the one ship that did not complete the journey?"

The miserable faces before him told him he was right.

"Well, then. Without a Charter, you have no authority. I will remain President until September 10th when my term expires. We shall pray that you are mistaken and that the *Sea Venture* will arrive before that time and we can proceed accordingly. Until such time, however, Captains, you have heard it all and know the proper course to follow. I have the allegiance of my men here who know these three of old and do not trust them as far as the nearest pissing tree. I will rely on you to follow my instructions for the care and discipline of our colony."

The ships captains, knowing that the stunned trio had been trumped by proper procedure, followed the angry President out of the church and into the chaos of the sick, the displaced and the bewildered.

Francis West spoke first. "He is not entirely wrong, you know."

Archer threw him an angry look. "Wrong enough. We all know the Charter exists and what it says."

"But Captain Smith does not, and as far as the Colony knows, the only patent they have is the original and it bears King James' seal and signature. I do not blame him for refusing to step down. It would be tantamount to disobeying the King."

"So we shall work around that. We let him be President until September 10th. Then instead of elections – there is no Council to choose from and Smith cannot be re-elected—we appoint a proviso Governor until Gates or other word arrives."

Ratcliffe brightened. "Let us ratify the Charter in absentia—right now!"

"Done!" cried Archer. "And who better than Lord De La Warr's brother to be Governor proviso?"

Francis West blanched at the idea. "You want me to defy Smith and the King?"

"Not defy. Succeed. As Governor! As the Charter requires! And since Gates, who was to be Governor in Lord De La Warr's stead till he arrives next spring, is not here, we need a substitute, someone that is here. Since you are the true Governor's brother and are here…you must see how it all fits together." Archer's pleasure was palpable.

West wasn't fully convinced but decided that the spirit of the Charter could prevail while letting the old Council rules naturally expire with Smith's Presidency. West knew his brother well enough to say he would likely agree.

"When do you tell him the Charter names him third in command of the new royal colony? That news might soothe his disappointment in losing the original charter." West looked expectantly at Archer, Martin and Ratcliffe who looked at each other.

"We cannot be certain that he was indeed so appointed, since none of us saw the signed Charter. Therefore, it is best not to say anything, in the case that he would take it to heart and then be unmanageable when he found out otherwise," Archer answered.

West, unsure that Smith would have been so slighted by the King's Council when his brother had written otherwise, was unwilling to argue the point. "So be it then. I will do as you prescribe, but I will not usurp Smith's power here at Jamestown. What fool would try?"

Within a week, steady footing and fresh meat restored most of the arrivals to reasonable health, and Smith decided to divide the unwieldy group for survival. Percy and Martin, along with sixty colonists, he sent south to the Nansemonds. West and one hundred and twenty others were to go north, to the Falls, where Powhatan's realm abutted the Monacans. That left three hundred or so with him at Jamestown, a manageable number considering the housing inside the fort and the tents set up in the field. Housing could be built in the autumn and palisades along the shoreline as needed.

Smith, seeing that Jamestown was in order and progressing, left ten days later to visit the Falls and see how West's group faired.

The barge with Smith and his five soldiers sailed up the King's River, the water smooth and shining in the early September light. Air less humid but still warm was easy to breathe, and deep inhalations cleared Smith's thoughts and lifted his spirits. Sailing even a short distance was a tonic that had been in short supply, and Smith happily cruised northward.

Finding the encampment on the very banks of the river ended the reverie. Smith stood amazed on the shore.

More haste than care had gone into the pitching of tents; someone had laid out the powder kegs and arms too near the fire; the very camp itself was on a flood plain, subject to even the normal rise and fall of the tide, and ever open to any canoe filled with armed Naturals. And not a palisade in sight.

Directly above was the village of Powhatan, situated on the hilltop, conveniently out of the way of invaders and yet remarkably handy for pelting arrows upon the encampment. Smith suppressed a growl, said nothing to the inhabitants who had said nothing to him, and trekked upward to visit Parahunt, Powhatan's brother, who Smith knew well and trusted.

Persuading Parahunt that the English would be useful in protection from the Monacans was not difficult; all of Powhatan's people were aware of the power of the musket and cannon and having them on the Powhatan side was a decided advantage. Parahunt agreed to Smith's terms and retired.

"So you have the entire village," Smith later told the colonists, "the fort, houses, fields, everything—at your disposal. Parahunt has agreed to pay a yearly tribute to Jamestown: every householder will give a bushel of corn in return for an inch of copper; all thieves will be sent to me and I will dole out punishment; and the entire village is ours for a proportion of copper. We have enough daylight left today to pack your tents and belongings and move uphill."

"Move? Why the devil should we move?" growled one of the colonists, a man of twenty with little of the gentleman in his voice or manner. "We know the gold lies yonder. You want us to give up our place and let any yokel pass by without so much as a By Your Leave? No, no. Gold is what we came for and gold is what we'll have!"

Smith tried logic. "There is no gold here, to that I can attest. We have found none in our two years here."

"So you say! But how do we know you can be trusted? We heard about you, Captain Smith, we know all about you. And it would be just like you to say it wasn't here, make us move, and poof! You find the gold yourself!"

Smith stared at the man whose words had drawn the entire company into hearing range.

The man continued. "You don't have no authority here, you don't. Master West is our commander! And he's the Governor, not you."

The crowd stepped forward with menacing eyes and suddenly several men drew knives, one for each hand, and others found pikes and hatchets.

Smith, seeing he was outnumbered and outarmed, withdrew to the barge in dumbfounded disbelief. The next day he returned to the hilltop village and stayed in the hospitality of Parahunt for nearly a week, thinking that he would rather enjoy his company than have to endure the company of English below.

Every day brought a new complaint. The English stole my corn! The English robbed my garden! The English ruined my house! And then the final insult: The English made our men prisoners!

Parahunt pulled Smith aside. "Your people are more dangerous than the Monacans. For your love we have endured these things. If you would lead, we will gladly follow you to fight them. But since you do not correct them, forgive us if we defend ourselves."

Smith declined. He could not lead natives against his own people, the King's people, not even the lubberly gluttons below. "I will try to reason with them again. But they are not willing to be guided by me or ruled by me, and I cannot lead without power. There are changes at Jamestown, my friend, and others have come who will destroy all I have accomplished. My time is coming to an end."

Parahunt listened intently and saw sadness in the Englishman's eyes that had never existed before. He understood. Life did not stand still, and the white man could be as ruthless with each other as with any enemy.

Smith tried to reason with the colonists, but they again could not be persuaded that his words had any merit. Seeing he could do no more and expecting West's return at any moment, Smith ordered the barge downriver.

Half a league gone, and the sounds of war whoops and screams turned their heads.

"Back! Back!" cried Smith and all aboard rowed as if Satan himself were on their heels. The encampment that had yesterday been a shaky, ill-conceived tent-city was now a flattened pile of canvas and smoldering ashes. Colonists stood or lay in shocked silence, some with their work still in hand— a cook holding a spoon in mid-air; a half-clothed infant on a blanket, his mother clutching the garments that needed to be changed; a smoking pipe dangling from the lips of a middle-aged man.

Smith appeared and no one moved until he spoke, asking what had happened.

"They came from nowhere!" exclaimed the pipe smoker. "Nowhere! They swooped in and freed the savages we had as prisoner, and then they all pulled down our tents and kicked our fires, a-screaming like no hellcats I ever heard. We heard them a-killin' out yonder but 'twas no use of our goin' out. No tellin' how many they've murdered!"

"How many did you see?" asked Smith.

"There must have a dozen, at least! All a-whoopin' and a-hollerin'! We didn't have a moment to fight back!"

Smith, hearing the pitiful numbers that had routed a company of over one hundred, felt the blood rush to his head and throb in his ears. His hands started shaking, he squeezed his eyes shut. His thoughts were a jumble of angry, unspeakable oaths. Finally, he roared as he had never roared before.

"Great God, by all that's Holy! You insignificant, cowardly, lily-livered pig herders! You couldn't find it in your sniveling little hearts to pick up an axe or hatchet? What about a pike or those knives you aimed so handily at me the other day? You threatened me well enough but when the real enemy assails you have not the courage God gave a gnat. I have never met such a disgusting display of soggy backbone in my life. Not here, not in England, not anywhere! The best that can be said is that you did not beshit your breeches – or did you?"

Smith kicked a barrel, then picked up a tent-stake and heaved it into the middle of the river, letting out a sound few humans could reproduce.

"Soldiers! Arrest the company officers, clap them in irons before I take a stake and drive it through their soulless hearts. The rest of you, pick up what you have left and carry it uphill. Anyone who argues will join the officers in leg irons and that includes women. I'll cuff anyone who makes mouths behind my back or even whispers dissent. Move."

Docile obedience reigned for the rest of the day, and by the next morning Parahunt's village had been resigned to the English, but not before restitution had been made in copper and bead and the swords and clothing stolen in the raid had been returned to the English.

Parahunt and his villagers left their two hundred acres reluctantly but leave it they did. With Smith's promises of protection from the Monacans and the power he wielded despite his claims, they had little choice but to move.

Smith was satisfied with the result although he was not expecting much in the future. These particular colonists had little to recommend themselves. They were criminals, do-nothings, and beggars. What was the Company thinking, sending the likes of them here? The news of six hundred colonists had elated him; now that they'd met, he was discouraged and angry.

At dinner, he was still seething, still nursing the anger and frustration of watching his hard work and discipline fall apart before his eyes. He did not hear the heavy boots approach nor did he notice anything until those boots were toe-to-toe with his own. He looked up and into the stormy face of Francis West.

"What in the name of Heaven are you doing *here?*" demanded West.

"The place you chose for plantation wouldn't sustain a rat. What possessed you to set up on a flood plain within arrow distance of Parahunt's village?" Smith rose as he spoke, putting his face within inches of West's.

"I thought the place fine enough, and we could draw fresh water easily without having to carry it uphill several times a day, if you must know. How dare you move my people without my knowledge or consent!"

"You were not here when the Naturals attacked and left your "fort" in tatters. As the President, I moved them to safety and sanity. Surely you are not complaining?" asked Smith, amazed.

West struggled to control his anger. "Complaining! From the moment I arrived here, nothing but complaints reached my ears. You caused the assault; you did nothing to save anyone while it went on; you have bullied every man and woman into submission. You have overstepped your bounds, Captain."

Smith's mind turned over the lies lain before him. "You believe I would not only stand by while Englishmen are attacked but that I would incite the riot? Surely you are not that gullible! I was nowhere near when the attack occurred, and I had just paid for the village you now inhabit. Why should I incite an assault against my own people? Think, man."

West, calmer now but resolute, said, "Please go, Captain. I will take care of all that needs tending at West's Fort. You have much to do at Jamestown, have you not?" He turned to a colonist hovering over the cook fire.

"You, Dyer, escort Captain Smith and his soldiers to their barge. Take your time and do not come back until you've seen them sail."

Smith, who had not noted Dyer before, surveyed the faces of the crowd that had gathered. Angry faces, hard faces, faces that did not want his help or his presence—and Dyer's face was fiercest of all.

"Very well. May God look after you and bring all you deserve." Smith then tossed aside his dinner in disgust, wiped his mouth with the sleeve of his doublet, and headed for the river.

Smith ordered the barge to stay till morning.

A lone firebrand burned on the corner of the barge. The sentry stood in sleepy vigil. Smith, his head cradled in the crook of his arm, fell into the deep sleep of the exhausted. Not three feet away, Dyer lay awake, his mind a whirl of plot and consequence.

Do it now, do it now. The voice in his head relentlessly beat the notion. *No one will know. It'll be an accident.*

The sleepy sentry had started to snore. His lighted match, glowing at each end beckoned Dyer. A short breath and the glow would turn to flame.

Dyer sat up. No one noticed. He crawled along the wooden deck, dodging humans and gear alike. From behind the sentry, he lifted his hand as if to lightly touch the man's shoulder. Reaching for the sentry's waist, he loosened the strap that held the match. Quickly, Dyer confiscated the glowing match and raised one end to his lips.

A flame sputtered and died. He tried again, this time blowing hard enough to make a little whirring noise. He froze, thinking the sound would awaken the sentry, but it did not.

The coil of hemp rope soaked in salt peter burst into a small fire and died down to a small ember, just enough to light a musket.

Dyer coiled the rest of the length of rope onto his fist in a loose circle and crawled to where Smith lay.

The powder bag, a leather pouch no bigger than a robin's nest, rested on Smith's hip. His arms were conveniently out of the way, the one tucked under his head, the other resting on his dagger sheath.

Dyer rested the burning match on the leather while he moved to the other side of the barge, crawling as fast as he could without disturbing anyone or anything along the way. Pretending to be asleep, he waited for the inevitable.

Smith's scream of agony woke everyone on the barge who saw nothing but the Captain jumping overboard into the cold river.

The shock of the water jolted Smith's mind to rights. The searing pain of the powder's ignition had rendered him near blind and gasping for breath; instinct alone had forced him into the water.

The weight of his clothing pulled him downward. Pain pounded at his brain. He thrashed his arms and kicked his legs, ignoring the excruciating wound at his side. His head hit a bodiless arm clutching under the surface and his hand grabbed at it. They clung together and soon Smith was on the barge again, wet, stunned, and in pain such as he'd never known.

He managed to look down his torso and saw that the breeches and doublet were sheared and in tatters around his thigh and hip. A scorched patch of skin nine inches square oozed blood and shredded flesh dangled from all sides. His powder bag was gone.

"To Jamestown! The fort!" he whispered in a strangled voice. His head fell with a thud on the wooden deck and his eyes rolled back as he lost consciousness.

Chapter Seventeen

Picking up the Pieces

Dyer stood on the shore, watching the barge disengage and set off downriver despite the darkness. His wet clothes did not hinder, but they were making him colder by the moment, so he began the climb back to Parahunt's village. Tomorrow they would all be on the riverbank again at West's Fort; tomorrow there would be no more John Smith to interfere in their affairs again.

Justice, thought Dyer, fingering the scars on his back. Justice and nothing more.

Sam, who had heard the sentry announce an oncoming barge, ran to the shore to meet it. Why is he coming back in the dark? the boy wondered out loud.

The barge approached with greater vigor than usual. This was not a casual return. The soldiers and sailors were doing everything they could to make the clumsy craft go faster. Doubt turned to alarm, and when he saw the Captain being carried off the barge, Sam almost panicked.

Sam trotted along side the cot. "What happened? Are you not well?"

Smith managed a thin smile and patted the boy's hand. "There was an accident and I will need a few days to heal, that is all." His voice was small.

"Will a surgeon help? Let me fetch Bagnall! How will you recover? What is to be done?"

"I do not know, exactly. I am not sure anything needs to be done," answered his friend from his bed, eyes shut and mouth grim. "Here."

As Sam wiped the Captain's brow with the handkerchief, he noticed the gaping wound and blanched. No one, not even the magnificent Captain Smith, could survive that sort of injury, Bagnall or no.

"I will leave for England, if I am blessed to live through the night. My time as President is over, and there is nothing I can do to help Jamestown now." Smith spoke with a calm that startled Sam.

"But you always fight! You never lose! Do not give up just as we need you most."

Smith's voice grew stronger. "No, I have always fought when it was right. Good men do not fight for the sake of fighting. You must decide for yourself if a cause is worth fighting for, worth dying for, worth other men's dying for. Until now I have battled to keep our company whole, to keep us fed, armed, protected, and in health. I have done what needed to be done to survive and thrive, God willing. But now—"

He winced as he shifted positions.

"Now I see that the opposition has the advantage. I am out of power in a few days and, if that did not prevent my leading, this wound surely will. I cannot rise from my bed, as you can see. Can a man lead from his sick bed? He cannot. The *Unity* leaves shortly for England, and I will go with her. I am not even fit to go on discovery. I have done what needed to be done and I have tried my best. No man can do more. I am grateful I am not dead and can return to England. Sometimes, Sam, no matter what you do, no matter what you've done, there's nothing more to be gained, and you just have to leave it all where God flung it."

Smith tried to sleep. His brain whirled with thoughts of the voyage to Virginia, the ungodly heat of summer, the fire that had consumed the original palisades, the hilltop village and Dyer's hateful face, till they all mixed together, and he dreamed Dyer was in the fort and setting fire to the cook's tent.

The sound of a pistol cocking jarred his mind to reality.

In the darkness he could barely make out a shape coming toward him. A sword lay by his side; he gripped the handle and cut a swath of air across his body. "Stop or I'll have your head!" The sword fell to the ground.

The shape halted, unsure of how to proceed. They had told him the Captain was out of his senses, that Smith would never know who had shot him. Now he could see that the President was all too aware of his surroundings. What if he shot and missed? What if the Captain recognized him? The gallows would be all he could hope for. No, it was not worth the risk.

The would-be assassin turned and ran out of the tent.

Smith faced the ship's bulkhead on his bed as the *Unity* prepared to sail. He had never felt so defeated, so persecuted, so alone. Rational thought assured him that he had nothing to be ashamed of, nothing to burden his soul, but regret tugged at his heart. He had come with such expectations; they all had. Now he could not even rise to stand on deck as he left the Virginia colony.

His seared body ached, and his head pounded with pain. He thought of Powhatan and the uneasy respect they had for each other. The coming months would be a trial; Powhatan would surely test the new leaders, and he wasn't sure if Virginia would survive until Gates finally arrived, if he wasn't at the bottom of the Atlantic.

What would become of the colony in the hands of Archer, Ratcliffe, Martin and West? Smith counted in his head all that he left behind: three ships, seven barges; commodities ready to trade, the harvest newly gathered, and ten weeks' provisions in the store; four hundred and ninety-odd persons; twenty-four pieces of ordnance, three hundred muskets, snaphaunces and firelocks, shots, powder, and match sufficient, cuirasses, pikes, swords, and helmets more than men; the natives, their language and habitations well known to a hundred well-trained and expert soldiers; nets for fishing, tools of all sorts to work; apparel to supply their wants; six mares and a horse; five or six hundred swine, as many hens and chickens, and several goats and sheep.

There seemed plenty for the colony to thrive, if the new leadership set about trading with Powhatan and continued the work ethic he had instilled. If.

What were the odds? Were he a betting man, he would wager against it. If Gates arrived before winter, the best could be hoped for. If.

Too many unknowns. Too much resting on the unlikely chance that a group of misguided, covetous, ambitious, self-serving men would suddenly translate themselves into worthy leaders. Now, if Lord De La Warr should come…If.

Smith heard feet shuffling cautiously nearby. When he opened his eyes, two friendly faces looked down on him with affection. Read and Sam did not say anything but stood in reverent silence as they waited for Smith to acknowledge them.

"You decided to go back to England, too?" asked Smith, attempting a smile.

"No, sir, no," answered Read. "I cannot leave until another blacksmith comes. You know that." He stopped. "I mean, not that I want to leave, not really. Now that my Anne and I are settled, it seems like home. And Sam here says he'll be my apprentice. Bein' the only smithies 'twixt the ocean and The Falls, why, we'll make a fortune!" Read and Sam had it all worked out. "But it will not be the same without you, sir. We'll never forget what you done for us, even the ungrateful amongst us. I jus' came to say thank you and God speed."

Read bowed his head and fingered his hat. Smith held out his hand. Read's eyes grew wide as he offered his grimy, muscular paw. They shook hands then, and Smith returned the compliment, "You proved yourself a worthy and honest man, Read. It was an honor to serve with you."

Read's meaty face and neck turned three shades of red as he stepped back.

"Sam." Smith's voice cracked.

"Captain. You were like my own father," whispered Sam. "I shall always remember you as the best man I have ever known. If I can be half of the man you are, I shall end my days well contented."

Smith forced himself to sit up. He winced as he drew the boy close and wrapped his arms around the lad's shoulders. The pain evaporated for the few seconds they hugged, and Sam squeezed his eyes to stifle the tears.

"Thank you for that, boy. Thank you. Now go to before we sail with two extra passengers. God bless and keep you safe."

Smith lapsed back onto the bed, watching them go, thinking of London, of the Company, of the mischiefs and miseries that had besieged them all in the last two and a half years, and that perhaps, just perhaps, he was leaving the Colony in the very best hands after all.

Epilogue

John Smith never returned to Jamestown, although he did visit the place the Virginia Company referred to as North Virginia—now Massachusetts—and that Smith later dubbed New England. While his departure could be interpreted as a punishment from the new leaders, I prefer to think he left willingly, injured and exhausted by the struggle, but clear-minded enough to see that he had little hope of any cooperation with Ratcliffe, Archer, Martin or West. On his return to London in 1609 he found that his letters had been published as *A True Relation* and that he had become a national hero. The King's Council had indeed appointed him third in command in the Second Charter, under Lord De la Warr, the Royal Governor, and Sir Thomas Gates, his deputy.

The ill-fated *Sea Venture* did shipwreck in Bermuda where Gates, Newport, Somers, and the remaining crew and passengers spent the winter building two pinnaces, the *Patience* and the *Deliverance*, on which they continued their journey, arriving at Jamestown May 23, 1610. In doing so they missed one of the deadliest chapters in the life of the new colony.

The Virginia Colony felt Smith's departure in ways they could not have imagined. The Powhatan Indians, seeing that the indomitable Captain had sailed away, unleashed attack after attack on the fort and any inhabitants that wandered from it. The result was the winter of 1609-10, the notorious Starving Time of the Colony, where of the two to five hundred colonists left when Smith departed (depending on which account you read) there remained but sixty in June 1610. Lord De La Warr's arrival brought the colonists' numbers back to five hundred. And if the veteran colonists had thought John Smith's tactics and regime were rough, they were in for a surprise with Lord De La Warr who imposed martial law after viewing the devastation of the colony.

In 1619 Smith applied to the Virginia Company to be Captain of the *Mayflower*, a job given to Miles Standish. Smith never married, dying poor in London in 1631, probably in the house of a friend. He is buried in London in The Church of the Holy Sepulchre, also known as St. Sepulchre-without-Newgate. As thorough as he was in documenting Virginia and his other adventures, he was quiet about his personal life.

What he did do was spend the rest of his life writing about the New World and promoting its advantages. The most important works cover his time in Virginia and New England, including the production of some of the most detailed and accurate maps of the region and the native inhabitants ever made. He died at age fifty-one, leaving behind his coat of arms, some land and tenements, eleven published works and a legend.

Every English and Powhatan name in this novel has come from the written record of Jamestown. For clarity, I combined the actions of several minor colonists into one or two minor characters, but every name named is someone who was there. I did take liberty with the wedding of Anne Burras to James Read. In truth, she wed a laborer named John Laydon soon after her arrival. To simplify the storyline, I arranged for her to marry James Read instead. In real life, she survived the Starving Time and bore a child in the spring, a girl she named Virginia, and later produced three more children.

What happened to James Read, Sam Collier and William Dyer is unclear. I have given William Dyer the dubious honor of lighting the fuse that injured Smith when the truth is no one knows how the powder ignited or who was responsible, if anyone. The three Dutch laborers—Franz, Jan, and Adam—who went to live with Powhatan were killed in the spring of 1610 at the hands of their hosts; apparently double dealing didn't sit well on either side of the Pamunkey River.

History shows that Gabriel Archer died in the months following Smith's departure, presumably in the Starving Time. Powhatan's men ambushed and killed John Ratcliffe after a failed attempt to trade for corn that same winter. George Percy returned to England after serving as temporary President following Smith and died the same year as Smith. Christopher Newport left the Virginia Company and went to work for the East India Company; he died on Java Island in 1617. Captain Francis West, brother to Lord De La Warr, abandoned the starving colony in the winter of 1610 with a pinnace full of food while his brother was still crossing the Atlantic. Despite that ignoble action, he later returned to Virginia and in 1612 followed Percy as commander. Eventually he became Governor of Virginia and married the widow of the very recently deceased Governor Yeardley, one Temperance

Flowerdew Yeardley. According to family legend, West drowned in Virginia in 1633.

Powhatan, already elderly when the first English arrived in 1607, commanded his confederacy of tribes until his death in 1618. When Smith left, Powhatan let loose his full power on the English and life in the colony was never the same. After Powhatan died, his brother Opechancanough inherited the power if not the throne (this he obtained in 1630 at the death of another older brother) and wrought his own havoc upon the English leading two massacres along the King's River, the first in 1622 and the last in 1644. He was near one hundred years old when he died at the hands of his captors that year.

Pocahontas, the little girl who charmed the English, was kidnapped in 1613 by Samuel Argall on an expedition near the Potomac River. She met and married John Rolfe of tobacco fame in 1614 after being baptized and taking the name Rebecca; she gave birth to son Thomas in 1615; sailed for England and died there, aged about twenty-one years, on the journey back to Virginia in 1617. She is buried at Gravesend in Kent County just below London. Her son Thomas was educated in England by his uncle, and he then returned to Virginia as a young man where he lived out his days. What little we know of Pocahontas' age comes from descriptions of her naked cartwheels from the early colonists which tell us she had not yet reached puberty in 1610 as Powhatan children wore no clothing until they were grown up. We know she was married to a Powhatan Indian named Kocoum in or before 1613. We assume she had reached puberty by then. The rest is mathematical and biological guesswork.

The first three years of the Virginia colony are generally unfamiliar to most people who focus on the fictional love story of Smith and Pocahontas thanks in part to creative filmmakers and storytellers. What they miss is the drama and conflict of everyday life that made those early days so remarkable—not because conflict and dire circumstances occurred, but because anyone survived to talk about it. John Smith's true legacy doesn't center on Pocahontas; his legacy is courage, leadership, intelligence and practicality in the face of terrifying odds and enemies, some of them in his own Company.

In researching this novel, I relied heavily on Edward Wright Haile's masterful *Jamestown Narratives: eyewitness accounts of the Virginia Colony*, which includes John Smith's work; Philip Barbour's intriguing *The Three Worlds of Captain John Smith*; and Ivor Noel-Hume's meticulous and enjoyable *The Virginia Adventure: Roanoke to James Towne*. All three works make excellent fireside reading although the first, being composed in the original colonists' own words, takes a willingness to decipher Elizabethan syntax. *The Chesapeake Bay in the Seventeenth Century*, edited by Thad W. Tate and David L. Ammerman, provided an excellent overview of the era's social history. For the Powhatan world, I turned to Helen C. Rountree's *The Powhatan Indians of Virginia: their traditional culture*. Since the Powhatan Indians had no written language, every account of their lives and words comes through English interpretations, and Dr. Rountree's analysis is scholarship at its best.

I hope this fictional account of Jamestown's early days will spur readers to visit the historic site, located just outside of Williamsburg, Virginia.

Historic Jamestowne is the location of an on-going archaeological dig that unearths (pun intended) something new every day, and where APVA Preservation Virginia and The National Park Service work together to interpret the site of the 1607 fort and surrounding environs. Jamestown Settlement, operated by the Virginia Department of Education, is an adjacent living history museum where visitors can see a recreated fort, Powhatan village, and replica ships. Come, enjoy, celebrate America's 400th Anniversary in 2007, and learn so much more than could ever be conveyed in one book alone; you'll be glad you did.

About the Author

K. K. Bruno is Karla Kraynak Bruno, a former educator and librarian, now a full-time writer in Williamsburg, Virginia, where she basks in the southern life with her husband and son and a houseful of books and quilts. An interpreter for Historic Jamestowne, she works at the archeological dig year round and spends her summers with the Virginia Shakespeare Festival. A graduate of The College of William and Mary (BA; MAEd) and The Catholic University of America (MSLIS), her next novel is the first in a series of murder mysteries set in Jamestown 1629.

www.kkbruno.com

Printed in the United States
203485BV00001B/262/A

9 781424 143672